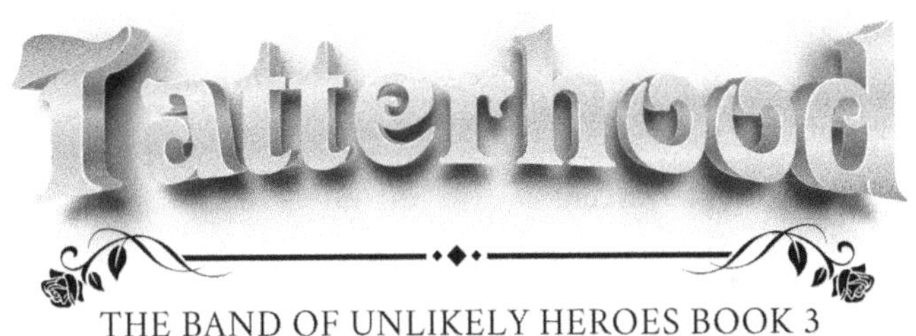

Tatterhood

THE BAND OF UNLIKELY HEROES BOOK 3

DAWN FORD

scrivkids

Published by ScrivKids,
an imprint of Scrivenings Press LLC
15 Lucky Lane
Morrilton, Arkansas 72110
https://ScriveningsPress.com

Printed in the United States of America

Paperback ISBN 978-1-64917-442-0

eBook ISBN 978-1-64917-443-7

Editors: Ann Harrison and Denica McCall

Cover design by Linda Fulkerson - www.bookmarketinggraphics.com

This is a work of fiction. Unless otherwise indicated, all names, characters, businesses, events, and incidents are either the product of the author's imagination or used in a fictitious manner. Any resemblance to actual persons, living or dead, or actual events is purely coincidental.

To my dedicated readers.
You make all the hard work worth it.

CHAPTER I

Beneath a canopy of tall oaks edging the Riven's boundary, Horra bent over the gnome girl she'd just shot with a slime bomb when a ball of toxic-smelling mud smacked her cheek.

Goo ran down her neck and clung to her thick red curls. "Rowan, stop shooting! You're hitting me again," she yelled at her druid companion.

Though a month had passed since her father returned with the grubby worm antidote from the swamp where he'd grown up, they were still hunting creatures the evil elf Erlking had infected with the magic-siphoning bugs.

Horra's shoulders pinched. Saving grubby-infested creatures had become an unending job. And being this close to the Riven, the mysterious land between the elven hidden kingdom and her kingdom of Oddar, put her on edge.

"Honestly, Rowan. It's the middle of the day with the best

light. How do you keep missing?" Frustration with the Erlking's plague and Rowan's inability to hit a single target flared in her gut. She made a mental note to get his eyes tested.

"Sorry, Princess. It must be the configuration—"

"It's a user issue, Rowan, not a technical one." She interrupted him before he could natter on and on about his newest invention, which he dubbed the *extermigrubber*. Frustration crept into her voice, and not only because Rowan had misfired a dozen mud bombs at her in just a few hours of hunting. Her target, a worq, had ducked at the last minute, allowing her large ball of swamp sludge to hit the innocent girl she was currently leaning over.

Horra captured the grubby worm squirming in the muck beside the girl and slid it into a jar she dug out of her knapsack. It was the third she'd gathered today alone. Pidge, her pet pudge wudgie and mighty huntress bird, would be in for a treat later.

The gnome girl moaned and then gagged. She rolled onto her side and coughed.

Horra couldn't blame her. The scent of their new repellent, a diluted mixture of swamp mud, was pungent despite its weakened mixture. She helped the girl sit up and swiped the goo from her face. "Sorry about that. You weren't my intended victim. Your abductor was. What's your name?"

A blank look crossed the girl's innocent, round face. The fact that she couldn't recall such a simple thing as her name was a sure sign of the worm's damage to her memory. Horra wondered how long the worm had been infecting the poor child. Her huge blue eyes filled with tears. She must've realized this wasn't where she was supposed to be.

Whimpers turned to loud wails as the child's face crumpled. "I want my mom!" she screamed between desperate gulps and sobs.

"Stupid Erlking," Horra muttered under her breath while waiting for the child's crying to die down. Saving the children was her newest mission in her battle against the Erlking. Her previous mission had been finding the trolls infected with the grubby worms that made them go insane. Though she was determined to face whatever magic trick the dark elf threw at them, Horra shuddered to think of what would come next.

Horra eyed the red-faced, wailing child awkwardly. No matter how many children she'd saved, the terror they experienced when coming out of the haze was the worst. And trolls were not normally nurturing creatures. They were fierce and formidable. She patted the child's back, hoping to give her some level of comfort.

Nimble, her gulgoyle pet, rumbled in the background, also nervous about the loud cries. He was already on edge from the scent of worq permeating this forest so near the Riven, though how the beast could smell anything above the swampy concoction was beyond her understanding.

"Princess? What have you done to that poor gnome girl?" Rowan stepped out of the brushy edge of the forest. His clackity voice had recently deepened to a low boom. It, along with his demeanor, had become more like that of her late instructor, Woodsly.

The similarity was unconscious on Rowan's part. Being Woodsly's seed and heir to the druid warrior race of woodgoblins, some kind of resemblance was inevitable. She wondered, not for the first time, why he couldn't have inherited Woodsly's nubby tail instead. She could tolerate that much better than his identical voice and attitude.

Dropping her claw from the child's back, Horra rolled her shoulders and tried to hide her frustration. "I didn't do it on purpose." She stood, leaving the gnome bawling on the ground. "The worq moved at the last minute and my bomb hit her instead of him. Now she's confused."

Horra glanced around the gloomy area, finding no sign of her target. They'd ventured into a well-known unsafe space close to the Riven, an elven danger zone, and there was no telling where the worq had gone. "The worq's disappeared, and now she's woken up to strangers in an odd place. I'd be crying too if I were her."

Horra walked back to Nimble and strapped her mud-flinger back in place next to her saddle. She turned and ran into a thick, mossy barrier. She let out a gasp. "Vinegar, Rowan! What'd I tell you about personal space?"

"That you are inordinately fond of it?"

Horra frowned as the moss on his bark tickled her arm. Had he actually just poked fun at her?

"Apologies, Princess. What do we do with the squawking child now?" Rowan stepped back and glanced at the sky. Though Springtide brought longer days, it was early in the season and the sun still set before suppertime.

The child shivered as a brisk breeze whistled through the tree limbs. She appeared to be wearing a thin nightgown, which was not suitable for the fickle springish weather they were experiencing.

"It will get dark soon," Rowan noted unnecessarily.

Horra perceived the unspoken meaning in his words and sighed. Dark spaces made him uncomfortable ever since their trek through the mountains. For a moment, the young druid warrior had seemed less wooden than normal, like he might even care about the gnome child instead of his own safety. It wasn't surprising that wasn't the case. He'd only unrooted a couple short months ago. Merrow, the druid's mentor, had warned Horra of Rowan's stunted emotional growth.

Still, Horra couldn't help but hope. "The worq is long gone

by now, so there's no use pursuing him. We'll need to bring the child back to the castle with us. We'll find her parents and reunite them like we've done with the dozens of other children we've saved."

"Where will we put her?" Rowan's eyes widened. The lighter chestnut color in his orbs was new, standing out from the mossy liverwort leaves covering his body.

"Between us," Horra said. "You'll have to sit on Nimble's back. Let's saddle up. We need to get going. I don't want to be out after the sun sets if we can help it." She knew Rowan understood her meaning. Night meant more worqs than they could handle together. Luckily, they were in the southernmost part of the area surrounding the Riven, and the ride back to the castle wasn't long.

Horra turned toward the girl, ignoring the unhappy tilt of Rowan's branchy crown. He would have to sit upon Nimble's hard-scaled back, something he wasn't overly fond of.

One of Woodsly's sermons came back to her. *Trying to please everyone is a waste of time and energy, Princess. Not even the most favored queen in Oddar's history managed that. The best you can do is please a few every once in a while. And even that is a fool's errand.*

"Isn't that the truth," Horra mumbled to herself as she helped lift the sniffling girl onto Nimble's back.

———

LATER THAT EVENING, Horra was shoving the last bite of greased grouse in her mouth as King Fyd stepped into the dining room. His face was grim, causing her to choke on her last swallow. "What's wrong?"

"Besides the fact you tracked swamp mud across the kitchen floor and are now sitting in the formal dining room still coated in the odious mixture? Do you need to go back to Etiquette Basics class?" Humor flickered in his clay-colored eyes.

First Rowan's joke, and now her father was teasing her. The pinch between her shoulders deepened.

She drank her spruce juice with as much dignity as she could muster before answering her father. It had taken hours to ride back to the castle after their failed mission, and she was famished. "You can thank Rowan for that. He isn't capable of hitting the broadside of a castle with his newest invention. It flies right or left each time, depending on which side of him I'm standing on."

Horra placed her utensils on her plate, picked up her goblet, and brushed the flakes of mud from her spot. She glanced up at the sound of laughter rumbling in her father's chest. She stood and made a face at him. "It's not funny. I think the grubby worm affected his eyesight."

King Divitri placed a claw on her shoulder. "I recall a certain princess who couldn't hit any of her targets with her bow and arrow just a few short years ago. Give the boy a chance. He's still green and growing. Even though he looks your age, and he's impressively smart, he's still a sapling inside. It's going to take a while for his rings to catch up to his size."

She stiffened. "I was never that bad of a shot." She headed for the kitchen with her dirty dishes.

"You were, and you could admit it if you set aside your frustration about getting stuck with Rowan," he said, following her.

"My frustration isn't with Rowan alone. We haven't caught any creature outside the Riven, even after I bombed them and removed the grubby worms. I figured—"

"You figured it would be easier to bring the Erlking down?

Wars take time. And unfortunately, we're fighting a defensive game at the moment." Her father's voice rumbled in a low octave, a tone he used when he wanted her to think harder about something important.

Horra's mind spun around what he meant. Her battle lessons on the impact of offensive versus defensive tactics weren't lost on her. Woodsly had been thorough in his training. She nodded. "Offensive is always a stronger position." Weariness crept into her voice so that it cracked.

"Exactly." The king crossed his arms over his chest. "You should let Rowan go out with someone else once in a while. Helping him does not have to rest entirely on your shoulders, Daughter."

"Merrow specifically told me I was the one to guide him." A yawn escaped her. She wanted nothing more than to crawl into bed and sleep for a day.

Horra nodded at the few hobgoblins remaining in the kitchen and placed her dishes in the marble sink. The evening meal had been over for a while, and the preparation for the morning breakfast complete.

The king stood in the doorway, an unreadable expression on his green face. "You will learn as a leader that some jobs have to be delegated. If not permanently, then at least temporarily. Burning out after one task doesn't do you or Rowan any favors. Now, go clean up and head to bed." He grinned, his tusks glowing white in the low light. He knew she would skip the shower if she could get away with it. "It will all seem better in the light of morning, I promise."

A FEW MINUTES LATER, Horra dragged her clawed feet as she made her way up the staircase to her bedroom. A wail from the guest corridor made her hesitate. "Must be the gnome child crying again," she mumbled as she yawned, grateful the servants would take care of the girl. The poor thing sobbed most of the way home until exhaustion made her fall asleep against Horra's back.

A hobgoblin's shriek followed the outburst.

Horra scrunched her eyes closed, debating whether she should get involved. When another shrill scream bounced off the stone walls, she moved to intervene if only to ensure she could get a restful night's sleep. "Vinegar!" Horra moaned.

She rounded a corner, where a lantern was lit. The light revealed a small hobgoblin woman coated with a fruity-smelling drink and sugared petals.

"What's going on?" Horra demanded, staring at Glory, the disfigured fairy princess who hovered over the servant in a menacing stance. "You're dismissed," she told the maid.

The woman exited eagerly, wiping the flowery-smelling debris from her clothes.

Princess Glory waved a hand in front of her gray tattered hood, her face hidden in its shadows. "You reek!" Her voice, which had been gravelly from the Erlking's hex, was now a surprisingly smooth, younger tone.

"Thanks, but I already knew that." Horra straightened her aching back to face the ungrateful fairy. Though Horra had sympathy for Glory after one of the Erlking's hexes had disfigured the princess, she had been more than a handful since they'd rescued her yet again from his clutches. And fairies, being conceited creatures, were already difficult without adding any other pressures. "What have you done to your voice, and what is the problem this time?"

A squeal barraged Horra's ears.

Princess Glory slashed at the air with fingers as crooked as a hobgoblin maid's hand. "This place is sucking the life out of me. I'm withering away."

"Not this again," Horra spat. Exhaustion pulled at her shoulders. She'd heard this argument at least a dozen times.

"Yes, this again. You can't keep me hostage any longer. I must leave this dreary castle. I need to return home." She squeaked the last sentence.

Horra narrowed her eyes at the fairy. Torren sounded like that once after he'd mixed together the wrong components of an elixir. The princess had obviously tried some sort of magic to reverse the hex the Erlking put on her. But since being hit by that spell, her magic had been wonky.

"There aren't enough resources to escort you home. We can't allow you to leave on your own, and we don't have the ability to form fairy paths. It's far more dangerous out there than you realize."

Fairy paths would allow the princess to travel the long distance to the Shining Kingdom safely. But the paths took strong magic to create. Trolls had no magic, and the princess's unstable magic made them impossible to project.

"You leave every day," Glory accused. "It can't be that dangerous."

Horra pressed her lips together. "I assure you, Princess, it is. Now, if you'll excuse me, I need a shower before I go to bed." She spun and headed back down the hallway.

"Wait." The derision had left the princess's voice. "Please."

Stiff-backed, Horra stopped and glanced over her shoulder. "What?"

"I propose a trade. That's what trolls like to do, right? Trade?" When Horra said nothing, she hurried on. "I simply need a few minutes outside the castle grounds to breathe fresh air. An hour, tops." She pulled a golden vial from her pocket. It glowed with light, much like the halo surrounding each of the fairies. At least the ones not hexed. So, Horra was correct. Princess Glory had been concocting an antidote to regain her beauty. "In exchange, I'll give you a potion to remove those dreadful warts from your skin. You'd be beautiful, well, maybe not so hideous, if you use this." She moved the small jar around in her bent fingers.

Her offer wasn't appealing to Horra in the least. Anger heated her face like a stoked forge. "How dare you insult me and my ancestors in such a manner? Warts *are* a sign of beauty to us." She fisted her shaking claws. "You fairies think your version of beauty is a standard all creatures should live by. You believe we are all inferior to your race. Let me make one thing perfectly clear. We trolls may not be fair-skinned or have magic embedded in our blood, but we are fierce and resourceful. Without us, you would still be under the Erlking's thrall or getting your magic sucked out by the grubby worm, leaving you a dry, glittering husk."

The princess shrunk back.

"You've done nothing but whine and complain since we rescued you, you ungrateful wretch! Do you honestly believe the Erlking would take pity on someone he deemed worthy of hexing in the first place? Surely you're not that dense."

Princess Glory straightened her bowed shoulders. Her gnarled wings crackled beneath the hooded cloak stretching tightly across them. "I have something he wants. Badly. He'd be stupid not to trade me for it."

Horra scoffed. "And what would that be? I'm all ears."

"You mean warts, don't you?"

Glory's snide comment hung in the air between them.

"Princesses? Am I interrupting something?" King Divitri's voice cut through the tense air.

Neither of them spoke.

The king seemed ready to wait them out. He crossed his arms over his broad chest, and his right eye twitched.

Horra wasn't ready to give in completely, though. She didn't care that her father expected nothing but her utmost civility toward another princess, especially one who was a guest in their castle. "Take a long look in the mirror, Princess Hideous," she said. "No golden potion or spell could even begin to make your selfish spirit beautiful."

CHAPTER 2

Glory waited for the king to spring to her defense against his daughter's cruel words. But instead, King Fyd stood, glaring at them both with an unreadable expression on his warty green face.

Horra leaned toward her, her face ruddy with anger and a sparkle of satisfaction gleaming in her mud-brown eyes.

Glory screeched as she spun away from them and stormed into her room. She glared at her bleak, prison-like bedroom as anger erupted inside her. "The nerve of that pathetic troll princess!" she shrieked. Magic, which she'd once so easily accessed, tickled her skin but fizzled out instantly. She screamed louder, tearing off the dingy, hooded cloak she wore to cover up her ugliness.

The troll princess didn't understand. Fairies couldn't survive without beauty. She was slowly going mad, and she couldn't do a thing about it. Glory threw the vial at the pocked stone wall. The magic she'd created formed a gold vein that bloomed in the crevices of the rock, beautifying the drab room. By morning, there'd be more gold than the trolls would know what to do with. But it was better than curing that horrible troll princess of her warts.

She sobbed. The potion worked on stone, and it would've worked wonders for the troll princess. Why wouldn't the potion work on her?

"You don't deserve to be beautiful. It's all your fault, anyway." Glory kicked a shard of glass away from her foot as tears streamed down her face. A gold vein spread on the wall and across the floor. She stepped away. A few drops of the gold had changed her voice earlier, and she wasn't sure what might happen if more touched her. Nothing good, she knew. The potion hadn't untangled her wings or changed her face back to its natural beauty as she had intended. The Erlking's spell was stronger than her magic, and nothing she came up with would overpower it.

Thinking of her wings, she attempted to flutter them, but the movement was painful. She grimaced, her mood darkening.

If it hadn't been for the trolls, she'd still be in her Shining Kingdom, celebrated as the brightest creature to exist in a lifetime. More beautiful even than her twin sister, Misty. Her life would be full of art, laughter, and most of all, music.

Music. She laughed, but there was no humor in it. She thought back to where it all began—the Erlking disguised as a dark fairy prince who loved melodies as much as she did.

He'd caught her eye with his pale skin and spiked black hair. He was everything she wasn't supposed to want but did. Her rebellion against her controlling mother and perfect sister had been sweet.

Except it had all been a ruse. He'd lured her with his dark enchantment like a fisher hooking an innocent glimmerfish.

He tricked her into mesmerizing her mother first, her sister next, and then used them all to invade the troll kingdom to gain access to the troll princess.

Betrayal and contempt warred for dominance in her heart. How could she have been so gullible? She shook her head. The Erlking knew a fairy's weakness lay in their beauty and love of artful things. He'd used that knowledge to his advantage.

Glory knocked the unwanted food off of a silver dining tray next to the lumpy bed and gazed at her reflection. Her eyes were fishlike—overlarge, with one lower than the other. Lumps protruded from her once-perfect skin. The sight was repulsive, worse than the troll princess's dreadful face.

Horra was right about one thing. Fairies were above other creatures. And Glory was already tired of being ugly like the troll princess. How the trolls had built such a powerful kingdom without beauty and music, she wasn't sure. But she also didn't care.

Her tears dried, but anger remained—a friend she didn't know she needed. "I'll find you," she muttered to the dark fairy ghost in her memory. Obviously only a figment of her imagination, but real enough in her heart. "And when I do, you'll have no choice but to trade me back my beauty."

She pulled out the book from beneath her bed that she'd stolen from him all those weeks ago when he wooed her with his edgy compositions. Beside it sat a golden kelpie bridle, which she set aside. Glory flopped onto the mattress, ignoring the uneven surface. "Somehow you figured out I stole them, didn't you? Otherwise, you wouldn't have disfigured me so badly."

The kelpie, which he'd used to spirit her away from her shining castle, had given her a taste of independence. His spellbook, though, had led to her downfall. Glory ran a gnarled hand across the cover. "You, my pretty, will be the weapon I use to gain freedom from his dark spell." She opened it and flipped through the pages. Her affinity for music drew her to the notes written in crisp penmanship. Each symbol contained magic, but not the light kind used by her kingdom. Dark and broody, the notebook practically hummed with it.

"Hobgoblin's Thrall. Trance of the Fairies." She ripped that page out, tore it into small pieces, and tossed them into the hearth. "Lullaby into Longing. Mind over Mouse," she read aloud, scouring the pages until she flipped to the only one she needed. "Aha! Taming of the Trolls." Her grin was maniacal, she knew. But she would be hex-free, and that was the only thing she cared about. It was time to take her life back.

The troll's spell page tore out of the book evenly, as if meant to be. Glory folded it and stuck it in her pocket. Both she and the troll princess would get what they deserved.

Glory used the extra sheets she'd hidden from the hobgoblin maids, tied them together, and in less time than it took to walk out the castle's front doors, escaped into the night with the sheet and the bridle.

~Rowan~

MASTER KNURL MUTTERED in his sleep. A shadow of a thought from the old rood fluttered like a leaf in the wind in Rowan's mind, leaving no trace of its substance.

Roods weren't supposed to slumber, but many things were yet beyond Rowan's understanding.

He called out and woke the dead druid spirit.

"Why do you disturb me?" Master Knurl's clackity voice creaked more than usual. The rood should've faded by now, but because of his bonding to the ageless Yew tree in Oddar's

Conservatory and the magic in the elven soil, he endured. Until the tree died as well, the rood would survive, untouched by the taint spreading across the Wilden Lands and disabling the rood network beyond these walls.

Rowan sensed a weakness in Master Knurl's voice. The sap in Rowan's veins stilled before flowing fluidly again. Rowan reached out and touched the tree. To comfort the rood? The druid woodgoblin didn't understand comfort beyond his needs, such as water, sunshine, and soil sustenance. The urge to aid pulled at him, though, in a peculiar way. "You were talking. It was incoherent but seemed important."

The tree split to form a face. "A dream, perhaps. I have no recollection of what I said." High branches rattled, and a dark figure leaped into the air from their depths.

Pidge, the resident pudge wudgie, scree'd and fluttered to the ground next to them. She bobbed her head at the newly formed creases in the trunk.

Rowan hesitated, ignoring the bird. "Roods dream?"

"In times of old, the Creature God would communicate to us druids in visions and dreams."

Rowan waited, but the old rood didn't continue. "Which was it? A vision, or a dream?"

Master Knurl hacked a cough, the Yew's limbs trembling.

Rowan jerked back as Pidge squawked. Was the tree ill? The thought of losing him, the last link to his ancestors, chilled the sap in his body.

"Fear not, young druid. I will be here for quite some time yet," Master Knurl answered his unspoken question. "It is only the resonance of the castle that affects me. I believe the fairy princess has left and taken something vital to your mission with her. I sense an unpleasant evil surrounding the item."

Rowan stroked Pidge's chin, his hands steadier now that

Master Knurl had assured him of his continuing presence. "What is it? Has she stolen something from the trolls?"

"No. She has stolen something from the second Erlking." The ground beneath the Yew tree murmured as if the rood were attempting to communicate. But to whom? He couldn't communicate with anything outside the Conservatory walls. The only tree inside the Conservatory with a live spirit inside it was a mute dryad living in the ropy Weeping Willow Welter tree who guarded a hidden entry along the back wall.

Rowan dug his roots into the soil, hoping to detect any connection to other roods the Yew tree might have. Silence. "How do you know she stole something?"

"When Princess Glory came to the castle last, I sensed she possessed an elven item. Its aura is similar to the magic in the Conservatory's soil, which, as you know, comes from the former Elf Lands."

"Yes, but the Conservatory soil is not evil." Rowan steepled his fingers as he often did while learning.

"The soil is neutral, that's true. But it is elven. Did Merrow teach you anything about the elves?" The tree puckered its lips.

"No, but he believed Woodsly left some of his knowledge in my seed's core. I knew answers the seedkeeper did not teach me, nor did he fully understand himself."

The tree grunted, rustling its leaves. "Woodsly was the best of our brotherhood. If anyone could leave knowledge behind, it would be him."

"But what do you know about elves?" Rowan prodded, leaning closer.

Master Knurl cleared his throat. "Our Creature God created our noble order after the elves relinquished control of their lands, removed all knowledge of their culture, then secreted themselves away. Thanks to the druid clans, we documented everything from that point forward. However, what we don't understand is why no additional information about them survived. It wasn't as if there weren't any intelligent creatures around. Besides the magic they left behind, it's as if they never existed. Until we discovered the Riven."

Rowan furrowed his brow. "The Riven didn't always exist?"

"It did not. It came into being a couple generations before the first Erlking appeared. At first, it seemed as if a scourge had taken over a forest we now know as the Riven. Two druid researchers went to find the source but never returned." The rood's voice cracked.

Rowan blinked at the face's outline on the trunk. "What happened then?"

"The trees died outside of that forest, and the druids realized it was more than a plague. It was a presence. Soon, we came to realize the forest shifted and grew like a living thing. Since then, we've been able to hold the borders, but with the Weald damaged and the roods' influence crippled, that too might change."

"What does this mean for the future of the Wilden Lands? What about the balance of good and evil we're supposed to maintain?"

"That, my young friend, is why you are here. Every period of terrible darkness allows for a set of heroes to rise and meet the challenge. You and your companions must be brave enough to stand in the gap between good and evil to fend off the flood the Erlking is sending upon the Wilden Lands. We are all counting on you."

Rowan stilled. The moss growing along his bark rippled. "You've given me much to think about. Thank you for your wise counsel."

CHAPTER 3

~Horra~

Despite worrying that her father would come knocking down her door, he hadn't. Horra had slept well and woken re-energized. She was now ready to face her father at breakfast.

The king's glance was brief when she sat down at the dining room table. Beside him sat a shining scroll, half-rolled up. Where it lay open, fanciful cursive writing filled the page. Fairy-like writing.

Horra eyed the gleaming document, her stomach twisting with dread. "Have they found Queen Toppenbottom?"

He didn't look up from his correspondence strung out beneath the partially rolled sheet. "No." His voice was a low growl. "Princess Misty has requested a meeting to discuss her mother and visit her sister. As you know, she's the only royal left to rule the Shining Kingdom at the moment. She apologized that because of some royal duties, it will be five days before she arrives." His words were like a hammer, striking her with meaning. "It's a reprieve." His eye ticked.

Horra recognized the fury simmering beneath her father's calm demeanor. More knots grew in her gut. She knew he'd be angry with her, but not irate. Grumpy though he could be, witnessing true rage within him was rare. She bit her lip to keep it from trembling.

A maid set a steaming bowl of gritty hash in front of her. She gulped back nausea. Her appetite had disappeared.

"Might I inquire what last night was all about?" Her father asked in a low voice.

Anxiety pounded a hole in her chest. She'd rehearsed how she would speak and what she would say, Woodsly style. However, she faltered after the news of the other princess's visit. She prayed silently to remain steadfast in the face of her father's ire. "Princess Glory insulted me. All trolls, actually. And I'd had quite enough of her attitude." Her words ended in an unintentional whine.

"Is that it?" His eyes remained unblinking. Cold. He wasn't a father asking his daughter about a disagreement. He was a king requiring information from a subordinate.

Vinegar and beans, but she'd stuck her claw in it this time.

Horra took a moment to steady her nerves before glancing back at him. It had been a while since her father was this unhappy with her. "No. She tried to bribe me first."

King Divitri swiveled his mug on the wooden table. "And that gave you the right to treat a guest in our castle, a royal one at that, so discourteously?"

Horra's heart sunk to her toes. How could she make him understand? She opened her mouth.

Sageel barged in from the throne room, halting Horra's speech. The maid twisted the apron she wore in her bony hands. Head bent low, she rushed toward the king. "Majesty, the princess is missing."

Horra waved her claw at her favorite maid. "No, I'm not. I'm right here."

Sageel shook her head. "Not you, Princess. The other one. Princess Glory. I went to pick up her breakfast tray—she likes it first thing in the morning—and it was untouched. So I knocked on the door. When she didn't yell at me for interrupting her, I knew something was wrong, so I checked her room. She's tied sheets together and escaped out her window."

The king frowned.

Horra groaned and dropped her head into her claws. This was so much worse than her argument with the insolent princess. This was a waking nightmare.

Not only was Glory's disappearance a political blunder, but if the fairy princess fell into the Erlking's hands, it might cause a war between the two former allied kingdoms. Especially with Princess Misty's promised visit only days away.

King Divitri turned his grim face toward Sageel. "Gather a search party from among the reinstated warriors. My daughter will lead them as Oddar's Queen Bearer."

His words were like thunder in Horra's ears, and lightning zinged through her blood as the meaning settled in. Her father had just declared her in charge of the kingdom, despite the fact she hadn't been coronated yet. She was queen in all but ceremony now.

Her father was essentially cleaning his claws of her actions.

Horra willed the tears not to fall as she asked to be excused.

Nodding, the king refused to look at her as he released her to her new fate.

Queen Bearer. Horra thought about the title as she made her way from the dining room to the Conservatory.

Only one other in Oddar's history had carried that title. During the War of the Warts, her mother became Queen Bearer while her grandmother and grandfather fought on the front lines. In her mother's words, "someone needed to run the kingdom during a war, and that was me." When her grandmother, Queen Petra, captured the first Erlking, her mother gave up the title and became princess again until her mother's early death.

It was why her mother was the best queen Oddar ever had. She already knew how to rule when she inherited the title for real.

Horra didn't feel like a queen at the moment.

A few minutes later, she walked down a sparkling-clean hallway and opened the Conservatory doors, her breakfast uneaten and her stomach tied in knots.

"Good afternoon, Princess." Rowan's clackity voice drifted over the rustle of the new leaves growing on the replacement plants the fairies had sown. "Is this a Pidge visit, or are we back on mission?"

"I brought Pidge a treat. But yes. We're heading back out for a different reason, though." She opened the jar of dried grubby worms she'd collected thus far. She'd had to dehydrate them in the lab. Live grubbies were too dangerous to make a mistake with, and the hobgoblin kitchen staff wouldn't come near them.

Pidge screeched in the distance, probably smelling the bugs the instant Horra cracked the lid. She spent the next few minutes tossing them in the air for her pet to snag and gobble up—a small piece of joy on an otherwise abysmal morning. "You're getting good at air catch, Pidge."

Rowan walked to the platform she stood on. He bent his

face toward the ceiling, where Pidge flew in happy circles. Though two steps below, he stood at eye level with her. "Her eyesight is better than most creatures."

Normally, Horra would mention his deficiency in that department. However, his inability to hit anything besides her backside was the least of her worries now. The king declared her Queen Bearer, meaning she held an equal title to that of her father. The title implied many things she'd rather not consider at the moment. "Did anyone tell you Princess Glory snuck out last night?"

Rowan twisted to face her, his brown eyes steady. "Master Knurl mentioned it. He said her leaving shifted the resonance of the castle."

Horra puckered her lips, her tusks poking her upper lip. She had no clue what that meant. Nor did she have the patience to ask Rowan for an explanation. "Did Master Knurl say which way she went?"

He shook his head, his wooden mouth creasing in a frown. "Once a creature leaves the castle, he can no longer sense them."

Pidge fluttered, then landed in front of them. She clucked at Horra.

"It's all gone, girl. You've eaten the last of them." She held the jar out so the bird could peck at the remaining crumbs. With another squawked complaint and a blur of black feathers, the pudge wudgie flew back to whatever she was doing before Horra entered.

"You are more tense than usual. What's on your mind?" Rowan asked. "Are you worried Princess Glory will get lost?"

"No. I'm worried she won't. If she finds the Erlking, or he finds her, then the queen won't be the only fairy missing." Horra studied the moss covering his bark. The sigils that Merrow had carved on the smooth surface a few short weeks ago were now hidden. She hoped they still carried power. They would need it. This was not their usual mission, and Rowan's safety wasn't a sure thing.

Melancholia struck her. Woodsly's poisoning, Torren's father's death, and the magical fire that destroyed the Weald were all the Erlking's fault. Why couldn't Glory have understood how dangerous the evil elf was? Did she even consider the political consequences her leaving would cause Oddar? Horra shook her head.

Rowan made an uncertain noise in his throat, a despicable crickety sound that broke her chain of thoughts. "And you want to go after her?"

Horra's laugh held no humor. "No. I am now Queen Bearer. It's my duty to find the princess and bring her back." Though her father hadn't said it in so many words, Horra knew what he meant when he'd given her the new title. Equal to him in rank, she was now in charge of their army. Any failure or embarrassing mistake would reflect upon her reign now. She was no longer a child or a princess to be coddled. An un-coronated queen, but a queen no less.

"I see. And you're not happy with this new title? Or is it the mission that troubles you?" Rowan's question was more of a challenge than an inquisition.

"I didn't ask to be Queen Bearer. I simply told Princess Glory the truth about the Erlking and herself. She's not only selfish, she's insulting and reckless. She's risked not only her life, but mine and that of anyone else assigned to hunt her down. With Princess Misty on her way here, this escape has put Oddar at risk of retaliation and war. For that, I can't forgive her."

Rowan rubbed a tuft of moss on his chin and hummed. "Would it not be in your best interest to lay aside your differences before searching for the other princess?"

Horra narrowed her eyes. "I don't see why that matters." Understanding formed in her mind. "Are you saying my attitude toward Princess Glory would cause me to fail my mission?"

He clacked his tongue and frowned. "Do not put words in my mouth."

She flung her arms wide. "Then what does it matter if I'm angry or not? It's not stopping me from searching for her royal stupidness. It certainly wouldn't keep me from bringing her back. I'm more than ready to drag her hide back here and lock her inside the dungeon for good measure."

A whisper of a breeze fluttered across the garden. Rowan closed his eyes as if listening to something she couldn't hear. When he opened them, he moved toward a potted plant, a vine that grew only a few feet and had sparse foliage.

"You brought this plant with us when we escaped the Weald after the fire. The vine had burned from around a Yew tree. The only signs of life were two green leaves." He stroked the spiky stem. "Do you know what this plant is?"

Horra tried not to show her impatience with the woodgoblin's ability to take the long way around a story. "It's in the fig family. Why?"

Rowan glanced at her then back down at the sad-looking vine. It hadn't thrived like other seeds and plants she'd brought back. "You're correct. It's a strangler fig, a *ficus mortuum totalis*—a deadly species that wraps around a tree and strangles it to death."

Horra blinked. "Why would there be dangerous plants in the Weald?"

"Because there is a place for all plants, but only where they're managed with an experienced hand. Merrow placed this vine next to a tree whose rood had passed on to the afterlife. Without its essence, that tree died. Druid tradition allows no spirit-bound tree to be chopped down, but instead preserved in honor of the rood who once dwelled inside it." Rowan left the plant and came back to stand next to Horra.

She crossed her arms, no longer hiding her impatience. "Okay. I'm still not sure what you're getting at."

"Bitterness and an unforgiving spirit are like this vine. They wrap around a creature's heart and choke out anything good within. Be careful, Princess, not to allow something this fatal to take hold inside you. For you will then become what you see in the fairy princess. And I need you to stay on the side of good, not evil, or we will fail."

CHAPTER 4

~Horra~

Later that evening, Horra sat atop Nimble on a hill, peering across Bough Valley and down to where Hobgoblin Pass crossed the Sterling River. It didn't look nearly as intimidating in the golden glow of the sun now that spring had arrived and green grass lined the deep ravines, creating a lush cover. Leaves had only just budded along the bare trees, and a light breeze rattled through the limbs.

A knight captain, three other recovered knight trolls, Torren, and Rowan accompanied Horra on this mission. Her other classmate and close friend, Murda, had been in the middle of taking her knighthood tests and therefore could not attend with them.

Murda had proved herself very helpful with the stolen children on their last mission together. And she was a good buffer between Horra and other creatures. Horra wouldn't admit to missing the female troll's presence as much as she did. As Queen Bearer, she needed to put up a strong front.

"Princess," a deep voice called.

"Yes, Captain Erast?" She turned her attention from the deceivingly calm view toward her meager army. This was the first time she was in charge of any real military action. She shoved the dread of making a wrong move out of her mind. "You have a question?"

"Is this where you wish to set up camp for the evening?" The captain's face barely concealed a condescending sneer.

She'd expected confusion since she hadn't shared a plan with them before they left. The only orders she gave were to follow her, though she'd told them they were hunting down the fairy princess. Her eyes flicked over to Rowan, who sat upon Pidge—a small accommodation she'd made for the druid, who didn't wish to ride on Nimble again. He alone knew about her misgivings.

He sat still. No twitch or flicker of leaves.

His solid support bolstered her. "No. We'll head to Bough Valley, find accommodations there, and eat at the Inn. We'll ask discreet questions about the princess and see if she's been here within the past day." Nimble quivered beneath her at the same moment Pidge fluffed her feathers. Horra glanced around briefly but didn't sense any danger.

Rowan peered around them before facing her. His lip twitched.

"And if we find out nothing from any of the locals?" The commanding captain lifted his square chin as if daring her.

Horra narrowed her eyes. They both knew she could have his head over any sign of impertinence. He was baiting her, seeing what she was made of. He was going to be disappointed. "Then I will give you new instructions in the morning." With a dismissive nod, she ordered, "I'll lead the way, Captain. You take the rear this time. Torren and Rowan, ride with me."

The captain looked as if he were going to argue with her when Rowan lifted his hand in salute. "Yes, Your Majesty, Queen Bearer Horra Fyd." He nudged Pidge and quickly moved into place next to her. Beside him, Torren guided her father's Stempner steed. Together, they formed a formidable wall.

Horra looked down at the troll captain riding atop a plain steed. Rowan's use of her full name was an effective rebuke. The captain's face pinched at being put in his place by the reminder of her new status. It would take some getting used to, but the troll wasn't ignorant. She held the seasoned knight with a piercing stare, praying silently to appear confident instead of showing the quaking inner troll she truly was.

He blinked first. Captain Erast steered his horse to the side and let her, Rowan, and Torren pass. She didn't look back to see if the knights followed as instructed. A good leader never questioned her knights.

"What is it?" Horra asked Rowan in a low voice once they were out of hearing range.

"Something hides here. Stay alert."

Torren guided his Stempner closer to her side. Whether from loyalty or fear, she wasn't sure. They'd already survived one magical trap, which left Rowan unable to communicate last year. It was possibly what set off the grubby worm infestation. Tripping any more of the Erlking's spells could have terrible repercussions.

They made their way down the grassy hillside toward Bough Valley and joined the road. Lanterns lit the area as the sun made its descent, and the air grew cooler. Hammering of new lumber replacing the hobgoblin business that had burned the last time she'd traveled this way faded as the day came to its end.

Horra rode by goblin carpenters packing up their tools. They stopped to stare at her and her entourage. She offered a regal nod and received grunts in return. No thumping of fists on chests. It was the most she could expect from creatures who weren't her subjects.

She recognized one laborer, though. "Halt," she called out, pulling back on Nimble's reins. "Good evening, Drungle. I'm so glad to see you made it safely back to your kind. I trust the rest of your trip back from the lower Iron Mountains was uneventful." Though perhaps unkind to single the naughty youth out, it didn't hurt to remind the goblins of her role in saving one of their own.

Drungle made a noise in the back of his throat and ducked his head.

"What's this?" A bigger goblin holding a sledgehammer strode up to the boy and shook his shoulder. "What's she talking about, and how does she know you?"

The goblin boy's blue face darkened, and the look he sent Horra could've peeled paint off of a wall. "It's nothing."

Horra laughed. "I found Drungle and another goblin girl captured inside the Erlking's lair and helped them escape. Did he not tell you?"

The goblin's wide forehead furrowed, stretching to the bald globe of his head. "He didn't, no."

"I found him to be quite determined to learn how to play the pan flute. In fact, one evening he practiced nonstop. It was quite a concert." Horra glared at the goblin, recalling how he'd followed them and then tortured them all night after she freed the children, including Drungle. She felt no guilt for pointing it out to his kin. The boy deserved something for his ungrateful attitude.

Nimble snorted smoke into the air as his stomach gurgled. She'd interrupted his morning meal before leaving, and it was past time for his evening meal. "It was good to see you again, Drungle. Good day, sir." Horra addressed the angry goblin, who must be his father, or possibly an uncle, then nodded at the other workers.

Drungle's shoulders drooped. All the goblins stared at him while Horra's knights stared at her. News that she'd rescued several children from the Erlking's clutches and then from the grubby worm invasion was now renowned. It hadn't, however, reversed the taint the Erlking left upon her kingdom after falling prey to his mesmerization spell.

Good. Maybe that earned her some respect in her knight's minds.

Torren laughed low. "That was priceless."

"I didn't do it only to shame the boy, though it felt good to put him in his place. Oddar is going to need all the allies it can get. Especially if we can't find the fairy princess."

THE INN WAS on the other side of Bough Valley. Most of the traffic through the village had decreased at the end of the workday, allowing her to drive Nimble down the center of the cobbled road without interference.

Small businesses with wooden walkways lined the smooth stone path. The town green—the village park—was now empty of the peddlers that set up during the day. The village was small, and soon they plodded along between quaint brick houses with small gardens and lawns in neat order. Hobgoblins were known for their tidiness. Finally, the small homes ended, and they reached the edge of town where the Inn was located.

The Inn was a large two-story building made from wood, not bricks. A porch wrapped around the building, and several windows lined each side to capture the most sunlight for the guests. Though impressive, the siding needed painting. But the roof was intact and the stairs looked sturdy. An equally worn stable jutted out of the bushes off to the right, the dirt corral contrasting with the new sprigs of spring grass growing amongst the winter-dead debris.

Horra arranged for their animals to be kept in the stables, not an easy feat with Nimble's size and Pidge's penchant for flying off to hunt.

She'd never stayed at the Inn before, but a large garden in the back promised many fresh herbs, and primitive wind chimes hung from every corner of the covered porch—a hobgoblin ward for fairies, something trolls hated because of the racket. Though a superstition, Horra couldn't blame the creatures. She and her hobgoblin staff had seen firsthand the pranks fairies could pull.

The chimes barely tinkled in the absence of wind, so she ignored them as she made her way onto the front porch and into the entry.

An elderly hobgoblin female welcomed her with a fist to her chest. "Princess, it's our honor to serve you'n. Nightly stay?"

Horra bent her head in a show of respect. The woman's nametag read "owner." "Thank you, yes. My knights are with me as well. How many rooms can I rent for the evening?"

"We're fairly booked, Majesty." The woman licked a knobby finger and flipped a page in her notebook. "I have the large suite available." Another flip of a page. "And two other rooms with two beds each. We also have a space above the stalls for a partial price if needed?"

"I'll take the three rooms and an extra bed for one of them." Though it would be fun to stick the captain out with the animals, it wouldn't do to heap further offense on him.

Horra paid for the rooms and headed up to refresh herself

before ordering a meal. Having not eaten breakfast, she was famished.

Her shoulders were tight when she sat down at a table in the Boarder's Hall only a few short minutes later. Her hair was slightly damp, but washing off the sweat coating her hide had at least been reviving.

Light music drifted from the pub side, where she could see her knights through the open doorway. That room was full, with nowhere to sit even if she'd wished it. She didn't. It was a relief not to have to sit with her men. She didn't want to make awkward small talk with them after the day she'd had.

Sparse furnishings filled the Boarder's Hall, though the quality of the tables and chairs was sound. No pictures or shelves lined the dark wood walls. There were lamps on the tables and candles placed on two large stag racks hanging from the ceiling, allowing plenty of light in the room. A menu card offered few options, mainly hobgoblin favorites since they were the Inn's main boarders.

"Well, if it isn't my favorite troll princess," a familiar voice said from the hallway to the entry, startling her. "Slumming it, are we?"

Horra glanced up to see Balk, her mercenary bocan friend. White paint glowed on one side of his freshly shaved head, and there appeared to be more marks on his arms. "Slumming it would entail an evening in a wagon outrunning mesmerized fairies." She grinned. "I see you're still alive. Who are your latest victims?"

Balk pressed a fist to his chest and bowed his head. "Only worqs, I'm afraid. I'm sure that's no surprise. May I join you? I'm starved from a long day's ride."

Horra held her claw out to an empty chair across from her. She wasn't surprised about the worqs. It did surprise her, however, that he survived searching for the Erlking after their last meeting. "Where have you come from?"

"Pine's Peak. I'd heard the Erlking had been making mischief there." He gestured for the busy maid. Theirs was the only clean table. The earlier crowd had already eaten and left the tables filled with dirty dishes.

The hobgoblin brought them goblets of clear water and took their orders. Horra ordered another water and stew for Torren, who was supposed to meet her after he finished cleaning up.

Horra gulped half her water and set it down before resuming the conversation. "And did you find him? The Erlking?"

Anger flashed across the mercenary bocan's face. "No. I keep missing him. I've chased him halfway across the Wilden Lands, but still can't catch him."

Empathy washed over her. Balk had been searching for the Erlking, thinking he was the one responsible for his daughter Floke's death. Or disappearance. Now that Horra had seen the children stolen by the Erlking's musical mesmerization spell, she wasn't so sure the girl was dead. Balk, for sure, believed her to be alive.

"Neither can I. Every time I think I have him in my claws, he slips away." Horra rubbed droplets of condensation off her goblet.

They both sat in heavy silence.

"Hey, Balk." Torren greeted him. They clapped each other's shoulders like old friends.

Though Balk had stayed at the castle for a short time after she'd returned from the Weald, she didn't know he and Torren had become so friendly. Chimes from outside the Inn clanged like two pie pans knocking together. The wind must be picking up. Horra hoped she'd be able to sleep through the racket.

A dark figure in the corner of Horra's eye caught her attention. But when she glanced over, there was nothing there. However, the hair on her hide rose. Something was amiss.

"Excuse me," she mumbled to her dinner companions. The stairs were in the same direction as the shadowy form she'd seen. She was on the steps before she drew another breath. At the top stood a dark, cloaked creature. "Princess Glory?" she called.

A bony hand protruded from the fabric, and a hazy ball of magic bloomed.

It wasn't the princess. It was the Erlking!

Before Horra could duck, the spell hit her and pain flared inside her body, stealing her breath. Her mouth opened, but no sound came out. She crumpled in on herself and fell.

CHAPTER 5

~Rowan~

Rowan stood beside a sneezewort plant in a corner of the Boarder's Hall dining room as the queen bearer and her knights sat down to dinner. Loose clusters of cheery white flowers atop dark-green stems with long, jagged leaves grew abundantly in the pot, brightening the sparse, mismatched furnished room. He sunk his roots into the soil and observed the lodgers of the Inn while blending into the wooden walls.

From his spot, he could see the front desk where the old hobgoblin owner checked guests in, the stairs leading to the bedrooms, and the tavern next to the dining area.

The maid trundled about, clearing tables and taking orders. Her skin had a gray pallor, and she had a terrible over-bite that gave her a speech impairment. However, he'd learned that hobgoblins, though small, were able-bodied even in their older years.

Sounds from the tavern filtered into the dining hall,

creating a humming din of voices and movements. It wasn't unlike the noise he used to hear nonstop in the Weald and was a great improvement over arguing trolls or the silence that remained in the space where roods had once been. Rowan closed his eyes, relishing the sounds.

Thunk.

His eyes snapped open.

Bang.

Oof.

The troll princess, in a blur of red hair, green Oddar uniform, and sparkling magic, tumbled down the stairway. A shadowy cloud snapped around her body where she now lay prone on the wooden floor.

Magic.

The sneezewort curled into itself, vying to escape the dark spell shooting through the atmosphere.

He unrooted and tried to make sense of what just happened. There'd been no warning of trouble. His roots had sensed nothing while resting inside the potted plant. How could this have happened?

When he reached his mind into the ether where the roods would communicate with him, he was met with only silence. Not a surprise. He moved closer to the princess to assess the situation.

After a stunned moment of silence, the hobgoblins raced around him in a frightened frenzy.

His stem tightened.

They were in danger. The Erlking was nearby.

~Horra~

Footsteps pounded across the wooden floor. Balk's face was the first Horra saw, followed quickly by Torren's. Her mouth remained open and her eyes wide as the lingering jabs of pain diminished. She couldn't breathe, however. Her claws darted to her throat.

Several of the boarders and their hobgoblin maid gathered around them, inquiring what happened.

Balk lifted her and slapped her back hard.

Once.

Twice.

A third smack and her lungs opened. Horra sucked in a glorious gulp of air. When her senses finally returned, she pointed toward the stairs. "The," she gasped, "Erlking."

Balk let her go and rushed up the stairs two at a time. He disappeared around the corner. Sounds of knocking and shuffling ensued as the disturbed lodgers emerged from their rooms.

By now, her knights had shuffled into the Boarder's Hall.

"What happened?" The captain eyed her dubiously.

"The Erlking attacked Queen Bearer Fyd on your watch." Rowan's voice startled Horra. He could be as silent as night when he wanted to be.

Erast's green face darkened, and he blustered out a breath. "And are you not under the same charge?"

Horra's head ached, as did all the spots on her body that had hit a step on the way down. She'd soon be covered in bruises, she knew. Their argument wasn't helping, nor was the ruckus coming from the rooming area one floor up.

Rowan steepled his stick-like fingers in front of him. "I am her charge. She is assigned to train me, not the other way around. I have to wonder who trained you. Why were you not eating in the same room where you could keep your future queen safe?" The gleam in his eyes hardened. "What will the king say once he hears about this?"

Torren helped Horra to her feet. It was rare to see Rowan so enraged on her behalf, and she wasn't sure what termite had bored into his crown. She shifted uneasily between the two males and lifted her claws in the air. "Enough. Captain, go check on our animals and make sure they're safe."

"And your personal guards?" the captain growled.

"Are not your concern. You have your assignment." Her tone was dismissive. In reality, she was more shaken by what had just occurred than defiant of the captain's ire. Though she'd known she was susceptible to some of the Erlking's magic, it put her on edge. As did all her injured spots, which throbbed to the beat of her heart.

After her knights departed, she turned to Torren. "Please go check on Balk."

He nodded and left. The maid tittered in a corner, probably frightened by her fall. "Please, some refreshments? And pack our food so we can eat in our rooms," she requested in a voice she used when Nimble was skittish. Hopefully, having something to do would ease the poor woman's nerves.

Horra took the coins from her pouch and laid them on the table. That seemed to break the woman's stupor. The hobgoblin snatched them up and hurried from the room with a bow.

Horra faced Rowan. "Were you in your room, or down here hiding when the Erlking came in?"

The woodgoblin wore an uncharacteristic frown. "In the corner by the potted plant, observing."

"And what did you sense about him?" She knew he would've noticed the caped figure before she did, especially if he'd had roots in the plant's soil.

Rowan clacked out a sigh. "That's just it, Queen Bearer. I

didn't sense him at all. You surprised me when you tumbled down the stairway. It was more startling when magic rushed across the room and disappeared."

Scuffling from the upper level quieted, and within moments, Torren and Balk came down the stairs. Neither of them looked happy.

"You missed him?" Horra asked, already knowing what their answer would be.

Balk rubbed a hand across his shaved head. "Are you sure it was the Erlking? Not some traveler?"

She tried not to take offense. The Erlking had a knack for disappearing at exactly the wrong moments. "Who else could hit a troll with magic that knocks them down a flight of stairs? We're supposed to be immune, remember?" Her eye twitched. That wasn't completely true, but she didn't want to parse the details of what did and didn't affect her at the moment.

Balk shook his head. He rubbed at the marks on his arms—a bocan's traditional record of their conquests—as though he longed to add another one for the Erlking.

"Here you are, Majesty." The hobgoblin maid produced two sacks, while another maid held out three mugs of differing contents.

Balk took the drinks, and Horra grabbed the food. With a murmured thanks, they all headed toward the stairs, Horra in the lead. She stomped up the steps as if to punish them for her assault.

Her room sat at the end of the hallway, as it was the largest quarters in the Inn. Balk hesitated when she headed that way. "Come along. I'd like to ask your advice on my current mission and what it means that the Erlking just showed up."

Balk couldn't turn back anyway. Rowan was a solid wall of a wood body behind him. At least Horra's wasn't the only personal space the woodgoblin druid violated. "Fine," Balk grumbled.

Her room was as sparsely decorated as the Boarder's Hall. The bed was bigger than the one she had at the castle, probably designed for a married traveling couple or a family of hobgoblins. Every inch was tidy, though, and smelled clean.

Horra set the sacks down on the round oak table accompanied by two mismatched chairs. She took her beet juice and handed Rowan the water. Balk grabbed his ale, sat on the bigger chair, and shuffled through the bags to find his order.

Her snail chowder steamed when she removed the sealed lid. A hobgoblin favorite, it wasn't Horra's preferred dish. It was, however, the best of the Inn's limited options. Luckily, the cook had seasoned it well with bitter root and garlic to overcome the earthy snail flavor.

"What advice did you need?" Balk asked around a mouthful of black bread dipped in stew gravy.

What kind of stew it was, Horra couldn't tell. She did note, however, that they'd seen no rats anywhere as they'd traveled through town. The bocan's history proved he would gladly eat any vermin. She took a deep drink of the beet juice to ease her gag reflex.

Horra finished her food and set the crock down. She filled Balk in on what happened after Glory escaped the castle.

Balk stopped with the spoon halfway to his mouth. Horra concentrated on his dark eyes instead of the stew's contents. "And you want to locate the first princess and bring her back, all before it becomes an inter-kingdom event?"

"Precisely. I don't know the first place to look for her. We came here because it's the closest large village, and I know she's looking for the Erlking. Logic says she'd head this way. Now that he's been here, I'm even more anxious to find the princess."

"I heard the queen is missing as well?" Balk finished his stew and set his crock aside. "Why would this fairy princess run away from your castle? Wasn't she almost comatose the last time I saw her?"

Horra frowned. "As far as I know, the queen is still missing." She didn't admit she knew the queen had gone looking for the evil elf right after she'd seen him last. "And the princess is no longer passively accepting her fate. She's desperate to reverse the effects of the hex."

Balk's eyes widened. "And she thinks he's just going to oblige her formal request? Maybe add some glitter to his reversal spell for good measure? Doesn't she know how dangerous he is?"

"I've told her more than once. She mentioned possessing something he wants badly." Horra shrugged.

He grunted and frowned. "And what would that be?"

"The princess has a personal item of the Erlking's," Rowan said, making them both jump. Horra had almost forgotten the woodgoblin was in the room with them.

"What?" Horra twisted to face Rowan. "Why didn't you tell me before?"

"You didn't ask."

Horra's claws itched to shake him. "I asked if you knew where she went. That's a clear invitation to offer me any information you might have."

The bark on Rowan's face shifted, curving into a thoughtful expression. It was the first time she'd seen any real emotion flutter across his face. "Duly noted for the future."

Horra dug into her hair and squeezed, which reduced her urge to choke the druid woodgoblin. "Do you know anything else about the princess you haven't told me? Like what item belonging to the Erlking she possesses?"

Rowan stared off into the distance. "Master Knurl

mentioned a notebook. However, he said she only took one page from it with her. He believes it to be the Erlking's since it has an elven aura. I'm unsure what it holds, though the rood thinks it's important."

Fatigue weighed on Horra's shoulders. "Probably holds his magic spells."

Balk leaned back in his chair, the wood creaking with his weight. "She'd be able to reverse the spell herself if it does."

"What could it be, then?"

A thoughtful expression crossed the bocan's face. "It must be something like a diary. Floke had one. She let no one read it, saying it was too personal. She wrote her deepest thoughts in it. Mostly about boys." Wistfulness deepened the creases in his forehead. "It was missing when I returned home."

Horra sobered. "Whatever it is, we need to find it. It might hold the secret of how we can defeat the Erlking."

CHAPTER 6

Again, Balk didn't seem convinced. "No one in their right mind would keep a running list of ways to destroy their own self."

Horra blew out a long breath. "You're right, but what could be so important, then?"

"It holds dark magic. Possibly, it's spelled so anyone else who comes across it can't read it or understand anything written on it." Rowan steepled his fingers in a move so like Woodsly, it gave Horra a twinge.

A knock on her door interrupted them. "It's Torren. Can I come in?"

"Yes." Horra stood to face him as he entered.

Torren stalked in, his back hunched. "He got away. We're not sure which way he went. It's like he was never here, though one hobgoblin lodger witnessed the figure lob a hex at you."

"That's the one who couldn't recall where the Erlking went after that, isn't it?" Balk pushed his crock into the center of the table next to a kerosene lamp and a vase holding decorative sticks. He pounded a fist on the wood, knocking the vase over. "Why is he so elusive?"

They all remained silent for several moments.

Horra was the first to speak. "What about the captain and the other knights?"

Torren stiffened his back like one of Oddar's knights. "I have them retracing our steps through Bough Valley to see if anyone noticed a hooded person traveling through. I'd like to see if he followed us or if it was just a coincidence. They'll report to me when they return," her former classmate said.

She nodded. "Good thinking."

Balk scraped a hand across his face, the stubble scritscratching as he did it. "Before we ate, you wanted to ask my advice on something? What do you have for trade?" He glanced at her pack, possibly remembering their first trade—her priceless jeweled dagger. His eyes gleamed, though dark circles enveloped them like bruises.

"Queen Bearer," Rowan interrupted. "I wouldn't advise you to bargain with a bocan."

Horra ignored Rowan's caution and snorted. "As if I'd trade that away again." She didn't mention that she had it in her pack. Horra sat back down calmly and faced Balk. "I believe you owe me a favor for directing you toward the Erlking last time we met. You help me, and I'll call it even."

The bocan sucked on his teeth, then frowned. He knew she had him, and bocans hated to be on the wrong end of a deal. "Depends how big an ask you need."

"Just advice. Where do you think the princess went? Where would she start her search for the Erlking?"

A smile tugged at the corners of his shadowed face. "I figured it would be harder than this. Are you getting soft, Princess Fyd?"

Horra held his amused gaze. "Queen Bearer Fyd, as Rowan stated." She nodded to the woodgoblin, who awkwardly watched their exchange. "And no. I've told you how important this is to my kingdom. Look. I don't know where to start and hoped you'd have some insight that might help." She didn't want to admit that her knights were reluctant to follow her. If she couldn't figure out where to go, she'd lose their respect completely.

Balk straightened his tunic, and dirt crumbled to the floor. "What knowledge has she on the elf?"

"She must know more than I realize if she has a notebook of importance. Maybe she took it from him when he captured her? She wouldn't have told me. I know she's aware of our run-in with him in the lower Iron Mountains because of the children we rescued. I planned on returning there if I couldn't figure anything else out."

Balk nodded. "He wasn't there, last I knew. You could try where he came from."

Horra jerked back and glanced at an unhappy Torren. "The Riven? You think she'd start there?"

"It's where I started. I couldn't get in, but it was my first point of contact when I realized I was up against an elf in my search for Floke. That's my advice. Take it or leave it, but we're even, yes?" He held out his hand in an unofficial acceptance of their deal.

Horra eyed his calloused hand and grasped it with her claw. A nod and a tight squeeze later and they were even again, though no magic sealed their deal.

Balk stood and stretched. "Good luck on your mission, Princess, er, Queen Bearer. I hope you find your runaway fairy in time to prevent any unpleasantness between your kingdoms. It would do no one any good if that came to pass." He saluted her. In three long strides, he reached the hallway and was gone.

"Except the Erlking." Horra sighed, suddenly more tired than before.

THE NEXT MORNING, Torren launched into his dozenth argument against heading to the Riven. "I don't care if that mercenary thinks it's the best place to start. It got him nowhere."

When Rowan cleared his throat, Torren lowered his voice. However, Horra was too tired and achy from her fall to listen to him. His voice became part of the buzz of boarder's conversations around them.

Horra choked down the last of her morning gruel devoid of any bacon grease, which had made her grumpy even before Torren joined her. The rest of the knights perched at different spots around the dining room, alert to any disturbance while they unhappily shoveled plain gruel into their mouths.

Horra leaned over the breakfast dishes, her mind on some dreams she'd had the previous night. In them, she'd found Princess Glory, but like in most dreams, which were actually nightmares, she couldn't reach her. Rats featured prominently in them to thwart Horra's ability to retrieve the princess. As time wore on, the images faded. She'd gone to bed pondering how the Erlking always escaped. Was her mind working out the puzzle? Or was she slowly going crazy?

After another bite, Horra missed Sageel's bracken bread slathered with bacon grease and their sour spruce juice. Stupid fairy princesses. She'd be home in the castle eating that very thing if it weren't for Princess Glory's untimely vanishing act.

A small dark flash along the baseboards startled Horra.

Gone in an instant, the thing darted around a corner and headed toward the hallway leading to the kitchen.

A rat? Her dreams the previous night put her on alert. She rose to her feet and turned toward the back of the room, signaling to Captain Erast.

"Yes, Queen Bearer Fyd?" Her lead knight approached her table and stood at attention. He'd been a bit more respectful since Rowan's dressing down the day before. She could tell it still grated on his nerves, though, as his face reflected what he didn't dare say aloud.

"Ask the proprietor if they've had any problems with vermin. Rats especially." She flicked her eyes across the room, searching for another critter.

Captain Erast hesitated.

Horra held back a sigh. "Do you have a problem with that request, Captain?" She needed to lose some of her opposition, and giving the captain something to do would ease her load.

Chimes outside the Inn erupted. Noise from the Inn's entry door opening and closing echoed in the room.

The look on the captain's face cleared. "None, Queen Bearer Fyd. At your service, Your Majesty." He turned and strode purposefully toward the front desk where he could request an audience with the Inn's owners.

Horra sat back down, glad the captain hadn't pushed her any further.

"What is it?" Torren inquired in a low voice, his food gone despite his unending list of objections about traveling to the Riven. Rowan, who stood along the wall near the potted plant, also turned his branchy head toward her.

"Just a hunch." She worked to finish her food. It had cooled and turned pasty. It stuck in her throat, and she drank all her water to force it down.

The maids came and cleared the dishes away, and still

Horra waited. After several minutes, she frowned. "The captain should be back by now."

"I'll go see what's taking him so long." Torren's chair squealed as he rose and left the Boarder's Hall.

Rowan approached her table. "What distresses you, Queen Bearer?"

"It's going to sound silly." She glanced around again. Her knights sat, awaiting her instructions. Most of the others, having had their fill of breakfast, trickled out.

"Please, go on." Rowan's face held no emotion. Not a crease of his bark was out of place.

Horra was glad the woodgoblin didn't have a sense of humor so he wouldn't laugh at her. "I saw a rat run by and into the kitchen hallway." She ground her tusks against her upper lip. "I had bad dreams last night about saving the fairy princess. There were rats everywhere, stopping me from getting to her. I'm not sure what it means, but it feels important."

"We encountered rats after leaving the Weald." Rowan's gaze drifted past her head.

"Yes, and I saw them after the fairies came to the castle and before Woodsly reverted to his seed." She waved a meaningful hand at him.

"I see."

Horra ducked her head. She could tell he didn't understand. How could he? She didn't understand what any of it meant. "I told you, silly."

"I find no humor in it, so it isn't silly." His forthright declaration helped to bolster her. "However, I fail to understand the connection."

"Horra?" Torren's voice entered the room before he did. "The captain has disappeared."

Several diners gazed back and forth between Torren and Horra.

Horra's stomach plunged to her boots. "What do you mean disappeared?"

"He's gone. He didn't stop by the front desk to ask questions. The owner said he walked straight out the door without a word."

The three other knights crowded around them, asking questions at the same time. A couple hobgoblins stood and left their full plates behind, shooting them angry glances.

Horra held out a claw. "Stop! All of you, go out and search for him. See if his horse is gone." She waited for Torren and the two knights to leave before digging into her pack and taking out her mother's dagger. Next, she unpacked her cloak and put it on. "Stay close to me and hidden," she muttered to Rowan. "Let's search the kitchen."

CHAPTER 7

~Horra~

Seconds later, Horra and Rowan entered the kitchen. Three hobgoblins bustled around the small space, cutting, stirring, and cooking. Steam curled out of a black pot, and the scent of gruel filled the air. A rat's tail dangled from a full trash bin. Horra had been correct about Balk's stew. She gulped to keep her breakfast from rushing up her throat.

She glanced around the room, her hood obscuring some of her vision. She moved slowly, keeping close to the outer wall, knowing Rowan was a step behind her.

One of the hobgoblins startled and glanced their way. Horra stopped and held her breath. She knew the cloak disguised her completely and that Rowan could camouflage himself as a druid, but it was a habit. The other cook yelled at the first one, and their attention shifted back to their work.

Horra continued to move through the kitchen, which was U-shaped with preparation tables in the open center, big enough for hobgoblins to walk around them. She shimmied past the last table where a pile of diced onions and horseradish had been left. The spice of the horseradish caught in her throat. She gagged to keep herself from coughing and hustled the last few feet to a shelf blocking the back entrance.

Once outside the door, she choked out a cough.

Rowan stood right behind her. "Are you all right?"

She swiped the tears from her cheeks. "Didn't you smell the horseradish?"

He held a twig finger up at her. "As I've told you before, I am incapable of smelling or tasting."

Another cough and her hood fell from her head. "Right. Well, I saw nothing except for the rat's tail in the trash. Did you see anything unusual?"

"I'm unsure what you classify as unusual. However, I saw nothing of concern."

Horra jammed her fists against her hips. "Let's go to the stables and see if we can catch Torren and the knights."

The sun shone down on them as they made their way around the overgrown garden to the stables. Since it was warm and there wasn't any wind, Horra removed her cloak. Light reflected off of the metal rods that made up the chimes at the end of the Inn's front porch. Horra stopped, staring at them.

Rowan stood next to her, close enough for his moss to caress her hide. "What is it?"

"There's no wind. It's deadly still."

He twisted his head around. "Yes, you're correct."

"But I heard the chimes earlier." Her mind flew back to the night before. There'd been little wind then as well, but she'd also heard the chimes before falling down the stairs. "And last evening, I heard them before I saw the Erlking. What could it mean?"

Rowan remained silent for a minute. "Master Knurl

mentioned the resonance of the castle changing after Princess Glory left. I thought the word odd for him to use, but I didn't question it. Doesn't resonance also mean vibration?" He glanced down at Horra.

"It can, yes."

They both turned to study the other chimes lining the covered porch, each fitted with different-sized pipes or strings with glass beads attached. One had a rainbow arc of bells.

"The ones I heard both times were pipes," Horra said. "The sound wasn't tinkly like it was when the mesmerized fairies first came to the castle. It was a deeper sound, but not too deep."

"Bigger pipes like this one?" He reached up and plucked the chime from its hook. It clattered, the sound reverberating.

She shook her head. "No. Smaller, maybe?"

Rowan replaced the chimes, and they walked around and up the front stairs. The chime nearest the door was smaller than the one the druid had held before. He unhooked it and ran a finger across the metal pipes. It was less clattery and more musical. "Yes, this sounds right." Horra took them from him and opened the Inn's front door.

Inside, the owner sat behind the desk. The hobgoblin looked up when the chimes Horra held made a noise. Her face pursed. "Those aren't for sale. Please return them."

Horra held them still so the owner could hear her question. "I will, but I wanted to know if you remember hearing them this morning?"

The owner glanced out a window next to the front entry. "There's no wind today."

Frustration gnawed at her gut. "I know." Rowan placed a hand on her arm, keeping her from continuing.

"What Queen Bearer Fyd is wondering is if someone came

in or out and possibly disturbed the chimes? Have you had any new boarders this morning, by chance?"

Horra sent him a grateful glance.

The hobgoblin eyed them both as if they were mad. "No. But now that you'n mention it, I may have heard them once. Probably when the troll captain went outside. Gave me the stink eye, that one. Slammed the door'n all."

Captain Erast hadn't been in that big of a snit, had he? Horra didn't recall him stomping out or grumbling. "Do you use these for security?" she asked, hoping to get a solid answer.

"Yes, especially after the Erlking," the hobgoblin owner said. She fidgeted in her chair, and her skin turned a paler gray.

Rowan's grip tightened. "Thank you for your time. We'll return these to your door."

Horra glowered but turned to follow him back through the doorway. "Why didn't you ask her more questions?"

He placed the chimes back on the hook and stilled them. The sound echoed long after he did. "I didn't recognize when the Erlking came the first time. I don't recall hearing these this morning, either. Something is muting the chimes' ability to warn the hobgoblins. I believe the only reason you heard them was because of who you are."

"What's that supposed to mean?"

"You are the only one who has effectively fought off the Erlking's musical thrall. Even in the caves, the music didn't seem to influence you. You are unaffected by his music magic."

"But he knocked me down a flight of stairs. I wouldn't say I'm immune to his magic."

"He is an elf. Therefore, he is powerful. But you and Murda are the only two creatures I've witnessed who have been able to resist the music."

Horra sat down on the steps leading into the Inn. "Not completely."

Rowan moved down the stairs to the ground, his roots digging into the soil. Sunlight gleamed on the green moss covering his bark. "How so?"

"After the fairies came and before I escaped the castle, I faced off with the Erlking in the kitchen." She frowned, remembering the pull of his music. "He had his pan flute on him and the music held me like I was moving through cold molasses. I couldn't move. If it weren't for Sageel hitting him with a pan, I wouldn't have escaped."

Rowan studied her face. Did he think she was lying? "What about the other times when you heard the music? Did it have the same effect?"

Horra thought back to each time she'd heard the music before and what happened. "No, just the one time, and he was there in person. It wasn't one of his flunky worqs sent to capture me."

He scratched his chin, his stick fingers rubbing against his soft green beard. "I've thought about the moment I became enthralled. I recall a single, beautiful tone that drew me out of the shelter of the mountain. It made my sap sing and my leaves tingle. Then I saw a noble, rare tree. It glowed like an ethereal ghost, beckoning me into the open. That's when the music changed. When my mind engaged in a hallucinatory vision."

Rowan continued. "When I spoke to Torren about his experience, it was different, but it started much the same way. He heard a song that he loved as a child, a tune so lovely it drew him. He said the experience afterward was like dreaming. My experience was similar. Vague and blurry. But that's not what happened to you."

The woodgoblin's last words whirled around her mind. "No, you're right. Nothing about the music calls to me. It's all rackety noise. And I didn't go into a vision state. I was lucid despite his music seizing control of my movements."

Rowan's hand was gentle on her shoulder. "And the magic that struck you yesterday should've done more than just knock you down the stairs. I sensed the strength in the spell. It could have deeply wounded any other creature, yet you ended up only bruised and winded."

She frowned. It hadn't felt like her troll immunity had saved her from the magic's power. She shuddered to think how much worse it could've been. "I hadn't considered that."

"You are stronger than you think, Queen Bearer. You are a formidable opponent for the Erlking."

When he removed his hand from her shoulder, the spot grew cold. Like her former instructor, Rowan understood how best to encourage her in the moments she needed it the most.

Torren strode up to them. "We can't locate Captain Erast anywhere. What are your orders?"

Horra's confidence popped like a bubble. She imagined what her father would think about losing Oddar's highest-ranking knight soldier under her watch. It wouldn't matter that the old troll had been surly toward her. The weight of her father's expectations bore down on her. "Gather the others and saddle up. We have more than one person to locate."

CHAPTER 8

A few hours after Glory escaped the castle, she stopped walking and bent over to ease a pain in her back. Pale pink bloomed across the morning sky. Her body already ached. As a regal fairy, she wasn't used to menial labor or walking.

She cursed the length of Oddar's borders. Though her Shining Kingdom was every bit as large as the troll kingdom, it wasn't nearly as wild with large ravines that forced her to travel a long way to get around them. Glory needed to pass Oddar's border so the Erlking's numerous rodent spies couldn't detect her.

She cringed at the thought of the vermin. Between their beady eyes and their squeaking voices, they were the most detestable animals in the Wilden Lands. And the last one she'd seen when she escaped the troll's castle had been the size of a trit-trot horse which came up to her mid-thigh.

Eyes on the bushes and brush, she glanced around but

couldn't tell if she'd gone far enough. She stomped her foot. "Without my magic, I can't tell where I am." Tears burned the backs of her eyes, not for the first time since the dark-magic hex had stolen what she loved more than life itself—her beauty.

With a heavy heart, she moved on. She meandered through a bent-tree forest where bottleleaf sprites lived in seed pods hanging from bowed branches. Smaller than a dragon's egg, the homes were tea-leaf brown and blended into the tree's bark.

Curious but mischievous creatures, one flew by laughing and tugged on her coat. "Hey!" she yelled, her hood falling off her head.

The leafy creature screamed and darted away, its wings whirring.

Anger burst in Glory's chest. At one time, the same creature would've stood transfixed by her loveliness. She would've at least expected the flittering sprite to dance around her. But this time it flew off, squawking in horror at the sight of her. "That's what you get for bugging me, you stupid creature," she screamed back.

Pods buzzed like a kicked hornet's nest.

Fearing retribution from hundreds of angry sprites, Glory hurried through the forest toward the road she'd previously avoided. Sprites, she knew, wouldn't breach their tree border to chase her. Out in the open, they were targets for owls. She yanked her hood back in place and clutched it tight for good measure.

Morning turned to afternoon. On and on she traveled. The dew on her hem dried, and soon sweat dampened her collar. "What I wouldn't give to create a fairy path." She found a large leaf and fanned herself. A shadow dashed by in the distance.

She hustled away again, fearing it to be a spy. Her feet burned with every step.

The purple sky faded to indigo as she neared a mounded dwarf village. Though her hand holding the hood cramped, she needed to keep her face hidden from anyone who might catch sight of her.

Outside the village, she spied a tree trunk lying next to a tall tree. The fallen tree lay rotten amid dried grasses waving in the breeze. Its stump sat an arm's length away from its base. Avoiding the spot where the tree had ripped from its roots, she flopped onto the trunk and rubbed her throbbing feet. Her shoulders ached. Each step sent a twinge of pain through her hips. "I can't go any farther."

The trolls would realize she was missing by now. Were they searching for her? Or did they write her off, as she had done to her mother and sister? It didn't matter. Her head start would help her stay ahead of them. Besides, they didn't know where she was headed. They might think she left to go home. She scoffed at that idea as she dug one of her treasures out.

The golden bridle gleamed in the sunlight. She was too tired to wait until she was beyond the troll's borders to call upon her secret weapon. With the leather straps held to her chest, she called, "Come, Calliope."

The gold on the metal flashed. Glory waited, unsure where the creature had gone since she freed it after stealing the bridle. The wind, which had been light all day and not strong enough to wick away her sweat, picked up and whipped her shoddy cloak about. Exhaustion weighed her body down. She could barely keep her eyelids open. Giving up, she closed her eyes for a moment to rest.

The next thing Glory knew, she leaned against the second tree. Something nudged her, and nickering woke her with a start. "You made it." She rubbed her hand across the horse's muzzle. Her hood had fallen away from her head in sleep, but the kelpie wasn't afraid of her. Fearsome itself, it didn't spook easily. Besides, it was the Erlking's pet, and he was gruesome to behold. "Thank you for coming."

Calliope snorted in reply, and Glory laughed. With a last glance around the wooded area, she stood. "Let's go find your former owner and get this deal over with."

<hr>

~Horra~

MINUTES AFTER TORREN announced he couldn't locate Captain Erast, Horra, Torren, and Rowan gathered beside the Inn's small stables. Pidge, bound by a rope and collar, danced around the corral. "I'm sorry, girl. I don't have a snack for you today."

Rowan pulled a wiggly worm from a pocket that Horra had never seen him use before. "I found this while we were searching earlier," he explained.

Horra studied him. The woodgoblin was becoming a man of surprises. "You have anything else in that pocket?"

Rowan scratched Pidge's chin. "No."

Nimble poked his nose at her nape and snorted into her hair. It was the first time in all the trips they'd taken away from the castle that he'd done so. She'd read in her library's *Extinct and Rare Species* book that some creatures snuffle their owners in greeting, leaving their scent behind as a type of warning to other creatures. It seemed more sophisticated in the pages of the book than in practice, though. "Ew. Did he leave snot behind?"

Torren snickered. "No, but you might want to shake your hair out before putting your hood back on."

Her other knights waited by their horses, stone-faced and ready to go. They did not appear amused by her gulgoyle's actions.

Her claw snagged in her long curls. "It's a sign of bonding," she said, then inwardly cringed. She didn't have to answer to her knights, even if their captain had just gone missing. And explaining might appear weak to them. "You three ride through Bough Valley and search for Captain Erast and the princess. We'll take the outskirts. Meet back here at nightfall." She hoped that would be enough time to find something. Even a small clue would be a victory at this point.

Horra waited for the knights to ride off before unhitching Nimble, climbing on, and joining Torren and Rowan who waited on their rides.

"Is it smart to allow your soldiers to wander off without you, Queen Bearer?" Rowan asked stiffly.

She jutted out her chin. "Having them around didn't stop the Erlking from creeping under our noses." With a snap of her leather reins, she guided Nimble onto the road leading north-west past the Inn. The path took them toward the Sterling River, which they'd tried to ride around when her father blocked off Hobgoblin Pass not so long ago. Horra's thoughts turned to Queen Toppenbottom. Was she safe? She could only speculate, but seeing the Erlking driving the grand fairy's carriage not so long ago had made Horra fear for the woman's life.

Sunlight dappled through overbearing trees on both sides of the dirt road. Their path widened as soon as they left the village's border. The only traffic they passed was a hobgoblin peddler wagon. Metal wares clinked from the inside and along the outside of the wooden box reminded Horra of getting captured when on the run with Rowan's seed. The peddler, somehow magicked by the Erlking, had taken her back to her castle where the Erlking and a mesmerized Queen Toppen-bottom awaited her.

She shivered at the memory and braced herself, shaking it off.

Pidge side-eyed the wagon as it rumbled by, possibly recalling the same event.

After traveling for a short while, Horra pulled on Nimble's reins. "Spread out through the woods and stay close enough to the road that you don't get lost. We'll meet back at the Inn."

Rowan raised a finger and opened his mouth to say something.

She interrupted him before he started. "I know it's not ideal, but we need to cover more ground in a short period."

The bark on his face puckered. "Then I shall travel on the same side as you."

Horra wasn't sure how that would be helpful. Though he now resembled a small oak tree size-wise, he was anything but savvy when it came to defense and violence.

"I'll take the right side." Torren spoke over his shoulder as he led his Stempner into the trees.

She glared at his back.

"You first." Rowan waved his branch-arm, allowing her entry on the other side of the road.

Vinegar and beans! Horra hesitated only a moment before giving in. She steered Nimble into the biggest hole between trees. The gulgoyle's footsteps crunched on the winter-dead grasses and brambles.

Rowan ducked beneath limbs as Pidge fluttered across a small ditch and into the forest. He sat awkwardly on the pudge wudgie, though the bird didn't seem to mind a large log riding atop her back. Soon, they would have to find another animal to fit the woodgoblin.

A flicker at the edge of Horra's eye had her yanking Nimble to a stop. Pidge halted too, landing on the grass next to her.

"Did you see that?" she asked, barely loud enough for Rowan to hear.

Pidge fluffed her feathers.

Rowan stood a few inches above Pidge's back, something that would've made her laugh at any other time. "I saw nothing, but I sense a dark presence."

Chills crawled across her hide. Nimble perked his ears and bellowed a hot breath. Smoke curled out from his mouth and disappeared into the air.

Horra waited.

A critter darted, scattering dead leaves.

Pidge screeched, but Rowan held her back from chasing after it by digging his roots into the ground.

Crunch. The sound came from the area the critter had scurried from.

Horra jerked her head around, searching for the source.

More crunching echoed through the forest. She twisted, confused about the direction of the noise, as nothing in her view moved and it seemed to be coming from more than one place.

In a blur, a midnight-black horse rushed through the maze of trees, disappearing before Horra was sure she actually saw it.

"It's Princess Glory on a kelpie," Rowan said.

Horra didn't have time to consider why the princess rode one of the most feared animals in the Wilden Lands. She bucked Nimble and took off after her.

CHAPTER 9

Frustration gnawed at Glory upon spying the troll princess and her woodgoblin companion. Why did she have to run into the one person she was trying to avoid? She clutched the leather straps, hoping not to fall off as Calliope raced deeper into the woods surrounding Bough Valley.

Earlier, she had asked the kelpie to hunt down her former owner's scent. Considering the direction she went, Glory thought they were headed to Hobgoblin Pass. The kelpie had turned last minute, though, and rushed past the hobgoblin village, bringing them to this forest instead.

She leaned over the black horse and whispered, "I can't get caught, Calliope. But don't go too far out of the way. I need to find the Erlking."

Calliope whinnied.

The Erlking's pet wasn't unlike the sea kelpies she'd grown

up with on the Shining Coast. Elves had trained this one in their hidden realm of Endwylde, giving it a deadlier temperament than her kingdom's milder-mannered changelings, which she had ridden in the waves instead of across forests. Both species were ten times faster and more powerful than any other creature, except for a full-blooded dragon.

She snickered. The Erlking thought he was so clever using song magic on her, a musical savant. Her instructor, Maestro Lyrie, used to quip that if one were to cut Glory open, an aria would spill out. Yes, the notes had drawn her to him, as had his rugged dark-fairy disguise. He hadn't fully enthralled her at first, which was how she stole so many objects from him without his knowledge. Tricking a trickster was an amazing feeling.

Until he'd turned the tables on her and found the right cadence to capture her mind. Glory frowned. He'd done it to her again after she escaped her mother's side when they left the troll castle. It was only after the trolls had covered her in the disgusting mire that she realized her mistake. If the music didn't reach her ears, he couldn't capture her. The sea-sponges inside her canals itched, but she was glad for them. They'd absorb anything the Erlking played.

Beady eyes flashed as they raced on. Glory shivered. If the Erlking had been anywhere near here—and Calliope would know if he was thanks to their former magical bond—he might have left some of his rodent spies. They'd spot her for sure. Probably already had.

She was ready. Her hand snaked to her pocket where she'd tucked his spell. It wouldn't be long now.

Something jumped out of a tree at the kelpie. Calliope balked. She rose on her front legs before a monstrous-looking creature, knocking her and the kelpie sideways. With orange-and-red fluffy hair, the creature resembled a giant but wasn't gigantic. The creature shrieked as they flew sideways and landed hard on the ground.

Glory scrambled to grab hold of the leafy mane to stay on the animal's back as Calliope dropped then stumbled back to a run. Heavy magic thickened the atmosphere with a familiar musk. She breathed it in.

He was close.

The kelpie abruptly stopped, lifted in the air, and zipped backward. Glory sailed over the top of her changeling horse. The orange creature swung the kelpie by its tail.

She landed squarely on her back. Her chest seized, and she struggled to breathe for a tense moment. The fleeting incident left her panting.

What in the Wilden Lands could catch a kelpie and swing it around?

The face that came into view was shocking. Tusks like the trolls, a snout like a hoar hound, and claws like a badger. Add the thick coating of fur covering the skin, and this creature wasn't like anything she'd ever seen. Standing taller than a worq, they were a cross between a yeti, a bear, and a giant. Glory was at a loss for words when suddenly the beastly creature screwed up their face and confronted her.

"Get out of my forest," they screamed. It was possibly a girl, but the voice was snarly and gruff.

Their forest? Glory stared wide-eyed at the creature. "What are you?"

A high-pitched squeal leaked out of sharp teeth. "I'm just a girl." Tears wavered in her brown eyes.

"Are you sure?" Glory asked. "You don't resemble any creature I know about."

The monstrous girl growled like a rabid animal. "Leave. Now."

Glory was unfamiliar with the forests edging the troll kingdom. One thing she was sure of, however, was that giants, no matter how furry or hideous, didn't belong anywhere near here. Their kingdom was farther north. Had the Erlking let a plague loose in the giant lands, creating a strange hybrid race?

Fury twisted the monster-person's face. "Argh!" she screamed, stomping into the trees and out of sight. Footfalls thundered, the sound scattering critters and birds everywhere until the forest fell silent once more. No birds chirped. Nothing moved.

Glory stared after the girl, ignoring the aches in her bruised body. Calliope stood close, her flesh quivering.

"Scared you too, huh?" Glory rolled over to stand.

"Glory?" the troll princess called from afar, too close for comfort.

Glory groaned. "Not again." No way would she allow the trolls to capture her and take her back to their dingy castle. Not when she was so close to finding the Erlking and getting her beauty back.

She grabbed the leather straps buried in the horse's thick, leafy mane and swung herself awkwardly onto her back. "Get me out of here," she told the kelpie.

With a snicker and a neigh, Calliope took off.

~Horra~

NIMBLE BOUNDED through the forest as Horra held on tight. They chased after the fairy princess. She screamed out Glory's name, hoping to stop the girl. How did a fairy get hold of a kelpie? Though she'd heard of them, she'd never seen one in person before. The kelpie was massive, bigger than the Stempner.

An enormous shadow darted through the trees ahead.

Horra squinted.

A flash of orange and red in the dappled light sent shivers down her hide.

What's a giant doing in this forest?

"Whoa!" She yanked hard on the gulgoyle's reins. Nimble danced sideways then slowed. He blew gusts from his nose.

"Grendel, is that you?" Horra yelled.

"Go away," came a wailing cry from the depths of the forest.

She was torn. Recalling how Grendel's parents had asked Horra for help in locating their daughter and then finding the scared children the Erlking imprisoned in that mountain gave her pause. Horra's conscience pricked.

Giants frightened her. But she couldn't leave a child, even a giant one, out in the open with the Erlking on the loose. "Dragon's fire. This way, Nimble." She flicked the strap left and they moved toward the area where the girl had disappeared.

Pidge's screech alerted her to Rowan's presence.

Horra glanced up to see the woodgoblin's rooty feet hanging from the pudge wudgie's sides. She wasn't sure how either of them were comfortable. "See if you can find a giant girl. We may need to help her."

She didn't hear Rowan's response, because Pidge darted ahead and to the left.

Cries broke out, and loud thumps echoed.

Horra urged the gulgoyle faster.

There, inside a break in the trees, Grendel stood surrounded by worqs. Six of them. She held out a tree in a menacing fashion, which should've convinced the bullies to leave her alone. But worqs were determined creatures.

Pidge scree'd above them, circling while a frowning Rowan

gazed down on the group. "Get your arrows, Rowan. Save the girl."

Horra reached for her bow. She nocked the first arrow and let it sail, but the worqs chased after the girl, who swung the massive log around blindly. Tinkling music followed in their wake.

The Erlking.

For a moment, Horra wished she would've broken all the instruments she'd found in that mountain room where she'd rescued the children. Maybe if she had, there'd be no more music to enchant anyone.

One of the worqs caught the tree Grendel wielded, turning the fight into a game of tug-of-war.

Horra pulled out another arrow and aimed, praying she didn't hit the girl.

It sailed true, hitting the worq in his chest.

He bellowed and let Grendel go. The tree fell to the ground as the giant girl panted with a lost and scared look on her furry orange face. She was obviously not used to anyone being stronger than she was.

Five worqs turned toward Horra, the sixth yanking the arrow from his body.

Pidge dipped down and Rowan jumped off. He landed behind the injured worq. Planting himself, he spread his arms wide. Roots blasted through the dirt and circled the worq's chest and arms. In the blink of an eye, the druid had him subdued.

The others were coming for Horra, however. She turned Nimble right, and they hooked a path around a large elm tree. Branches behind her broke as the group followed. Low limbs tangled in her hair, so she jerked her hood back over her head.

Together, she and Nimble dodged trees and ran in circles to evade the worqs. She glanced over her shoulder to see what

Rowan was doing and saw him wrapping another of the creatures in woody roots.

She continued her errant race, keeping to a tight enough circle so the worqs would follow her. Rowan picked them off one by one until only one remained. Horra spun Nimble around to face the brute, aiming her final arrow at him.

It flew through the air and hit the worq low in the knee. Though short of her goal, it did stop him.

Rowan walked over to him and dug his legs into the ground again. Dirt flew as more roots busted through the dirt and dried leaves, wrapping around the worq.

Horra steered Nimble to stand by Rowan's side. Once the gulgoyle stopped, she slid off. "Wow, Rowan. I didn't know you had that trick up your wooden sleeve."

He glanced down at her, his bark unmoving and his moss fluttering in the wind. "Nor did I, Queen Bearer."

The worqs grunted and made other noises as they struggled to break free from their root prison.

"Thank you. I'm not sure I could've fought them off much longer." She patted Nimble, who was panting as smoke curled from his nostrils. The space between the gulgoyle's scales glowed. "Good boy," she crooned. "But now what do we do with them?"

Rowan whistled, and Pidge fluttered down next to him. He looked the bird in the eyes and let out a series of clicking noises.

The wudgie warbled and darted for the first worq.

"What did you do?" Horra watched her pet circle the worqs like a predator.

"I told her to find the grubbies." He turned toward her, his moss parting into a smile. "It's one of the ways I've exercised her. Hiding her treats so she has to find them."

Horra's mouth hung open. "That's genius."

"I know."

Pidge yanked at the first worq's neck, detaching a fat grubby worm from the creature.

The others, having seen what the bird was doing to their companion, started yelling in worqen.

Rowan glanced around. "What about the giant?"

"Oh no." Horra had forgotten while running from the worqs. "Grendel?" she yelled as she raced back through the forest to find the girl. The trees were tall and wide enough to see through, and the midday sun dappled the area with plenty of light. She should be easy to find.

After several minutes of searching, Horra stopped. The girl obviously didn't want to be found. And she had other priorities other than a lost giant child.

All the worqs were de-grubbied by the time she returned to Rowan's and Pidge's sides. Nimble grazed not far away.

"Grendel's gone," Horra told Rowan.

Shushing noises echoed from behind them as if someone moved through the dried underbrush. She turned, half afraid and half hopeful it would be Grendel.

It was Torren instead.

"I heard Pidge's screeches and came to check on you. I didn't think I'd find you with a hoard of worqs tied up with roots." He shot Rowan a surprised glance. "Well done, Mossy-coat Man." Torren used the title the children had given the druid after escaping the Erlking's mountain. Though it had been a joke at first, it stuck.

Rowan ignored the teasing. "We need to bring them back to the village, but I'm unsure how."

Torren walked to the closest worq and spoke in stilted, broken worqen.

The worq answered in smooth, heavily accented words.

Torren frowned and glanced uneasily at Horra.

Foreboding twisted her gut. "What'd he say?"

"The Erlking is heading back to the Riven and is taking Queen Toppenbottom and her daughter Princess Glory with him."

CHAPTER 10

At Torren's declaration, dread sank like a rock in a pond inside Horra's gut. "What? He has the princess *and* the queen?"

Torren frowned, and his tusks stuck out further. "If my translation is correct and if you believe a worq's word."

"What would they gain in telling us something that wasn't true?" Rowan asked, his brushy brow creased.

Torren raised his claws and gestured wildly. "To get us off their track so they can go free. Or to get us inside enemy territory. Worqs aren't known for their truthfulness, wood boy."

Rowan stiffened.

"Enough. Torren, I know you don't want to go to the Riven." She placed a claw on his arm. "But everything so far is telling us to go there to find some, if not all, of the answers we need about the Erlking. By avoiding it, we could lose the war."

Torren turned stony eyes on her. "I'm not going, and that's final. Remember how spooked you and Rowan got when we traveled around Hobgoblin Pass with the children? Nobody. Returns. From. It." He crossed his arms.

Rowan held up a finger. "Nobody that we know of. It's all hearsay and possibly the Erlking's scare tactic to keep people away from what could be his headquarters."

Torren blew out a disbelieving breath. "You're kidding me right now. Were you or weren't you freaked out when we were there?"

The druid calmly held Torren's stormy gaze, though Horra noticed a leaf or two twitching. "I did some thinking and talked with Master Knurl in the Conservatory. The voices were too real to be actual roods. He mentioned how dryads used to live in the forests near what we now think of as the Riven."

"What does that have to do with anything?" Torren glared at Rowan.

"When I became mesmerized, I saw a spirit tree in my vision. It was lovely to behold, and I immediately knew it was an elven tree, native to Endwylde. The knowledge came to me unbidden as if I could link up with the being mesmerizing me —wood creature to wood creature." Rowan steepled his fingers. "Before the magical fire burned the Weald down, Woodsly told me of a poison spreading across our kingdoms, tainting the roots in such a way as to hinder our communication. Though elves might have the kind of power and knowledge to perform such a plague, as the first Erlking proved with his withering warts, it is more likely something a forest creature would create."

"Like a dryad," Horra stated, thinking. Dryads, she recalled from old books in Oddar's library, had disappeared long ago, around the time the elves had. They had become legends, and no one was sure if they existed or not. "The fables state that like the roods, their life force is directly connected to the trees of sacred forests. Could they leave their forest, then? The roods cannot go beyond their borders. How could one appear and entice you if they are away from their woodland home?"

Rowan nodded. "That is a question I need the answer to. I sense if I can reach the bottom of it, many of our other questions may be answered."

"Until then, we have to do something with these lunks." Torren gestured to three of the worqs who were working to break out of their rooty bonds.

"They have been more patient than I thought they would." Horra unsheathed her mother's dagger tied to her belt.

The worqs all stopped moving and stared at the dwarven-made item. Nearly unbreakable, it was made of marbleized kobold and onyx, both rare and strong metals. The handle was inset with a sapphire, a ruby, an emerald, and a diamond. Balk, with his metalmagic and addiction to metal objects, had salivated over it when she traded it to him for her safety. Thanks to the mesmerized fairies, he'd broken his vow and it had returned to her. They'd used it to create the antidote for the mesmerization spell, so it was more than priceless.

Remembering her initial interaction with Balk gave her an idea. Though trolls had no magic to create binding spells, the dagger itself was infused with magic and quite useful in a pinch.

She pointed the razor-sharp blade at the closest worq, which grunted and leaned back. "Tell them I'll let them go if they agree to a blood oath. They have to promise not to act against Oddar or trolls again, even if they fall prey to the Erlking. Their lives will be forfeit if they commit or participate in any act against us."

Understanding dawned on Torren's face. He spoke in confident worqen, adding a couple tongue clicks for emphasis.

None of the worqs looked happy about it. They eyed her with distrust.

"Leave them, then." Horra replaced the dagger and turned to walk away.

Protests broke out.

Horra grinned.

She dropped her smile and turned back, eyebrows raised at Torren.

"They agree."

~Glory~

LATER THAT AFTERNOON, Glory's stomach grumbles became too much. Beneath her, the kelpie's stomach rumbled as well. Not an ideal situation to be in with this animal. Hungry kelpies were dangerous. It had been a long day and there was only one thing for it.

"Head toward water," she told Calliope in a grim tone. The kelpie would track out the nearest river, stream, or bog and lead her straight to it. And hopefully not drown her alive in the depths and eat her for dinner to sate its own hunger.

The animal had lost the scent of the Erlking hours ago when she escaped the troll princess. Now the sun lowered in the sky and shone like a beacon across the landscape. It would soon be too late to continue, and they'd need to camp. Her body twitched, her eyes drooped, and she wasn't sure she could stay atop Calliope much longer. She thought finding the Erlking would be an easier task, especially using the kelpie to sniff him out.

Minutes later, the kelpie's head jerked up and down. Scents of loam and running water tickled Glory's nose. The animal cantered faster. The reassuring trickle of rushing water broke through the hushed air. Goosebumps broke across Glory's cursed body as longing for a dip in the stream washed over her. Though it would be cold, like the showers she suffered through in the troll's castle, it was better than staying sweat-laden and stinky.

Willow trees grew along an embankment, something locals used to keep their water source free of contamination. The area where the stream broke free past a field and meandered crookedly into the distance was large. An owl hooted from a far-off tree. Nothing tainted the clean air, which assured Glory the stream was sound.

She stopped Calliope and walked them both through the drooping layers of limbs. Dry weeds and leaves crunched beneath their feet.

Once past the trees, Glory removed the golden bridle and let the kelpie roam freely. Inside the circle of willows, cattails grew wild in groupings of long, blade-like leaves. They were bare but still green, their seedy fluff long gone, and they rattled when the kelpie stepped through them into the fresh stream. After a long drink, the horse chomped on the bottom stems of the cattail plants.

Glory ran her hands over a long strip of leaf before breaking its stem off. With no flowers in sight and no ability to magic them into existence, Glory had few options for nourishment. However, this particular water plant had many uses, and some parts of it were edible, if not enjoyable.

Between the few Glory picked and ate, Calliope finished a small swath, clearing a space where she could walk into the stream. Glory removed her hooded cloak, frowning at how shabby it had become since racing through the trees, where limbs had tangled with it and torn holes. It was now more tattered than ever. Not that it mattered. Everything she tried on turned dingy and worn within a few hours, thanks to the hex.

She hung the hood on a broken limb, tucking the bridle beneath it in case a critter showed up and saw the gold. Under that, she tucked the Erlking's spell sheet. Everything she wore needed to be washed, as did her reeking body, so she entered the stream fully clothed. The cold depths were bracing. The dirt and grime ran from her body as she scrubbed, leaving her not completely fresh but much cleaner than when she'd started.

Back on the shore, she took her clothes off to wring out before putting them back on. Besides not having a change of clothes, waiting for them to dry before redressing was too risky. Rats were the least of her worries, as worqs also traveled in wandering bands. She didn't want to come across any alone and without magic for support.

After gathering several limbs and sticks, she created a fire. Though stripped of magic, a meager thread remained, helping her manage that small task easily. Soon she sat before the warm flames, and slowly, her clothes started to dry.

A stick broke in the distance.

Glory startled.

The kelpie jumped up from her prone position and nickered.

Glory rushed for her cloak, flinging the tattered hood back over her head. She grabbed the spell and the bridle before darting back to Calliope. As long as she possessed the golden bridle, the horse would defend her against any creature, including the Erlking. She placed the bit in the horse's mouth and clung to the reins.

She tucked the musical spell inside the hood, the least-damp spot on her body since the breeze and the fire had dried her hair. She re-situated the small sponges she'd placed in her ears for protection against the Erlking's music, then faced the area where she'd heard the noise and waited. The sky had darkened to indigo, and the moon and her fire were the only lights by which to see.

Tinkling musical notes carried on the breeze.

Glory stiffened. *She* wanted to find *him*, not the other way around.

More noises came from beyond the trees. The shadows from the vines made the darkness more eerie than it should be. Voices sounded next. Glory shivered against the cool night air. She clutched the leather straps. If things went wrong, she had an escape.

But they couldn't go badly. She needed her beauty back. She wouldn't survive without it.

A bent figure emerged from beneath the heavy canopy of willow limbs. A female, by the look of it, as they wore a long dress made of grassy plants—green despite it being the early onset of Springtide. The dress flexed with her every movement as if alive. She carried a carved wooden lamp emitting a golden, flickering glow.

Golden, like piskie light.

Glory squinted to be sure, but it was true. Three of the deceitful creatures fluttered wildly inside the glassed-in center of the lantern. They'd once been loyal to the fairies, but the whiff of magical power that came from the Erlking had changed their allegiance. With no mesmerization needed, they'd flown willingly into the elf's web. She took a step back, coming in contact with the kelpie's warm hide.

The figure, tall with a fine bone structure, stood and faced her. Her skin bore markings like bark, but unlike woodgoblins, it was smooth. Limbs with dried leaves covered her head, tumbling down her back in a ponytail, not unlike an upside-down limb. Her bare arms held the same markings as her face, still smooth, and her hands were bone thin and stick-like.

She smiled at Glory, but there was no warmth to it. There

was, however, enticement that tickled Glory's mind. "Ah, yes. There you are. We've been watching for you, fairy princess. Bring her," she called.

Bring who? Glory didn't really want to know, but she couldn't seem to muster enough energy to jump onto Calliope and race away from the stream.

Another creature was dragged into the small clearing. They jerked, struggling to get out of the hold.

She recognized the captive when the moonlight hit her silvery dress and crystal shoes.

Her mother, Queen Toppenbottom, stepped through the ropy limbs, a set of golden braces on her wrists pinning her arms in front of her body. No sign of her powerful scepter. The Erlking had probably absconded with it just like their crystal carriage. And she knew how keen the fiend was to obtain magical objects—like his instruments.

Glory blinked at the glowing restraining device. It was the same pure gold as the kelpie's bridle, used to control and manipulate the unfortunate victim.

Two of their male fairy escorts held the queen's arms in a tight grip. They shoved her out from beneath the tree's canopy and into the open. Glory could now see her mother's bruised face. Something white covered her mouth, which kept her from screaming.

A surprised glance back at the fairy guards confirmed the Erlking had mesmerized them. Their inner lights were dim, and their faces twisted in anger instead of showing their usual haughty disinterest.

Her mother simply shook her head before shifting her gaze away from Glory.

Glory's stomach dropped. Her odds of bargaining successfully with the Erlking just lowered.

~Glory~

Glory turned to face the dryad. "Where is he? And what does he have of yours to force you to move against a royal fairy?"

The dryad showed no emotion. "I'm authorized to offer you a trade. Your mother's life for yours. What shall it be?"

Glory clutched the leather strap tightly and clicked her tongue. "No introductions or pleasantries for a princess of the fairy realm, dryad? Do they not teach you etiquette or common courtesy in Endwylde?"

From the corner of her eye, Glory noticed her mother twisting in the male's grip, but she couldn't free herself. Glory refused to glance her way, because it would show her weakness and erode any bargaining power she held. If she held any.

"What is your choice?" The woman's voice didn't change, nor did her expression.

Glory could talk herself out of most situations and make

most creatures wither with her disdainful attitude. It was rare to find someone she couldn't influence. The Erlking had been one such creature. The annoying troll princess was another. But with this dryad, she needed to change her tactic.

"I don't know. What would you do if you were in my shoes?" Glory caught her mother shaking her head at her. Her mind flew through the few things she knew about dryads, which she'd learned from the forbidden section of the Shining Land's library.

Dryads were usually female, their male counterparts being oreads. Oreads were the forest-keepers of yore who tended the first woodland where the fabled first fruits grew. Though the males could travel from forest to forest, the females held a spiritual connection to their trees and could not leave them or live without them. On rare occasions or in an emergency, they could transform from their woodland form to a more ethereal one, having the voice of the wind itself.

When the dryad gave no reply, Glory sent her a sympathetic glance. "Why do you wander so far from your home, tree spirit? Has he taken it like he's stolen so many other things? I can help you retrieve it. I have the means to force him to obey me."

A terrible shriek exploded from the dryad, scaring some sleeping birds out of the trees nearby. The shriek pierced the air and drilled into her brain like an ice pick, even with the sponge in place.

Glory shoved her hands over her ears, and Calliope jerked at the reins. She held on tight, hoping the powerful horse wouldn't drag her on the ground. If that happened, she'd most likely be killed.

When the sound ended and she glanced back up, her mother and the male escorts were gone. Calliope snorted and danced as far as the reins allowed, her eyes wide and terrified. Glory shushed the horse.

The dryad was the only creature left standing beneath the trees. Fury twisted her face into an ugly scowl, and her mantle of leaves waved though there was little breeze.

With the thrall of the woman's beauty gone, Glory dropped her arms to her sides. Her stomach roiled. Though she'd detested living beneath her mother's thumb, she didn't wish her to be injured. What would the Erlking do with her now?

No amount of refinement training would help her out of this mess. The dryad was not someone to bargain with. Not normally one for praying, Glory sent up a silent plea that she hadn't just sentenced her mother to death or worse because of her insolence. One thing her formal training had taught her was that the way to appear confident was to fake it. She knew well how to do that.

She nodded at the dryad. "Tell the Erlking I have what he needs. If he's willing to conduct a true exchange and not just give me an ultimatum, I'm sure we can come to an arrangement we'll both be happy with. He has until the next full moon to meet me, or I'll destroy everything."

She jumped onto the kelpie's back, and with a smack of the reins, they raced downstream and away from the dryad. Tears spilled from Glory's eyes and vanished into the air.

There was no sign of her mother or the male fairy escorts. The only thing she saw was the cold blue residue of the fairy path clinging to the treetops and glowing bright against the darkness.

~Rowan~

Rowan stripped the roots from the worqs minutes after Queen Bearer Horra sealed their blood oath. Unlike the worqs they'd freed at the castle, these six creatures ran off as soon as the last root detached. The ground still rumbled from their retreat. "What is our next move?" Rowan asked.

Wrinkles broke out across the troll's face, some above her brow and others running along the edges of her mouth. She returned the cleaned dagger to its sheath before answering. "We have to keep searching for the captain and the fairy princess. We've almost lost a whole day, and time's wasting." She sighed. "Between the captain deserting us, the giant child interrupting our hunt, and battling the worqs, we haven't accomplished much today."

Rowan raised a finger. "That isn't true. We did all those things, and we figured out that dryads could be involved with the Erlking's efforts in taking over the Wilden Lands. That is valuable information. We just need to think it through rationally and come up with a plan. Then we can head to the Riven."

Torren stomped over to his horse and mounted. "We should return to the Inn and see what the other knights found out first. They and the captain might be there waiting for us. It's already too late to head out again, even if everyone is back at the Inn. We'll eat, rest, and start fresh in the morning."

"You seem agitated," Rowan said. Trolls' emotions always confused him. Helpful one minute, abrupt the next.

Torren didn't answer. Instead, he steered his horse toward the road and rode off in silence.

Horra brought him Pidge's rope. "Don't mind him. He doesn't want to go anywhere near the Riven again, and it's making him testy."

"Testy?" Rowan climbed onto the pudge wudgie's back,

thankful for the soft feathers to sit upon. With a swing of her long wings, they took to the air.

Horra climbed onto Nimble's back. "Meaning he is not happy about it and he's showing his grumpiness."

They followed Torren. Sunlight streamed through the breaks in the trees, warm enough that critters moved about and chittered to one another. Life was returning where winter had created a vacuum, offering a balm to Rowan's senses.

Rowan kept Pidge fluttering and floating at a height where he could still speak with Horra. "What if Torren refuses to come? Will we still go? The answers we seek may be on the other side."

She glanced at him. "I know. But I can't make him go."

Rowan cleared his throat, eliciting a dark look from her. "As Queen Bearer, you have power over all of Oddar's subjects, especially those who have vowed to fight for the Crown."

"Yes, but at what cost?" Her eyes narrowed as she glanced ahead, straight at Torren's back. "He's terrified of the Riven. I'm not sure if it relates to his father's death or not. After Mother passed away, there were times I'd get scared over nothing. Grief does weird things to you, and I don't want to traumatize him any further."

Horra patted Nimble's head. "We can do it without him. And it might be best if we leave the other knights out as well. Less complicated."

Pidge ducked with the current then rose again.

"What I'm really telling you, Rowan, is this: You were born to take on the Erlking. I am your mentor. It's our job to keep the balance of the Wilden Lands in check. I don't recall Merrow or the roods setting the responsibility of this war on anyone else's shoulders."

"I see." Rowan contemplated what she said. It made sense

if one took in the broader picture. "The odds of two novices defeating such an evil as the Erlking are not in our favor." He glanced at her silhouette, darkened by the shadow of the trees. "I don't have confidence in the two of us alone accomplishing that goal."

"Neither do I, Rowan."

CHAPTER 12

~Horra~

By the time they returned to the Inn, orange light dimmed to dusk and the scent of prepared food permeated the air. There was no sign of Horra's knights. Her claws itched to tear something apart, piece by piece, and then tear it into even smaller pieces. "Where in the Wilden Lands did they go?" she asked the stable manager, a half-goblin, apparent by his small size and facial features.

The man shrugged. "They never returned, Your Royal Troll-ness." Though goblins bore no allegiance to Oddar, his hobgoblin heritage would place his loyalty at least partially in favor of Oddar.

"Gah!" Horra screamed, startling the gulgoyle. She patted her pet. "Sorry, boy. I'm just frustrated. Why does everyone keep disappearing?"

Rowan handed Pidge's rope over to the hobgoblin attendee and made a loud clackety noise in the back of his throat. "It is not a good use of our time to run after everyone who goes missing."

Horra rounded on him. Merrow had warned her about how green he was about certain things. "But it's okay to leave my knights out there, ripe for the Erlking's picking? I don't think so."

The druid raised a finger to argue, but Torren thumped his back. "You won't win this argument, Rowan. A good leader never leaves her troops exposed."

They left the stables behind and walked to the Inn. Besides the noises of diners eating inside, the night remained quiet.

Her neck ached, giving her a headache. She noted the chimes she and Rowan checked out that morning were no longer hung outside the entry door. However, she was too hungry and tired to care much about the superstitious items.

The owner sat on a stool behind the desk. She thumped her chest and bowed her head. "Your Majesty. Are you'n back for the night? We've just sold out the Inn. Only the room above the stables is left."

Horra wanted to cry. "We'll take it. Can we have some food delivered? It's been a long day."

"Just the three of you'n?" the woman asked as she signaled to one of her servers.

Horra nodded, unable to speak around her tightening throat. Nothing was going as she planned. And now they were forced to stay in the stables. Not that she minded being with the animals. She preferred it over a tent in this instance. Made from rare wyvern skin, they blended in with the environment, be it trees or rocks. She wasn't sure how they would work out in the open and so close to the village.

What she was more worried about was her budding reputation as Queen Bearer and word getting out about being put up in the lowliest of accommodations. Especially when all the residents of Bough Valley would know she'd lost her knights by morning if that piece of gossip hadn't already made its way around the village. This wasn't something she was used to worrying about. But after suffering her father's ire, she now must think about such things.

Horra paid the owner, giving them a nice-sized tip, and led the other two back outside. The half-moon shone brightly from a cloudless sky, and several stars poked through the darkness. A hint of rain scented the air, boosting her gladness over not having to camp outdoors.

"Look on the bright side." Torren bumped her from the left. "At least wood boy here doesn't snore."

Rowan stood taller. "I don't. But you certainly do, and loudly at that. We may need to use those earplugs again, Majesty."

The earplugs had kept the music magic from mesmerizing them when escaping the Erlking's mountain. Horra's mouth quirked at the lighthearted banter, though she could tell Rowan hadn't meant his comment to be humorous. His seriousness made it that much funnier. She thumped Torren's arm with her clawed fist. "Thanks, guys."

They approached the stable door, crouching to get inside. "Let's get settled. We have some decisions to make, and I'd like to rise bright and early tomorrow to find my knights."

~Rowan~

AFTER THE QUEEN bearer and Torren had fallen asleep, Rowan dug his roots into the soil next to the slumbering pudge wudgie and a boulder version of the gulgoyle. The half-gargoyle creature had immediately changed to stone after the half-goblin manager scrubbed him down and fed him. It wasn't the first time he'd noticed the queen bearer's pet shifting to his less-vulnerable state, but he wondered if the creature knew something he didn't. Nimble could be skittish, but it was probably due to being boarded outside the stables in an unprotected area.

The night was cool and fairly bright. Sitting beside the animals, Nimble especially, allowed Rowan more than adequate warmth. He scratched the moss on his chin. It itched, detecting a rain shower coming soon. He couldn't tell how soon, but the moisture content in the air grew with every passing moment.

Rowan appreciated the still calmness though he also desired to listen to the murmurs of roods that used to fill the Weald in the evenings. He'd found that time especially helpful to his learning. The dead druid spirits were always active, even when Merrow, being a full woodgoblin and not a druid, needed to rest and rejuvenate. They were always eager to answer any of Rowan's questions, offering him detailed explanations.

Pidge made a soft noise in her sleep, and Nimble's boulder shuddered. Caught in a semi-doze, Rowan snapped his eyes open and dug his roots in deeper. There, past the taproots, he found what he was looking for.

Except it wasn't what he wanted to find. He quickly withdrew his roots, rushed to the fence, and tumbled over it. Torren's snores greeted him before he opened the door and climbed the wooden ladder to the loft room.

Horra had set up her sleeping bag on some hay bales on one side of the loft while Torren slept on the dusty floor on the opposite end.

"Queen Bearer, wake up."

Neither troll moved. Was something wrong with them? No,

Torren was still snoring, and Horra smacked her drool-laden lips and rolled over.

He reached out and shook her shoulder.

Horra screamed and jumped, rolling off the bales and onto the floor.

"Gah, Rowan! Warn someone before you scare them out of their sleeping bag." She dug something out of her ears.

Rowan stepped away so she could get out of the bag. "My apologies, Queen Bearer. I didn't realize you took my advice about plugging your ears seriously."

"I didn't need you to tell me how loud he is, but yeah, I listened to you." Horra sat on the bench and pulled her last plug out. "What's going on? I know you wouldn't wake me unless it was important."

Pidge's alarmed screech echoed.

They both swung their heads toward the doorway.

"We're being invaded, Your Majesty. The rats are coming."

Horra blinked. "Rats?" she asked dimly. "You woke me up for rats?"

Rowan wrung his hands. Visions of the enlarged vermin they'd seen after escaping the Weald were still sharp in his mind. "The animals grew restless, so I dug in past the topsoil and found a massive group of rats coming our way. Remember the one at the gnome's house, and the ones after that? They have the same magic signature. They've already breached Bough Valley's borders and are spreading out. I'm not sure what their intentions are, but it can't be good."

Horra hissed out a breath. "Why not?" She strode over to Torren and kicked his leg. "Wake up. We've got company." To Rowan, she said, "Get the animals ready in case we need to leave."

He raced back to the corral but only got as far as the doorway when he spied several pairs of beady eyes glowing in the darkness, all headed their way. Rowan slammed the door and stood against it.

"Your Majesty. They're already here." The door moved, and he twisted to keep hold of the wall.

Scuffling sounded from above, and the animals housed inside, including Torren's horse, tramped around and snorted alarmed noises. Sniffing came from outside the door, which, to their disadvantage, opened in. Unless he dug his roots in to hold the door shut, the critters would get inside.

One rat jumped at the door, moving it enough for another to get their pink foot inside. Without thinking, Rowan dug in, spreading his roots deep into the dirt to block the entrance. He reached his arms wide and clung to the wooden wall like a vine. However, he wouldn't be able to reach the windows along the far side of the wall.

Torren slid down the ladder without using the wooden steps, and Horra quickly climbed down after him.

"Rowan? What's happening now?" Horra asked, just as another rat smacked against the door.

The chimes on the Inn clanged, the sound exploding into the night.

Her eyes widened. "Dragon's fire."

Torren ran for the tools hanging on a wall on the other side of the horse stalls. He grabbed an axe and swung. "This'll do."

Horra quickly donned her woodencloak. "The Inn's residents are in danger. Did you see how many there were?"

He'd dug his roots in as far as they could go. The rats were stronger than he'd given them credit for. "I saw at least a dozen, if not more. Each the size of a trit-trot horse. The odds of us successfully defeating them all are low." His voice wobbled as the door kept shaking.

Horra pulled out her dagger and held it up. "Low, but not zero. Let's go."

CHAPTER 13

Horra stood, waiting for the druid to move out of the way. "Rowan, we have to get outside. It's the only way to attack them." She yelled to be heard over the chimes that clanged like a child shaking a rattle. She pulled at Rowan's arm, which was steadfast against the wooden wall.

His wood creaked with the effort of holding the door shut.

The druid's eyes opened wide. "My roots won't pull up. I'm stuck."

"Should I chop through the door?" Torren shouted into her ear.

"Might injure him. Let's try the windows." She nodded toward the far wall. "Rowan, we're going to leave you here. Try to blend into the wood so they don't recognize you." Horra didn't wait for him to reply.

Torren had already made it to the first window, which was

too small for him to get through, and was moving on to the second, larger window. When she reached the first window, she glanced out. The rats were everywhere, chewing on the fence posts, the trees, and anything they could get a hold of.

"What in the Wilden Lands?" She gaped. Cool air washed across her hide when she opened the window. The clanging grew louder. None of the rats paid her any attention. Climbing up the belly-high window, she balanced on the sill and observed the vermin.

Screams joined the clanging chimes, bolstering her into action.

She jumped down and raced toward the closest rat, which chewed on a fence post where Pidge had been resting earlier. It stopped gnawing a second before she pounced. With one swipe of her dagger, it didn't move again.

Torren had made it out and was chasing another out of the corral. A dark shadow swooped above him. Pidge's screech joined the rest of the noise. The rats were too large for her to gulp down, but it didn't stop her pet from hunting them.

Horra attacked the next rat, and then the next, and the next, until she reached the Inn. Several of the hobgoblins stood on the front porch, but she could hear the sound of something breaking inside. With her woodencloak on and the hood over her hair, they didn't see her as she ran past them and through the open front door. She followed the racket to the kitchen, where two rats had opened the icebox and were chomping through the Inn's food.

With a mighty scream, she charged after the ravaging duo, taking care of the first one before it even knew she was there. The second hissed and rose on its haunches, locking its gaze with hers.

It shouldn't be able to see her with the cloak on. When she attacked, it moved in reaction. "Why is it you can see me?"

Horra motioned right then jabbed left, faking the rat out and landing a solid hit.

Huffing from exertion, she stepped back and listened. The clanging grew less raucous. She made her way back through the hallway between the pub and the Boarder's Hall, out the front door again, past the huddles of hobgoblins, and back to the stables.

Nimble remained in his boulder state while Pidge feasted on one of the rat carcasses. That would keep her pet bird satisfied for a while. At least, Horra hoped so.

Rowan opened the stable doors as Torren killed the last of the rats, his roots intact and his arms back to their normal size. Some of the moss on his face dangled, having been scraped while he held the door shut. The animals inside were quiet now that the threat was over.

Torren cut off the tails of the rats they'd dispersed as he made his way back. At least ten of the creatures lay in the dust around the Inn's property.

Horra flipped her hood down so he could see her. "What're you doing that for?" she yelled at Torren.

"Spoils of war, I assume," Rowan replied. He rubbed the bark on his arms. "Some armies in the past have taken pieces of their enemies as an outward show of brutality meant to keep their foes from rising again."

Horra screwed up her face. "I know that. But still. I didn't think Torren, of all trolls, would do something like that. How did you get loose?"

Rowan lifted a leg. Several of the roots on his feet were splintered or broken off completely. "The old Slippery Elm Tree in the corral helped push my roots out of the ground. Otherwise, I would still be paralyzed by the Erlking's spell."

Before Horra could question him further, Torren trudged over.

She made a face at the tails he held up.

"We'll hang these around Bough Valley to deter any other intruders who wish to harm anyone." He hesitated. "That is, if it's okay with you, Queen Bearer."

"Ew, whatever." She spun around, glancing at the aftermath of their battle. "What do we do with the bodies?"

"Butcher them, a'course."

Horra recognized the hobgoblin cook from her trip through the kitchen. He hadn't been cowering on the front porch like the other servants and boarders. Her stomach pinched at the thought. "But they're full of dark magic. Aren't you afraid of the effects of eating them?"

"I'n't the first time and won't be the last." He grabbed the rat by a foot and dragged him toward the Inn.

Horra held up a claw and swallowed hard. "I'm not eating anything for breakfast tomorrow." She watched the smallish cook drag a creature twice his size as if he'd done it many times before.

Perhaps he had. Bough Valley was bereft of vermin each time she'd visited. Even her castle wasn't that free from pests.

She couldn't think too deeply about the implications, or her stomach would lurch. "We need to check the Inn. I killed two in the kitchen. Seems to me if they were after the boarders, they would've gone upstairs."

Rowan steepled his fingers. "Maybe that wasn't their mission. We need to figure out why they attacked so soon after the Erlking visited the Inn."

"Yes. We know it has something to do with him, at least. But why now? The bands of rats have been roaming across the countryside, leaving the villages alone until now. What's changed?" Horra stopped to look Rowan straight in his mossy face.

The green foliage crinkled with his frown.

Torren sighed deep. "I suppose that means we head to the Riven."

Having a plan usually calmed Horra, but this time was different. Her heart raced and her gut told her it was danger-ous. But she was Queen Bearer. Making the hard decisions was her duty. "As soon as the sun rises, yes."

<hr>

HOURS LATER, Horra wiped sleep from her eyes after dozing lightly for the remainder of the morning. Only the rain dancing on the stable roof had allowed that sweet indulgence. Torren slept with the rattails since Pidge took every opportunity to snatch them away.

She joined Torren as he saddled his horse. The tails dangled over the animal's back.

Nimble nudged her shoulder, and she scratched his chin. She spoke to Torren. "I need you to scout out the area and then head back to the castle if you don't find the captain or the knights. Gather another search party and hunt for them."

Torren stopped what he was doing to stare at her with an unreadable expression. "You don't want me to go with you to the Riven."

She'd expected some relief, not the flatness in his voice. "You don't want to go to the Riven. You've made that abun-dantly clear."

He jerked the last buckle into place, then stared into the distance. "We're in the middle of a war." Tears glittered in his mud-colored eyes when he turned to her, confirming Torren knew what she was doing and why. "Would you give any other knight the same consideration?"

Horra sucked in a breath. "Maybe, given the same circum-stances. I don't want to hurt you, Torren. I'm trying to, I don't know, keep you safe. Whole, for you and your mother." She closed her eyes against the pain in his expression. "You told me once that Woodsly treated me differently. I never saw it that way. He was always punishing me. But looking back, I see how he was protecting me."

She opened her eyes. "He taught me that the best thing to do sometimes is to safeguard something precious. Though I hate to admit it after competing with you for years, you are meant to be a knight. You have the instincts and the strength to carry out missions. You can take a punch and keep going. I need you here to search for the others and keep everything going while Rowan and I head into the Riven."

"But what if you don't come back?" His voice was raw and ended in a crack. "What do I tell your father? That I let you go with a green woodgoblin into a land so dangerous everyone avoids it at all costs? He'll skin me alive if you don't make it out."

Horra placed a claw on his arm. "He put me in charge when he made me the Queen Bearer, for better or for worse. He'll know it was my choice to have you here, keeping our knights and our kingdom safe. I can't be everywhere at the same time. Someone has to stay and find our missing army. There are few I trust to have my back. You've proved yourself time and again. I believe in you."

He sniffed and blinked. When he glanced back at Horra, his tears were gone. "I'll do my best to honor you, Queen Bearer." He thumped a claw to his chest and bent his head.

Horra squeezed his arm and bit back her own tears.

He swung himself onto his horse and, with a nod, rode off with the rattails on his lap.

"That wasn't easy for you to do," Rowan stated from behind her.

"No." She turned to find him holding two sets of wooden bells. "What's this?"

Rowan held them up for her to inspect. "I know you have doubts about my ability to craft tools that will function correctly. However, I assure you these will warn us of danger when we enter the Riven. I carved them from the corral's tree. It seems your eighth great-grandmother, Queen Ruby Fyd, blessed them, henceforth establishing the village of Bough Valley. She blessed the stones as well and buried them with the roots." He waved his arm at the sprawling elm growing on the opposite side of the fenced-in area. A large tree, it provided the only shade for the corral on the far side.

He'd mentioned the tree when she asked how he got free. She stared at him. "How do you know that?"

"When my roots dug deep enough past the spell's parameters, I made contact with the tree's roots. It told me its history, and it mentioned the toxic spell that's been spreading across the land, which targets the younger trees, petrifying them. Older trees whose roots sink deeper than the Erlking's toxins are protected from the effects."

Horra studied the large tree. Three trunks grew from the center of a sturdy base, forming a split, rounded top. Its wide trunk was green-gray with rough bark. "Why would the Erlking petrify trees?"

"Tree roots are the links roods use to communicate. Was not Woodsly one of the first creatures targeted by the Erlking?"

She glanced back at Rowan. "After the fairies, yes."

"That was no mistake. The Erlking got rid of his biggest threat first. When that didn't stop you from getting my seed to the Weald, he needed to come up with another plan, or plans, as I now see it, to hinder me."

Understanding sunk into Horra's mind. "The petrification

and the fire, both to keep you from accessing the wisdom of the roods."

"Yes. But not only me. You as well, Queen Bearer. As I see it, had Master Knurl in your Conservatory not hidden his presence from everyone, I don't doubt the Erlking would've destroyed his tree as well. And that's where the dryads come in use. He couldn't have forged past the Weald's spells without another wood creature's help."

"Do you think we'll find dryads when we enter the Riven?"

He nodded.

Horra took a chime from him, the fine wooden tubes tinkling with the movement. Inside the wood barrels were clear stones—crystals if she weren't mistaken—which produced a pleasant sound. Much better than the ones the hobgoblins had hanging around the Inn. "Then we'll need all the help we can get."

"I agree." Rowan took his chimes and made his way over to Pidge.

A chill worked its way up Horra's spine at the concern in his words.

CHAPTER 14

Hours after leaving the dryad behind, Glory steered the kelpie as far as the fairy path led. After the blue trail disappeared in the morning light, she continued westward toward what she knew as the Riven. Every instinct bolted at the idea of entering foreign elf terrain. Rumors had reached the shores of her Shining Land, and she knew it to be a dead end. However, the Erlking's old pet needed no prompting to follow her mother, even after the glowing path turned invisible.

The horse knew the way.

"That's where he'll be," she muttered to Calliope under her breath. Wind rushed through Glory's hair, which hung free from her hood as they raced. It whipped and spun for the first time in too long. "It's his home. He used you to travel between his cursed land and into the Wilden Lands. It's how he's hidden so well." She was sure of it. There could be no other way for him to remain untouched. No one would willingly follow him to such a dangerous place.

Only the Erlking's former pet could find him there now.

Glory's mind warred with her fear. She knew enough about fighting to understand it wasn't wise to put oneself inside enemy territory. Before she lost her magic, it never occurred to her to be scared. The Erlking changed that. Given her few options. She wasn't patient enough to wait him out, to believe he'd listen to what she told the dryad. He was anything but predictable, except when it came to revenge.

She'd use that to her advantage.

Calliope slowed. Glory sat up straighter on the horse's back to see where they were. The sun was cresting, which meant it was mid-morning. If she wasn't mistaken, they'd ridden around in circles. The Erlking thought himself so clever for throwing her off the trail. She sniffed at his arrogance.

In her former life, she'd be sitting down to tea in their grand flower gardens. Glittering, lush bushes with their teacup-sized sparklebud blooms would scent the air with a sweetness that rivaled no other, and whimsy birds would call to each other across the plush expanse. She lifted her face to the sun to capture that memory, but the air suddenly grew cold.

And instead of the warbling song of the whimsies, unintelligible voices whispered as if carried on the wind. Chills raced up her arms, and she flipped the hood back over her head in defense. She spurred Calliope, but the kelpie didn't respond. They came to a halt in front of a nondescript elm. Open brushland with trees growing sparsely in odd formations spread as far as she could see.

Death had occurred here. She didn't know when, only that the land emitted sorrow.

Glory peered closer at the trees until a sensation like ice

raced down her spine. Was this a dryad cove? The trees appeared to be in mid-stride, leaning away from where the kelpie had been heading. She sensed no life in the husks of wood. Nothing but a barren wasteland surrounded her.

The back of her neck prickled as if she were being watched. "Keep going," she said, kneeing the horse.

Calliope's flesh rippled, and she blew air out of her nose. The kelpie stamped a front leg, shook her leafy mane, then stilled.

Glory dropped her head and sighed. The horse would go no farther, even if she had the golden bridle. But why? "Why can't one thing go right in my life?" she whined, her lips trembling. Deep down, she knew the answer. But she never liked to be the one at fault.

She flounced off the horse. It skittered sideways, away from her. "Give me," Glory ordered, removing the golden bridle, then tucked it inside her cloak in a hidden pocket she'd sewn. She checked to make sure she still had the folded music spell. It crinkled under her touch.

The whispers grew to murmurs. She'd hoped to have the kelpie with her to keep her safe when she faced the Erlking, but that wasn't to be. She squared her shoulders and slapped the changeling's hindquarters. "Go on. You're of no use now. I'll call you if I need help later."

Startled, the horse raced off into the distance, disappearing from sight before Glory could regret her choice.

Glory closed her eyes and gathered her courage. With a deep breath, she took the first step toward the Riven.

~Rowan~

GOLDEN SUNLIGHT SPARKLED on water droplets left behind after the rain ended. The moisture made the moss on Rowan's bark spread into a thicker blanket, warming him against the coldness of the mid-morning air. A faint tinkling from the bells accompanied Nimble's clomping steps across Hobgoblin Pass.

Rowan's legs dangled over Pidge's sides, but the pudge wudgie had no trouble keeping them both afloat. She was strong and determined, much like her owner, which at this moment he was grateful for. Though his splintered roots didn't exactly hurt, they were more sensitive to the elements.

Once again, he wished he had some of Merrow's tingleroot paste. But that formulation was lost when the fire snuffed out his mentor's life.

Horra's saddlebags bulged with provisions she'd purchased from the local vendors at the village's square before they left. Nimble had no trouble with the added weight. The queen bearer sat bent over a crudely drawn map she'd made this morning before inquiring of the locals where they believed the border of the Riven to be. Everyone they'd questioned offered different answers.

"Do you think it's the magic that keeps the locals from knowing the exact border? None of them had any real experience finding it," she said as they left the travelers on the main road behind. They chose instead to go through the open meadow on the far side of the bridge and toward the snaking Sterling River's ridge.

"Either that, or they're so superstitious that whatever they're told becomes tainted with each retelling." Rowan gazed at the horizon. A calm blue sky perched above a blurred landscape. The sun's heat burned off the moisture left from last eve's rain, creating the haziness. The day would be warm. "I don't think we'll need a map. We certainly didn't the last time we traveled near it."

Horra scrunched the paper in her claws. "That's true. I can still feel the creeps it gave me."

"I'm unsure what creeps are, but I did sense something menacing." Pidge dipped and rose back up. The bells hanging from her neck tinkled with the movement.

Horra laughed. A smile spread across her wide green lips. "That's kind of what the creeps are. You sense something dangerous or off about something and it makes your hide crawl."

He glanced at her to try to understand what she found humorous this time. Nothing he said had been the least bit funny. Perhaps she took pleasure in explaining things to him? That, he could appreciate. Imparting knowledge to others was pleasureful. "Ah, I see. Once in a while, my bark does tingle or quiver."

Horra motioned with her claw. "See, you're not so bad after all." Nimble's chest rumbled beneath her, his scales emitting a dim glow and his bells chiming.

Rowan hesitated, first because of the threat of fire, and second, because he didn't comprehend the meaning behind her words. The wind picked up and Pidge rode a wave until they flew next to their companions. "I don't understand. When was I bad?"

Horra opened her mouth but hesitated. "Never mind. It's just a phrase trolls use."

Though he still didn't grasp her explanation, he nodded to let the subject go, which he'd found to be a useful tool with the queen bearer and some of the other creatures he'd dealt with. The moss on his face tightened across his bark. He glanced around. "Is it getting colder?"

She gazed up at the sun, which shined brightly from a cloudless sky. "It shouldn't be. We should be growing warmer as the sun reaches its peak, not the other way around."

His roots tingled, particularly the maimed ones, throwing him into deeper alertness. "I believe I am experiencing the creeps."

Horra visibly shivered and clutched her woodencloak tighter around her neck. "I'm with you on that. We're still in the open, though. I thought we'd be farther in before sensing the Riven. Didn't it seem that way to you last time?"

"I admit to not being as attentive as I should've been on our last trek through here. I was rather freezing and using most of my energy to stay warm." Whispers preceded the wind, spoken so softly he couldn't catch the words. "Did you hear that?"

"No, but I can tell the wind has shifted. Instead of blowing west to east, it's coming from the north now. That usually means a storm is heading our way, but there are no clouds or dark horizons in sight."

Pidge's dangling head-feather whipped back and smacked Rowan in the face. Her bells chimed.

He lifted the rope, which had lain slack against her neck. His bark quaked. "Maybe we should stop and walk?"

Nimble shuddered, causing his bells to ring.

"There, there. We're perfectly safe." To Rowan, Horra spoke in a soft tone. "That would be a good idea. Let's slow down." She pulled on the reins and her gulgoyle stopped immediately, jerking her forward. She gasped but kept upright.

Rowan signaled for Pidge to land. They circled the area, and she swooped down, landing solidly.

Both of them dismounted and gazed at their surroundings. The wind swirled about them, but not as wild as it had when they were moving. The chimes stilled.

"Do you think the Riven will let us in? Balk couldn't enter." Horra's claws were on her hips, the leather straps dangling from one fist. Nimble shuddered and belched, sending smoke into the air. She ran a comforting claw over his scaled neck.

Pidge fluffed her feathers.

Sap rushed through Rowan's trunk. "The air feels ... odd," he said, unsure what he sensed.

"It's charged. Like the moment after lightning hits and the air snaps at you. Like it's alive and could bite you if it had a mouth."

Rowan wasn't sure that was quite what he meant. He said nothing, though, as they studied the area, which was familiar. "Did we travel through here before?"

Horra crinkled her nose. "I think so, when we had the children in the wagon. We would've been close to here to get where we ended up." After a moment of silence, she continued. "Let's keep heading north. That's what we did last time, and we found the barrier near that sheer cliff. The chimes should warn us in time if something dangerous is near, yes?"

He recalled the tree assuring him the bells would work. "Yes."

They walked in silence, leading their animals. Pidge was the only one who made any noise, and then only because she caught the scent of some small animal. She'd feasted well that morn on the defeated rats. However, Rowan had no doubt she would soon grow hungry again and her huntress instincts would take over.

Pockets of cold air hit them as they traveled high above the Sterling River's bend. As soon as they moved into a frigid zone, their next step would bathe them in the sun's warmth. It was quite disconcerting to Rowan's mind.

Since the bells only made noise when their animals moved their heads, he was certain they were safe. He just needed to remain vigilant.

Without the snow, the area seemed bigger than before.

Different. Though he'd detected new grass budding around Bough Valley, this area wasn't close to a spring bloom. No hum of life waiting to burst through the soil reached his roots as he walked. All was quiet except for the air, which rushed in bizarre bursts from every direction. The elm trees growing in patches were mute, no spark of life within.

"This is it," Horra said as she glanced over the edge. She stood several steps away from the crumbling cliff, but her boots sent small rocks tumbling over the side. "Gah. It was scary enough with snow piled everywhere. It's terrifying to see what lay beneath it all."

Nimble rumbled nervously. His chimes tinkled for a moment before quieting.

Rowan steered Pidge closer to ease the gulgoyle's fear. "I'll trust your opinion on that."

As she stood peering over the cliff, Horra's long red curls bobbed with the waves of air pluming out of the valley. Her cheeks were ruddy, and when she glanced at him, her eyes sparkled brightly. "I wonder how far a scream would echo."

Rowan frowned. Of course that would be her first response to such a sight. "I wouldn't try—"

Horra opened her mouth and let out an ear-piercing shriek. Echoes immediately followed.

Nimble shuddered and turned to stone. The chimes went quiet beneath a layer of rock.

Pidge squawked and jerked, breaking loose from his hold, tearing the cord holding her bells. They tinkled as they fell to the ground. Pidge flew off in a rush of wings.

Rowan's sap heated, but before he could respond, something dark blurred by him, grabbing his trunk and jerking him away from the queen bearer.

The last thing he saw was Horra's back as she giggled, her eyes trained on the Sterling River valley below.

CHAPTER 15

Horra giggled, her voice bouncing around the canyon. Every once in a while, she did something unexpected for fun, to see how Rowan would react. This trip had been so full of strain that she wanted to ease the tension. She glanced behind her to watch Rowan's response, but he wasn't there.

"Rowan?" She spun around. A boulder sat where Nimble had stood before, and Pidge was nowhere to be seen. No chimes sounded. The echo was gone. No birds chirped and no critters moved. There wasn't even a whisper of wind. "What in the Wilden Lands? Where'd everybody go?"

She slapped a claw to her head. "I scared them all. Come out, Rowan," she called. "I was just playing." She walked around the brushy area. The only places to hide were a few spots where the trees bent into strange positions. "Okay, I'm sorry I screamed over the cliff. Rowan?"

The first odd patch of twisted trees stood in a mounded circle, all of them dead. Horra touched one of the blackened trunks to peek around to the other side and see if Rowan was hiding.

"Go away!" a voice screamed in her mind.

Horra jerked her claw back and stumbled away, out of the circle of trees.

"What was that?" It wasn't a rood. The voice hadn't been clackity or low like a male's. She turned back to make sure she still had Nimble's boulder in her view. The trees didn't move. They were all quite dead, but there was something unnatural about the small grove.

"Rowan?" Her call was lighter now, more reticent. What happened in the brief moment when she'd turned her back? Surely he wouldn't run away because of a simple childish prank. "Pidge? Here, girl."

Silence.

"Drat and vinegar!" Horra stalked back to Nimble's side. How long would it take before her pet decided he was safe enough to turn back into his regular form? She sank to the ground, her back against the warm, solid gulgoyle rock.

Seconds turned to minutes while Horra waited for Rowan to return. What was taking him so long?

Horra glanced up when she heard crunching footsteps, hoping it was Rowan. She stood and peered around Nimble.

A hunched figure walked around one of the tree groupings, heading Horra's way. Clad in a dark but faded cloak, they looked familiar.

The tattered hood was the final clue. "Princess Glory?" Horra yelled.

The figure stopped, hesitating. With a stamp of a foot, she raised her head, though her face remained hidden in the depths. "Why can't I get away from you?" Glory shrieked.

Nimble rumbled, his stone hardening.

Horra stepped away from her pet and removed her hood so the other princess could see her. "Trust me, you're not who I was hoping to find either."

"What're you doing here?" Glory asked, still standing in the same spot.

Horra crossed her arms. "You first."

They stood, neither speaking, for several minutes.

With a jerk of her arms, Horra broke the standoff. "Stubborn fairy. I don't have time for this."

"I'm stubborn? Have you met yourself?" Glory waved a bony hand her way.

Horra refused to answer as she turned back to Nimble. "C'mon, boy. We have to find Rowan. We can't leave him out here on his own."

The stone shook but didn't break open. She tsked in frustration. This wasn't what was supposed to happen. Head turned to the sky, she whistled for Pidge instead. If she could get her pudge wudgie back, she could coax Nimble out of his protective shell. Then she could find Rowan.

A scree overhead drew her attention. With a claw over her eyes to block the sun, Horra spotted Pidge circling a grouping of stones. The stones were too far to leave Nimble alone with the fairy but close enough to hear the bird. She whistled, to no avail. Pidge wasn't listening, because her concentration was on the area below.

"Argh!" Horra glared at Glory. "Don't do anything to Nimble before I return."

Glory's hooded head shifted back and forth as if looking for the gulgoyle. "I don't have a clue what you're going on about."

Good. If she didn't know what Nimble was, she could do him no harm. "Never mind. I'm going to get Pidge." She flipped her hood back over her head and tucked her hair inside.

The fairy let out a disgusted noise. "That bird?"

Anger rushed through Horra's body and her heart beat faster. Clenching her fists, she ignored Glory's insult and walked past her toward the spot where Pidge circled and scree'd.

The instant her toe hit magic, Horra knew she'd made a mistake. Not only did it feel like stepping into thick molasses, but the sensation of bugs crawling over her hide enveloped her. The only question was, had the fairy princess set the trap, or was it something the Erlking orchestrated?

She couldn't stop once she started. The force had a hold of her like when Nimble jumped over the log and the trap affected Rowan. She moved in slow motion, and as she crossed the threshold, the magic finally let her loose.

Horra's foot thunked down on the ground, and the rest of her followed in a swift motion. Her new surroundings were nothing like the previous area. Buzzing music filled the air as green grass danced to the notes.

The trees moved too, as if in conjunction with the rise and fall of the hum. Unlike the music the Erlking used in the castle when he took it over, this music washed across her scalp and rushed down her body to her toes in prickling tingles. It echoed the swamp, with the bugs and frogs all competing for dominance. It called to her as no other sound could, urging her to close her eyes and rest in peaceful bliss.

She held her breath, unsure what to do. For an eternal minute, she stood transfixed by the perfect unity of the plants' dance and the swampy symphony. Then something hit her. Glory. She bumped into Horra, knocking them both to the ground, where they fell in one great heap onto the lush grass.

"Brgfff—" Horra grumbled from beneath the fairy princess, her face pressed to the ground. For a moment, the drone of the swamp ended and her head cleared. As the fairy princess moved, though, the humming started again.

"Get your warty legs off me," Glory screamed.

The delightful buzzing stopped, and the motion of the plants and trees halted. Trees swiveled in their direction, creaking as they moved. The droning music suddenly began again. But this time Horra's heart pounded to the rhythmic beat of an angry susurration.

Crack!

Pop!

A tree bent over them, a limb reaching out. This was nothing like when Kryk came to her in a tree, animating the bark and limbs. This one seemed alive.

Or enchanted.

"Look out," Horra squealed, unable to move with the other princess still atop her.

The tree grabbed Glory, lifting and dangling her from its branch. It shook her, and she screamed. Then the fairy went silent.

Horra rolled sideways and stared up into the treetops. Glory wasn't the only thing moving in the limbs. Bulbous-bellied spiders crawled out of the tree's branches and pounced on Glory. In moments, they had her spun in a cocoon up to her head, her hair and one shriveled wing stuck out of the end.

Horra gulped down the terror, but it rushed up to tie itself into a knot at the base of her throat.

Alarm pounded in Horra's ears, drowning out the buzzing notes of the music. Her eyes widened at the other bundles dangling from the trees, just like Glory. *So, is this why when you enter the Riven, you don't return?* She was aghast. There were too many to count. Some were only bones with tufts of hair sticking out.

Something nudged Horra's ankle. She jerked her foot away.

Yanking her hood back in place, she recalled the rat in Bough Valley. Horra whispered a quick prayer to remain hidden from whatever was at work here. Immediately, the ground shifted. Buggy little black objects crawled beneath the fallen leaves. She held back a choked squawk. The ground was alive. Was she sitting on top of some type of insect colony or a hive?

Horra's stomach roiled at the thought.

The humming drone died down again, and the trees slowed to a rhythmic sway. The roiling creepers under her feet calmed. Everything almost seemed peaceful, harmless. With her hood on, the buzzing didn't entice her like it had before.

Had the Erlking found a song that would appeal to trolls? Horra hoped not. She'd not take the hood off again while she was here, just to be safe.

She frowned when she glanced back up into the trees. No matter how annoying the fickle fairy was, she couldn't leave Glory hanging. She'd have to climb up the tree to save her. The music must've mesmerized the fairy. Otherwise, she'd be screaming like a banshee to break free. Horra checked her side, reassured to find her mother's dagger still in its sheath.

A few bones littered the ground as she trod lightly, making her way toward Glory's tree. When she was two trees away, the ground rattled. With a whirl, everything around Horra pivoted and swirled. Dizzy, she fell to the ground, inhaled, and choked on something that flew into her mouth. She prayed it wasn't one of the bugs. Luckily, it tasted only like dirt and debris, not insect carcasses.

She staggered to a standing position, her head still spinning. "Gah." Her knees knocked, and it took a moment for the wooziness to clear. She clasped her head to steady herself as she glanced around. Glory wasn't in sight. None of the trees were there either. The forest had swallowed her and spit her out into a completely new area.

Horra's eyes widened as her stomach dropped. "Oh no."

CHAPTER 16

Instead of a forest, Horra stood in a perfumed meadow. Flowers grew one upon another, creating a carpet of blooms that spanned across an endless horizon. The air smelled like fairies with their oversweet, cloying scent, but worse.

She sneezed and slammed a claw to her nose to keep another from escaping. When the urge to continue sneezing stopped, she let go, breathing shallowly. "What in the name of pickled juniper berries?"

Whimsy birds dipped and darted about, happily chirruping as their long tail feathers trailed after them. Upon closer inspection, the birds flying above her were much too large to be regular whimsy birds, which could rest on her arm. They flickered in and out of sight like ghosts, blending in with the sky before blinking back into existence.

Horra shook her head. What was wrong with her eyes? She wasn't woozy, but something was off. She closed them and pinched the woodencloak tighter around her neck, ducking her face further into its depths.

The fog cleared from her senses, and she opened her eyes. It wasn't whimsy birds soaring above her. "Wyverns?" she whispered in shock. Her instruction manuals about rare and extinct animals had photos of the creatures. Horra knew they existed because troll's survival tents were fashioned from wyvern hides. However, she had never seen a live one.

Or possibly she had and never realized it. These creatures were there one minute and gone the next, only to reappear somewhere else altogether.

"Scree!"

Horra jerked her head up. Pidge flew above all of them. But that wasn't possible. She'd been too far from Pidge when she entered the Riven. She put a hand against her heart. Nothing seemed real. This was all too wonky to be true.

"Queen Bearer?" Rowan's voice was thready.

She glanced around. "Rowan? Where are you?"

"In the air to your far left."

He sounded as if he was being flung around.

There. She caught sight of him, then the wyvern holding him flashed into view. It vanished just as quickly. The creature had Rowan curled in his tail and was one of the larger flying creatures. The woodgoblin was indeed being whipped through the air as the wyvern moved.

Horra's stomach clenched as she remembered being swung back and forth in the giant girl Galumph's hand. "Good grouse, Rowan. How am I supposed to rescue you from that thing? I can see it one minute and then it's gone."

The wyvern dragged Rowan in an S-curve as the other wyverns winked in and out of sight. It was all rather confusing.

"I don't know, but I'd be eternally grateful if you did." His last word was high-pitched and trailed off as he sailed away from her, disappearing and reemerging several feet away.

Horra blinked. What did she know about wyverns? They were in the dragon genus and had two legs instead of four, like Nimble's class of gully dragon. Much more serpentine in nature, their tails had venomous stingers, powerful enough to kill a giant. Hunted to near extinction, there had only been a handful of wyvern sightings in the past few decades.

Dragons, too, were rare. Almost nonexistent. They'd only found Nimble when the trolls raided the dwarves in the upper Iron Mountains after the war. The dwarves had been inching closer and closer while illegally mining in troll mountain territory using the war to cover their actions.

Horra touched the dagger, which had been created for the dwarf king from jewels mined in troll mountains. The weapon, along with several other items, including Oddar's golden sword, had been seized along with the arrested miners. After the raid, Queen Petra had dethroned their king. Under troll threat of subjugation, the dwarves bargained a large sum of restitution in exchange for their freedom and made a blood oath to never trespass on troll soil again. Now dwarves were rarely seen except in one of the village pubs.

Somehow, the dwarves had acquired the half-dragon. Now, on elf land, she'd found wyverns. Was there a link between the dwarves and the elves?

"Princess?"

Rowan's one-word plea broke through her troubled thoughts.

"Right. I'm figuring it out. Give me a minute." What did she have that a wyvern would want? Pidge was snack-motivated. But Horra had no treats large enough to offer. Nimble needed other animals to make him feel safe. She didn't think that was the case with these creatures, even if she could pin one down.

And if the music was mesmerizing them, could she break the spell?

"Ah! This is impossible!"

Pidge scree'd again and dodged a couple of the wyverns that suddenly blinked into sight in front of her. If her pudge wudgie was having trouble keeping track of them with her precise instincts and eyesight, Horra had even less chance of reaching the one holding Rowan.

"Be careful, Pidge," she called. Horra checked her pockets. If she had some sort of snack, she could entice the bird to the ground. Then maybe with Pidge she could figure out how to reach Rowan.

In her back pocket, she had a chunk of dried pig's ear. The butcher hadn't been able to sell it to the locals in Bough Valley, but it was a nice delicacy to have on hand. Horra had happily bought it and stuck it there in case Pidge needed a crunchy snack. Good thing, since the rest of her supplies was unavailable within Nimble's rocky exterior now.

"Here, Pidge. I've got a treat for you." She broke off a piece and tossed it in the air as far as she could throw it. It arched and fell back to the ground.

With a shrieking blast, Pidge spread her wings wide and dashed after it. She bumped into some wyverns on her descent, but nothing stopped her. The creatures didn't even seem to notice the hungry bird. Pidge swooped in at the last second and gulped the chunk down before it hit the ground.

"Good girl." Horra tossed another piece on the ground, hoping to get her pet to land.

True to her huntress nature, Pidge obliged.

When the pudge wudgie bent down to snatch the dried chunk, Horra jumped on her back, grabbing hold of the rope reins. Her pet was large enough now to hold her weight, and her legs didn't dangle nearly as much as Rowan's longer ones did.

Pidge twisted her head in a questioning manner. It was the first time since leaving the castle that she'd ridden the bird. "Let's go get Rowan," she said.

Wings wide, Pidge jumped into the air, thrusting Horra back. She grasped the rope tighter, which bit into her claw's softer side. An expert flyer, Pidge dodged the flickering animals as best she could. In only a few moments, they found their way to the large wyvern holding the woodgoblin.

"Now what do I do, Pidge?" she asked as her pet fluttered around the creature, following its serpentine motion when it disappeared. When it blinked into sight, she could see that the creature had a tight hold on Rowan with several layers of tail wound around his trunk. Freeing him from its clutches wouldn't be easy.

"Get me out," Rowan clacked out as he soared through the air.

Horra held herself back from rolling her eyes in frustration. She dug out her dagger. "I don't want to stab it."

"Do it." Rowan darted by her face before dashing away again.

She took a deep breath and firmed her hold on the jeweled handle. Pidge floated near Rowan, and Horra took a wide swipe at the air near his body.

At first she hit air. And then something solid.

The wyvern's loud squeal startled Pidge. Horra, having only one hand on the ropes, fell off the side of the pudge wudgie.

Horra clung to the rope, but her weight teetered Pidge sideways and they both dipped. Rowan dropped out of the sky at the same time. She reached to catch him with her free claw, but between her dagger and the wyvern's motion, he spiraled away from them. "Vinegar!" she yelled.

Still several feet in the air, Pidge struggled to keep them afloat. Wyverns darted nearby. It was only a matter of time before they got bumped by one. With a last-minute determination to keep her pet safe, Horra let go of the rope. Below her, Rowan landed and his body turned into a pile of sticks.

Just like Woodsly when he'd died.

Horra screamed before she, too, hit the ground. Though the grass and flowers were lush, they did little to cushion her body, and her back took the brunt of the impact. Horra lay stunned for a moment, staring up at the wyverns winking in and out of sight. For an instant, she wondered how their small wings could keep their large bodies airborne. And why they only had two legs.

The ground shifted again, rattling her bones and unsettling her stomach. Horra closed her eyes and held her breath to keep her stomach from lurching. When the movement ended, she opened her eyes and blew out a choked gasp.

This was not where she'd just been.

She was used to her swamp at the bottom of Oddar's castle. What surrounded her now made her swamp seem like a puddle.

It took more strength than she liked to flop to her stomach and stand up. Humidity made it harder to breathe. Her head reeled until she blinked several times. When she could finally see, Rowan—or his remains—was nowhere to be seen. Nor was Pidge.

"Not again."

~Rowan~

MOMENTS AFTER BEING FREED from the wyvern, Rowan lay on the ground, thankful to be out of the horrid animal's grasp. He'd never been comfortable around Nimble, even though the gulgoyle was quite docile. The half-dragon was enormous, breathed fire, and acted unpredictably. After being flung around by the snake-like dragon, Rowan gained a newfound appreciation for the gulgoyle.

Before he managed to stand, the troll princess screamed, and the ground reverberated, rattling him to his innermost core. Eyes wide, he watched as the Riven tore itself apart and reassembled into something different.

Rowan stared at a forest, first in awe. But when he realized the troll princess was nowhere to be seen, he panicked. "Horra?" he called in a feeble voice. He cleared his throat, attempting to push his apprehension aside. Nothing he'd imagined about the Riven had come close to its reality so far.

What would happen next?

He sat up and tried to gain his bearings. The moss in his ears tickled his inner fibers. He stuck a finger in his left canal and moved it about, hoping to get rid of the sensation. When he removed his finger, a deafening buzzing barraged his earhole. Not quite music, but louder than anything nature normally provided. He quickly re-fluffed the herbage to mute the sound.

"Ah," he muttered. The moss had been protecting him by blocking the sound. He would leave it alone and live with the annoying prickle. When he stood, his roots detected dark magic at work in the soil. The ground wasn't solid like it should be. He bent to inspect it closer and realized he was standing on a field that moved about like ants in the dirt. His finer roots stretched and then recoiled. For the first time, he could almost taste the toxic nature of the spells. His fibers shrank from it.

Bending over, he sought to identify the substructure. The sight before him wasn't reassuring. Hundreds, thousands, possibly millions of brownish bugs with bulging eyes and membranous wings crawled about. Though they were moving, there were enough of them to make the ground appear solid. That's why the sound had been so loud—they were all "singing." This piercing racket was the call of the chitterbugs, which were among the loudest insects in the Wilden Lands.

Rowan flinched.

Emotions washed over him. He couldn't parse each feeling, but they were overwhelming. This was perhaps due to the disorienting effect of the Riven as it shifted and recreated itself. However, he had more reasons to be repulsed. First, he knew the insect to be a parasite to trees. Chitterbugs burrowed inside a host tree for years at a time, hibernating and feasting on sap to live until their larva emerged in swarms. The sounds they made would attract other chitterbugs so their life cycle could start anew.

A shiver wracked Rowan's body. The grubby worm that had infested him was bad enough. Chitterbugs invading his trunk was downright incomprehensible. He needed to get out of this place, and fast.

Rowan glanced around and stilled. Bundles hung from tall limbs, waving slowly back and forth like catterwump chrysalises, only these were much larger than any catter critter's would be. With the Erlking's penchant for vermin of many kinds, he could almost believe them to be giantized versions.

But no. They were shaped more like bodies than insects.

All of Torren's warnings of creatures going in and not coming out drifted into his mind. Could these be the doomed visitors? Rowan's bark tightened around his trunk. Were any of them still alive?

His gaze circled the area before he spotted one bundle with long auburn strands dangling from the bottom. He squinted, then gasped. One shriveled diaphanous wing gleamed beside the head. It was the fairy princess, Glory, whom they'd been searching for.

She dangled several tree lengths away from him. Slowly, he followed a path toward her that avoided all the possibly infested trees. He caught sigils carved into the bark, ones he didn't know or understand the meaning of. Had the elves used charms like the Archdruid clan did in the Weald? He made note of the different symbols in his mind in case he needed the information later.

He was one tree away from the fairy when the ground rumbled, then shook, and the world shifted again. The motion brought him to his knees, and everything swirled in a confusing blur.

Not again.

CHAPTER 17

~Rowan~

When Rowan glanced around, he was in a grassy field. The trees, along with Glory, had disappeared. The ground wasn't alive here, though his roots confirmed it wasn't solid either.

Tall grasses dashed about in a rhythmic motion like wind flowing through hair. How would he get back to the fairy princess now? His inner fibers cramped, the water in his system rushing in a bewildering manner. Sap spewed out of his mouth, an action he had no control over. After several moments, his system calmed. He spat out the rest of the offending liquid.

He rubbed his head, taking comfort in the moss's softness. Questions darted through his mind, starting with how they had all ended up inside the Riven. The wyvern had grabbed him, but how did the princesses end up here as well? If he kept shifting around to different areas, how would he ever rejoin Horra, Glory, and Pidge?

The Riven was dangerous for far different reasons than he had imagined. No grisly monsters guarded it. No dark-magic-wielding elves greeted him. This magic was far more insidious. But if the elves placed magic here to keep the foundation safe, there had to be a way to remove it.

Just like Merrow taught him, he thought back on what he knew about magic in particular. Even dark magic had parameters. One could only perform certain acts. Fairies could take one object and charm it into becoming something entirely different. Diseases, such as the last stages of the Crud, were fatal no matter how many spells one used.

The druids had laid forty stones in the Weald and etched sigils on them and the trees along the border to hide the space. Each sigil represented a different magical seal. He believed it was the same with the troll castle's Conservatory, though he hadn't researched enough to prove it. Merrow had taught him that the Creature God had placed his fingerprint on the Wilden Lands in much the same way—setting the rules of nature into place in an orderly fashion.

If that held true in the Riven, dark-magic spells and chaos or not, some type of magical signature would hold the spells in place. If he could find them, he could find a way out of the Riven safely.

That, however, was like hunting for a small weed in an enormous field of tall grasses.

"Which would be next to impossible," Rowan muttered into the wind.

~Horra—

At the Same Moment~

HORRA STARED bleakly at the swamp she now stood in. Frogs trilled and clicked, filling the air with a symphony of natural song. Again, something tugged on her senses, pacifying her like a lullaby. She flung her hood back over her head.

Turning in a circle, her boots sunk into the mud. Dampness along her backside soaked through and registered in her stunned mind. "Ew." She swiped at her bottom as if that would make it go away.

Her mood darkened. "What kind of wonky magic moves you from place to place?" She trudged over to a drier spot. Reeds and thick-bladed grass stuck out like spiky hair from the ground. A few mature trees stood sentinel in the distance.

Horra squinted. Their trunks were twisted oddly, as if the trees spun as they grew. They wavered like the wyverns had, only they didn't fully disappear from view.

"This place is so strange," she grumbled.

The sky was bright blue with no clouds, and the sun shone brilliantly across the green expanse. The scent of swamp water sat heavy in the too-warm air.

Frogs jumped out of her way as she walked toward the closest tree. Maybe she could communicate to Rowan through the tree or its roots. It was her best hope of reuniting with him, unless the Riven shifted them back together again.

Though the tree wasn't far, walking in the sucking muck and dodging the croaking critters slowed her progress—something that had never happened to her before while wearing the woodencloak. Usually, she was able to glide wherever she walked, and she blended into the atmosphere so well that even animals avoided her. "Out of my way, you clod-hopping nuisances."

An unusually large toad jumped, smacking her in her stomach, leaving a wet splotch on her cloak that soaked through to her clothes.

Horra stopped. Though she'd been cold while wearing the woodencloak, she'd never gotten wet before. The woodencloak protected her from the elements. Now it didn't. "Why isn't it working?"

Was the dark magic in the Riven responsible?

The area rumbled as she took her next step. "Oh no, not again!"

A whooshing sensation tugged at her until she was dizzy. She closed her eyes and fell to her knees. One moment she was in brackish water. The next, she kneeled against a rocky ridge.

"Oh, bother."

~Glory~

Sometime after Being Hung in a Tree

Music filled her mind, and the rumbles only added to the refrain. She didn't even mind that the same chorus played again and again. It was wondrous.

Glory had never believed in Heaven before. She now knew how wrong she was.

The tree's shuddering made her feel like she was lying in a silken web, rocking back and forth, not a care in the Wilden Lands. Could this go on forever?

Glory hoped so. She never wanted it to end.

CHAPTER 18

Rowan grew tired of the shifting scenery. After the grassland, he ended up by a rocky stream where different types of birds filled the branches of the trees lining the waterway. By the looks of it, they were all calling and chirping, creating a sort of symphony. He didn't dare listen to confirm his suspicion.

Next, he found himself on a rocky cliff where he slid and almost dropped off the side. On and on it continued, without repeat.

Now he was in another forest, unlike the first forest with the hanging corpses. This one had glowflies, flying beetles with light-producing organs on their abdomens that blinked in unison under a moonlit, star-laden sky. He assumed they danced to another of the Erlking's charmed songs. However, the tree before him completely distracted him from that line of thought.

It was *the* tree.

Rowan recalled the magnificence of the Ghost Tree from when he'd been mesmerized. The tree was ethereal with its silver bark and rounded white flowers. It was everything he remembered and more, standing regally in the center of this grove with its radiant canopy stretching across a grand expanse.

He desired to reach out and touch it, even though he couldn't hear the music. Its glowing aura drew his eyes, filling his mind with its beauty. Many trees were grand and resplendent in the Wilden Lands. The Yew trees were one such variety. But this tree? It was beyond anything else.

Flickers of the glowflies darted about his head, disrupting his view. They moved around the Ghost Tree in the same manner.

Rowan walked closer to inspect it. He'd known immediately what the first tree was when he saw it in his music-induced stupor. This one was identical, which couldn't be an accident. Woodsly, his predecessor, must've left that knowledge behind for a reason. But why?

Another puzzle to untangle.

With the instability of the Riven, he needed to figure it out quickly or he might lose his chance. The tree pulsed, startling Rowan. He stood frozen for a moment until it became apparent the area wasn't shifting.

Yet.

Spurred on by fear of missing a valuable opportunity, Rowan stepped closer, leaving the glowflies behind, and touched the massive silver trunk. A jolt traveled through his timber, holding him fast to the Ghost Tree.

Voices filled his mind. Too many to separate and too much to take in. But he couldn't move and wasn't able to halt the barrage. "Stop," he demanded, his voice cracking.

All noise ceased, but the hold persisted. Carefully, so as not to dig into the poisoned land, he reached out along the tree's roots to see what the intrusion was.

The tree was alive, bursting with spirits. He'd never experienced so many clinging to one tree before.

"Who is this? Why do you detain me?"

The voices rose in a raucous riot.

"Quiet!" Rowan waited for the clamor to die down. It took longer this time. The spirits were anxious. Not only did they shout at him, but they seemed to be arguing amongst themselves. Their agitation put him on edge. Finally, a hush fell. "Is there a rood among you?"

"*Yes,*" the voices answered as one.

"I will speak with them directly." Rowan gathered his thoughts. "Why are so many spirits linked to this tree?"

A pause.

"*We are all prisoners here. If we leave the tree, we will be destroyed.*"

"How?" he asked.

"*He has set traps. It is different for everyone.*"

The ground around the tree rumbled, and the atmosphere wavered, shifting once more. This time, it didn't take Rowan with it. It did, however, release him from the hold the spirits of the tree had on him. He shook his leaves, glad to be moving again.

He glanced around. Was this tree an anchor? If so, was this what he was looking for? Could he unravel the magic spells using the Ghost Tree?

But who was the "he" they were referring to? "He? Do you mean the second Erlking?"

"*We do not know him by that title. Music is his medium. Some call him Piper. Others call him the Conductor. All agree that he is evil.*"

"Music magic? It is the Erlking, then," Rowan confirmed. "How many are you, and how did you end up in the Ghost Tree?"

"We are hundreds. Dryads, roods, bogeys, spirits, fray folk, and a banshee or two. There once were more, but some died trying to escape. This fair tree is an island, sheltering us from the darkness and poison that has seeped into the land. It is from before, and its roots go deep enough that the magic hasn't penetrated the tree. We cannot move past its border, though. Elves established the Riven centuries ago, but the one you call Erlking changed the magic and added illusions."

Rowan considered the information. "I know every creature except for the fray folk. Who are they?"

A different person—a woman by the sound of the voice—responded. *"We are elves banished from Endwylde to the Riven by our Sylvan Council. We are not lawbreakers except in the eyes of our leaders. Our only infraction was to speak up against them. Only those who practice the dark magics are truly criminal."*

"But if you are elven, can you not use your innate magic and free yourselves?"

A murmur of voices rose and drifted off. *"We cannot."*

Rowan was curious about what they were hiding. From the little he knew about them, elves were exclusionary, secreting themselves behind an impenetrable wall. He mentally shook himself. The wall wasn't impassable, just impossible to escape.

"I'm trying to find the magical underpinnings so I can release the Erlking's hold on the Riven. Can any of you help me do this?"

"Some have tried before. But we do not recognize his spells and thus cannot remove or counter them."

Rowan frowned. "There must be a way."

"We will help you in any way we can."

"Then let's get started."

~Horra~
Even Later

HORRA BRUSHED her cloak off after crawling out of the rocky ravine. She was used to mountains of all kinds. She'd climbed on rocks before she could walk. And she'd survived being eaten by ballasts when the Erlking overtook her castle with the help of the mesmerized fairies. But she had never been swallowed by a mountain before.

Especially with the magic of the woodencloak disguising her.

The Riven was entirely too strange. None of it made any sense.

Mountains didn't come to life and gobble you up.

But this one had attempted to.

When she finally shook off the last of the debris, she jammed her clawed fists against her hips. "What in the name of dragon fire is going on here?"

The ground rattled again like it had minutes ago when she lost her footing. Horra rushed backward and away from the crumbling edge above the ravine. It curved like a smile, mocking her.

She tucked her head further inside the hood. "I need to get out of this forsaken place, and now."

A noise pricked her ears. She glanced up briefly, not wanting to take her eyes off the ground, which was currently solid.

A dark figure flew in circles some distance away. Another scree. "Pidge!" she yelled and took off running toward the bird. There wasn't much time between shiftings, so she didn't want to miss the opportunity to get her pet back.

Large rocks littered the ground, and scrub grass poked out of the gravel. She paid no attention, knowing her boots were sturdy enough to keep her from twisting her ankles too badly. "Pidge!" Her screams caught the bird's attention at last.

The pudge wudgie stopped circling and swung in her direction.

"Good girl!"

Horra's foot caught on a stone and she fell, tumbling along the hard surface and skinning her hide. Undeterred, Horra stumbled to her feet and kept running, her boots crunching against the pebbles.

She'd almost reached her pet when she slipped, but only momentarily. Eyes on the sky, she ignored the mountain's attempts to thwart her.

"Here, girl." Horra raised her arms and caught Pidge's claws in hers. The ground shook just as they rose into the air. When the shifting started, it didn't yank them into the swirling, changing landscape. They flew through it, untouched.

"Do you see that?" Surprise rushed through Horra. The mountain blurred for several moments before stopping and settling. Dust clouded the ground. Pidge continued flying.

Horra kept a tight hold on her pet's feet as they flew over the rocky plain. Her eyes were on the hazy horizon, and her mind spun. Why didn't they get sucked into the vortex of the Riven and change places again? Was it because they were in the air?

That must be it. But they couldn't remain in the air forever.

They drew closer to the blurred area.

Horra held her breath and, with a mighty swing of Pidge's wings, they flew beyond the mountain portion of the Riven.

Darkness enveloped them as they entered a large forested section. She groaned. This was the place where she'd entered the Riven. Luckily, they weren't flying high enough to soar past the cocoon-like bundles hanging from the limbs. Minutes passed, and Horra's claws cramped. Pidge dipped, growing tired. "Land on a limb, Pidge."

Pidge scree'd in response. She swung harder up and found a tree with lower limbs. In seconds, Pidge hovered over a large branch and Horra let go. She dropped and landed, sprawling across a tree's bough. Leaves shook and rattled above them. Pidge circled and landed a couple limbs away from her.

Horra sat up, careful not to teeter or fall off. Though the tree's limb was big enough to support her, it creaked beneath her weight. Horra took a deep, cleansing breath. "Thank you, friend. You saved me."

Her pet crooned before side-eyeing their surroundings.

"Wish we were home in the Conservatory." Horra leaned against the tree's trunk, and it hummed against her back. "Now we just need to find Rowan." When she closed her eyes, an image of Glory appeared in her mind. "Oh yeah. And rescue the fairy princess."

Frustration bubbled in her gut. "It's all that stupid fairy's fault. None of this would've happened if she hadn't run away from the castle in the first place."

Pidge glanced at Horra as if questioning her logic.

"Don't give me that look. She's the reason we're stuck in this mish-mash maze. I wouldn't have come near the Riven had she not run away. And now I've lost Rowan." She blustered out a breath. "Fairies are nothing but trouble."

The pudge wudgie clucked in the back of her throat and turned her inky black head away.

Horra fought the urge to stick her tongue out at the bird. Maybe she could try to contact Rowan instead. She placed her claw firmly on the buzzing trunk. "Rowan?"

The tree creaked, and the bark snapped. *"Queen Bearer? Where are you?"*

Relief flooded Horra, and she grinned. "Back where I entered, thanks to Pidge. We're up in a tree."

"In what part of the Riven?"

"A forest. There are … things … hanging from the limbs."

A crack came from the trunk. *"Those trees are not safe. Can you find another, safer place?"*

Buzzing hummed to life beneath the bark as if to verify Rowan's words.

"Pidge, we need to go—"

The tree moved, not like when the scenery shifted, but more like something was emerging from the bark.

Or a bunch of somethings.

The wood rippled, and rounded bug heads appeared. Hundreds of them. It was as if the tree itself was nothing but a hive of creepy-crawlies. The critters were as long as one of her claws, with shiny, hard shells covering everything but their squirming heads.

Chitterbugs. An invasion.

Horra squealed, startling Pidge. Before her pet could fly off, Horra rushed over and grabbed hold of the rope. She climbed onto the bird's back. "Let's get out of here!"

CHAPTER 19

~Horra~

The same moment Horra and Pidge flew off, the tree they'd taken refuge in collapsed. A branch snagged Horra's hood as it fell. Immediately, the drone of a thousand chitterbugs assaulted her ears.

Holding the rope in one claw, Horra jerked her hood back in place. A chitterbug dropped from the fabric onto her face. She screamed and slapped at it, praying there wasn't more than one on her.

Spurred on by Horra's shrieks, Pidge darted upward.

Right toward one of the dangling bundles.

Horra jerked the rope, and Pidge grazed past the hanging bag of bones. "Lookout, Pidge!"

The bird straightened out her flight once Horra resettled on her back.

With her hood back over her head and the noise now muted, Horra focused on where they were going. Pidge dodged another bundle, but there were so many. "Fly lower, Pidge."

The bird dropped, taking Horra's stomach with her. She gulped to stop the churning in her gut. "Vinegar and beans! You're going to make me sick. Try to keep steady."

They flew beneath several bundles. Ahead, though, Horra spotted Glory's hair. "That one, Pidge. I'll try to cut the princess off if you fly close enough to her."

Pidge sent her a trilling cackle.

Horra drew her dagger and wrapped the rope around her free wrist. At first, Pidge swung wide around the princess. Then she darted in.

Horra stuck the dagger out and swung.

And missed.

"Again, girl."

Pidge swooped down and back around. With a mighty push of her wings, they neared Glory again. Horra leaned out, holding tight to the rope for balance.

Success!

The dagger cut through the threads holding the cocooned fairy like a hot knife slicing through bacon grease. Horra tried to catch the bundle, but they were moving too fast.

Glory fell.

"We have to get to her before the chitterbugs." Though normal chitterbugs didn't attack other beings, Horra wasn't sure what spells the Erlking had placed on them. She held on while Pidge spiraled down, straight for Glory.

The only way to get the fairy was to land and snatch her away before anything else could reach them. Pidge flung her wings wide as she landed near the princess. Horra dismounted. "Don't leave. I'll be right back."

Pidge squawked.

Holding her hood tight, she rushed to Glory and picked her up. Though not as heavy as the castle's pins that secured the passageway's doors, the fairy was nothing more than dead weight. "Good thing trolls are strong," she muttered as she stumbled back to the pudge wudgie.

Dirt flew in the air as chitterbugs crawled out of the ground. Horra hurriedly threw Glory over Pidge's back and climbed on behind her. Meanwhile, Pidge eyed the creepy crawlers but made no move to eat them.

Strange. The bird had no qualms about eating skeezes, which were disgusting. And it wasn't as if Pidge ever skipped a free meal.

But Horra knew how smart her bird was. It wasn't a good sign she didn't eat the bugs. "Let's go."

Pidge sprang into the air.

Horra grimaced. Of course the fairy princess would take up most of the room on the bird's back. Mesmerized or cocoonized, the girl was a thorn in Horra's hide. Horra held tightly to the rope and prayed to the Creature God for their safety.

"We're coming, Rowan," she promised.

~Rowan~

ROWAN'S LINK with Horra ended. He hoped the queen bearer was able to get away from the chitterbugs. His roots had sensed darkness in them—some sort of hex—while he was in the same forest. The moss on his face tickled as he frowned deeply.

He turned back to the Ghost Tree. "Does anyone understand how music magic works?"

The elf woman replied, *"It is a rarely used form of magic in my culture, deemed simplistic or elementary. Many children's tales are written about music, mostly to dissuade them from the medium. Fairies are more likely to use music magic."*

"I am confused. Why is music deemed simple in your culture?" Rowan inquired.

A titter echoed in his mind. *"Elves prefer science and engineering over the arts. Anyone can play a musical instrument or sing with a modicum of talent. We believe that using your intellect to advance your surroundings is the highest form of enlightenment."*

That piqued his curiosity. "I see. Yet a man using a lesser form of magic has locked you in what is essentially a prison."

Outraged voices broke out. He didn't stop them. "Master Rood?" he whispered into the noise, leaning into the tree's fibers to establish a separate connection.

"How can I help you?" came the reply. The enraged voices faded into the background.

"What are the weaknesses of music magic? Is there a counter-magic I can use against it?"

"If it were simply music, that might be easier to undo. However, I've sensed this magic is multilayered with many anchors and fail-safes. And contrary to what the elf stated, there is science behind it. We would not remain captive if it weren't sophisticated. If you can break through his snares, unraveling the threads of the music will be, as the elf said, simple."

"So, it is just what I thought." The weight of the task settled in his stem. He was no closer to an answer than he was before touching the Ghost Tree. "Thank you, Master Rood."

"You're welcome, young druid."

Rowan let his hand fall to his side. He'd thought trolls were stubborn and unyielding. Elves, it seemed, were just as bad.

The ground rumbled, and Rowan's view distorted as if it were breaking apart and then reforming. He was safe inside the circle of the tree's roots. But where would he go once he left its protection? How would he find the magical anchors before the shifting started again?

Dismayed, he sunk his roots into the soil, reaching for nourishment to replenish his energy. He closed his eyes and welcomed the silence.

His mind spun, trying to work out a solution. He'd seen the Erlking one time during the battle with the swamp bombs. However, he hadn't gotten close enough to glean much information. All he knew was what the troll princess had shared with him and what the roods had told him before the Weald was destroyed. One thing Horra had said stuck out to him.

Rowan reached out to the Ghost Tree once more. "Why would the elves remove the Erlking's ears?"

Screams filled his mind.

"*Dark magic.*" A new voice rose above the rest.

"*Cursed,*" another shrieked.

The rood shushed them all. "*The druid needs information. Please explain.*"

"*Only the worst offenders have their magic stripped. Those convicted of the most gruesome of crimes. The Sylvan then marks the criminals by removing their ears, which is a symbol of honor and pride for elves. It is the highest disgrace an elf can suffer,*" the female elf stated.

Rowan considered this. "Would doing that take away their ability to hear?"

"*Yes. That is part of the punishment. Silence makes an elf go mad.*"

"If he weren't already insane to begin with." Rowan contemplated for several minutes. "Is there a way to reinstate the ability to hear? I've been told the Erlking has held conversations, and he continues to use music to target and torment other creatures. How would he do that if he's deaf?"

"*The Sylvan rarely make mistakes.*"

"What if they did? Is it possible to hide a magical ability from your leaders? Could it be they didn't sense the danger in his music magic and they didn't fully remove it?"

Silence.

"You might be on to something, young warrior." The rood spoke this time. *"Use this knowledge wisely."*

Rowan removed his hand from the bark one last time. He retracted his roots from the rich soil at the base of the tree. "Now I just need a good plan."

Scree'ing in the distance caught his attention. He stepped away from the trunk as far as he could without leaving the tree's sanctuary.

Pidge circled in the blue sky above him. He spotted Horra on the bird's back, and something else—he couldn't tell what. "Over here!" he called.

The pudge wudgie screeched, arched, then headed his way.

Rowan waved, not wanting them to miss him. "Land inside the tree's shelter. It's safe here."

"Rowan?" Horra yelled. "Is that you?"

"Yes."

The ground rumbled. Rowan's sap rushed through his fibers. He reached out a hand, but they weren't close enough.

The area shifted, blurring and shaking.

"No!" he screamed.

This couldn't be happening again.

~Horra~
Moments Earlier

HORRA SPOTTED ROWAN BENEATH A MAGNIFICENT, sprawling silver

tree. Glowflies danced around the tree, their lights pulsing as if to the strains of a song. "Let's get Rowan," she told Pidge.

Rowan called out, his branchy arm held up to greet them.

They dashed toward the flickering lights and the tree. The ground rumbled, and the air moved around them. Another shift.

"No!" Rowan's shout startled Horra.

The trees and land below were indiscernible.

"Dragon's breath," Horra muttered, praying the magic wouldn't toss them about again.

When everything came back into focus, Rowan and the tree were still there.

Pidge snapped at the first glowfly they came across, jerking Horra from her perilous sitting position. Her heart hammered in her chest as her feet dangled off of Pidge's tail. Though she'd done this once before, she didn't relish repeating it.

"Stop that, Pidge. I'll give you a thousand glowflies if you drop us next to Rowan. I promise." Horra spoke around the lump in her throat.

Pidge squealed, probably in protest at her request. However, she did as Horra asked. Glowflies pelted her head as they rushed through the swarm.

The impact of the landing jarred Horra's body. She let go of the rope, disentangling it from her arm, then rolled over to stand up. "Ugh. Never again. Nope. I refuse to dangle off another bird for the rest of my life."

"Queen Bearer, are you all right?" Rowan's calm voice helped her gain her bearings. Between the Riven's constant changing and the flight through the dangling graveyard, nothing was stable.

Pidge shook her feathers, knocking the fairy princess from her back. Glory came to rest at Horra's feet.

"Never been better." Horra dusted herself off, trying to disguise the tremble in her claws. "What is this tree?"

"It's a Ghost Tree." He turned to gaze up at it. "Also known as a Dove Tree, named after its gray bark. I saw it once before when I was mesmerized."

Horra blinked. "*This* is the tree that lured you into the Erlking's mountain?" She didn't understand the attraction.

"A vision of it, yes. And it wasn't just the tree, but the music as well." Rowan turned back toward her. "There are refugees inside this tree. I've been speaking with them."

"Really? What have you learned? Something to help us get out of here, I hope?" Horra ignored her pet zipping around the tree's base and gobbling up all the glowflies.

"Yes. And no."

Horra stared at his moss-covered face that gave away no trace of emotion. The spark of hope he'd given her wavered. "What is that supposed to mean?"

"It means I'm not sure how to get out of here. We're stuck in this rotating, cursed land for now."

CHAPTER 20

~Horra~

Horra glared at Rowan while stifling the urge to stomp her feet and scream. "That is not what I wanted to hear."

"Is that Princess Glory?" Rowan asked, bending over to inspect the bundle at her feet.

"Pidge and I cut her loose, yes." Now that the rush to escape the graveyard forest was over, Horra needed to check on the fairy. She knelt.

If she didn't know any better, it would seem the girl was asleep. Horra swept the dirty brown hair from her face and tried not to cringe at seeing her disfigured features again. She'd seen the damage the Erlking had inflicted, of course, but not close up.

Empathy warred against the anger she held against the girl for fleeing Oddar's castle. Her chest constricted. Glory's snore ended with a hoggish snort erupting from her piggish nose. "Let's unwrap her."

"Did you see what kind of creature did this?" Rowan asked, not moving.

Horra's claw stilled over the body. "I think it was a big-bellied spider. Why?"

"I shouldn't have to remind you who we're dealing with."

Pidge landed next to the fairy, startling Horra. A glance up revealed a starlit sky devoid of glowflies. "Full?" she chided her bird.

The pudge wudgie fluffed her feathers, let out a cluck, and sat down next to the tree's trunk.

Horra pulled her dagger back out of its sheath. "I'll be careful." Slowly, she sliced through the silky web one layer at a time. After each layer, Rowan took the threads and placed them outside the tree's shaded canopy. She didn't question his reason.

Soon, only a couple layers remained, and they could see through the nearly invisible strings. "Almost there."

Horra raised the dagger to slip it through the remaining fibers when she saw it. She jerked back and pointed to the small black spider resting on Glory's chest. As if sensing it wasn't covered any longer, it wiggled, revealing a bright-yellow violin mark on its back. She shivered and moved farther away. "Is that what I think it is?"

Rowan leaned over her. "If you mean a combatis rigoralia, also called the death bringer, then yes."

Horra sputtered. "Now what do we do? If I uncover it, the critter might bite Glory. Or me."

The spider squirmed again, flexing a long black front leg.

Pidge's head popped up.

"Don't—" Horra cried before the bird pecked the spider out

from the last vestiges of the web. She shook it, knocking off the threads clinging to her beak.

With a gulp, the spider was gone, as was the threat.

"Uh," Horra stammered. She stared into the pudge wudgie's golden eyes. "Rowan? Please tell me that won't harm Pidge."

"Pudge wudgies are capable of digesting many poisons and toxins without effect. She should be fine." Rowan scratched the green fuzz on his chin. "Have you noticed, though, Queen Bearer, that the Erlking uses a great many critters in his quest to take over the Wilden Lands?"

Horra retrieved her dagger and sliced through the final webbing covering the fairy. She glanced up to catch the serious tilt of the woodgoblin druid's head. "Yes. What are you thinking?"

"I'm not sure yet." Rowan filled Horra in on his conversation with the tree spirits.

She swiped her claws in the dirt at the base of the tree, removing the clinging remnants. "He can't be deaf. I talked with him myself. Sageel heard him discussing the door troll with the fairies. I mean, I saw the scars where his ears should be. I guess I never considered he should be deaf."

The ground rumbled, signaling another shift. Horra closed her eyes to keep from getting dizzy as the area broke apart and reassembled itself.

Pidge fluffed her feathers.

When the disorder died down, Horra's glance fell on the prone fairy princess. "Do you think figuring that part of the puzzle out might help us defeat the Erlking?"

"Something about the link nags at my mind. It won't leave me alone. I don't understand. I can't describe why—"

Horra held up her claw. "What you're sensing is what we trolls call a gut feeling. You might know it as intuition."

"Ah. A perception of something that's not physically manifested." He stoically contemplated the idea, his eyes on the moonlit sky. "What do you do when this gut feeling comes upon you?"

"Mother once told me that her gut often knew things before her mind did. I wonder if she knew she was going to die before—" Pain pierced her heart, remembering her mother's suffering at the end.

"She was afflicted with the Crud, was she not?" Rowan's voice lowered in a rare show of empathy.

Moisture gathered in her eyes and she clamped her jaw to keep control. "Yes. She hid it from me, how sick she had become close to the end. There was never any sign that her condition was fatal. But looking back, I can see that she knew. We took several trips before she wasn't able to travel anymore. She was always so active, so it never occurred to me it was her way of spending as much time with me as possible and imparting all the lessons she could before she died." Her voice cracked on the last word, and she coughed to disguise it.

Horra swiped away the troublesome tears. "You know Woodsly was just as brave when the Erlking poisoned him. He placed the Medicinal Curse Book in my knapsack, then rushed to find me before he gave in to death."

Rowan stilled. "From everything Merrow has told me and all that you've mentioned, Woodsly appears to be a legendary figure."

Horra swallowed the emotion clogging her throat. She still missed the stodgy stick that was her instructor, no matter how many times he had enjoyed punishing her. Carrying the responsibility lately of keeping so many safe from harm, she keenly understood the weight he'd been under to train her after her mother's passing. "He was and will always be a hero to me. Merrow told me he left some dregs of knowledge within your seed. Trust your intuition, Rowan. Even if you can't prove what it's telling you with facts and evidence. It's a rare thing for it to fail."

Rowan nodded, his eyes steady and serious. "All that remains, then, is to find the link between everything."

"Easy sneezy." Horra grinned, hoping to lighten his mood. He'd grown too sober.

His mossy face creased with a frown. "Indeed."

Delighted to receive the reaction she'd hoped for, Horra turned to the next important matter. "Right after we wake the sleeping princess. You wouldn't have a handsome prince hidden somewhere in those branches, would you?"

"No, why would I?"

Horra snickered. "No reason."

~Rowan~
In the Same Moment

THE FAIRY PRINCESS was pale upon his first inspection after Horra removed all the poisonous spider webs. Her chest rose and fell, revealing she was still alive and breathing. Rowan ran through the varied remedies and antitoxins he knew. "How do we wake Glory if we don't know exactly what her ailment is?"

"Well, one thing usually wakes most people up." Horra lifted her claw, and the slap that followed echoed across the strange forest.

The fairy princess jerked upright. She cradled a hand across the now reddening spot on her cheek. "Ow! What was that for?"

Horra snorted. "Where do I even begin?" She stood and walked over to Pidge. "But seriously. Rowan, Pidge, and I just rescued you from a death bringer, its web, and from hanging forevermore in a tree-bound graveyard full of the bones of the Riven's victims. You're welcome."

"I didn't thank you." Glory's voice quivered, and her face scrunched with what Rowan assumed to be anger.

Rowan stood and brushed himself off. "Ladies, there is no time to argue. We must figure a way out of here or we'll all end up like the bags of bones in that shifting forest."

"I have no idea what you both are talking about." Glory's gaze whipped from him to her arms, where some of the web still clung to her pale skin. "What is this?" she shrieked.

Rowan grew weary of the fairy princess and the drama that always accompanied her. "You were seized by a combatis rigoralia spider when you entered the Riven. It spun you into a cocoon and hung you from a high tree in the forest you landed in. That"—he pointed to her—"is the remains of the web Queen Bearer Fyd removed from your body after Pidge ate the spider hidden inside said cocoon."

Glory twisted her head from him to Horra and back to him again. "The Riven. A spider? Wha—?" She rubbed her head. "I thought I was in music heaven. It was such a wonderful dream."

"Whatever spell she was under is still probably befuddling her." Horra took something out of her back pocket and fed it to an eager Pidge. "I should've let her sleep until after we got out of this place."

Glory sighed.

Rowan noticed the queen bearer's shoulders stiffening at the fairy's reaction. "We're safe here," she said. "And I just proved I can get two people on Pidge's back." She glanced at Glory with narrowed eyes. "And though I'd vote to leave the princess behind if worse came to worst, it would be best if we could all make it out of here alive."

Rowan agreed. "If the Riven does indeed have some sort of magical underpinning, and the Ghost Tree is not affected, reason would dictate there must be something close by to anchor the magic."

Horra scratched Pidge's neck. "What is the common factor in all the places you landed in?"

He considered. "The graveyard forest had chitterbugs. The meadow where you found me had wyvern." He ignored Glory's snicker of disbelief and continued. "This forest has glowflies. Well, it did until Pidge ate them."

Horra joined in. "The mountainous terrain tried to eat me alive—like a ballast, and the swamp had attack frogs."

"Every time I would get close to you or a tree I could link up to, except for the Ghost Tree, the Riven sent me to another area different from the one I'd just been in. The only common distinction is that he uses creatures he can control."

They fell into quiet contemplation.

"You're both mad." Glory rose, flipped her hood over her head, and started to step out from beneath the tree.

Pidge screeched and dodged in front of the princess.

"Hey!" she yelled.

"Don't scream at my pet." Horra rushed to stand in front of Pidge. "All she's trying to do is save your stupid hide."

Rowan pinched the space between his eyes, squishing the soft peat that grew there. "Will you both stop arguing? We wouldn't be here now if you two could get along."

Horra stomped her foot. "Fine. Go ahead and step outside the tree's boundary. See if I care."

The ground rattled, and the air blurred.

Horra grabbed Pidge's rope and jumped closer to the tree, pulling the bird with her. Rowan also moved away from the root's outer border, but in a calmer manner.

When he turned around, the fairy stood transfixed as the area split open, broke apart, then came back together again.

"What. Is. Happening. Here?" The fairy's voice pitched so high, the liverwort growing in his ears expanded, blocking the shrill noise. Though Torren liked to tease him about being Mr. Mossycoat man, there were many moments he was thankful for the protection.

Horra crossed her arms over her chest. "We tried to tell you."

Pidge clucked her agreement, then fluffed her feathers and settled back down against the tree's trunk.

Glory shook her head, the hood's ragged hem waving back and forth with the motion. "I don't understand. One moment I was walking along, and the next moment, I'm in a surreal nightmare."

"Welcome to our new reality," Horra mumbled as she moved closer to the pudge wudgie. Though spoken too low for the fairy to hear, Rowan caught it.

Rowan wasn't versed on how to make two different female creatures get along. Merrow had only briefly touched on diplomacy in his rush to impart a century's worth of druid knowledge. He almost wished Merrow had focused less on the Wilden Land's history and more on creature relations, especially those involving females.

The bark between his shoulders tightened. Rowan wasn't sure if he was going to survive being the only sane creature in their group.

CHAPTER 21

~Horra~

A minute later, Horra plunked down beside the tree, anger boiling inside her. The sulky, uncooperative fairy princess got under Horra's hide in the most abrasive way. If only it were as easy as leaving the girl to her own fate.

She bit her lip, knowing what her father would say if she told the princess off.

Look what happened the last time she'd done that.

Instead, she sat and stewed in the juices of her anger and waited for the Riven to stabilize once more to continue her conversation with Rowan.

Glory stomped away from the root's edge and settled on the other side of the tree. Thankfully, she was now completely out of sight.

Horra picked at a spot of lichen on the Ghost Tree's bark. "How is it possible this tree remains free from the elves' spells?" She hurried on, knowing the druid would turn informapedia in the blink of an eye. "I mean, as big as the tree is, it could have already been established when the Riven was formed. But even so, how?"

Rowan tented his fingers, proving she was correct about him turning all instructorish at her questions. "Most tree roots will only go as deep as the water table they grow on. Under the right conditions, such as loose, rich humus, their roots can penetrate farther down and beyond anything that would soak into the upper levels of terra firma. When I sank my roots in before you appeared, they sensed a treasure trove of nutrients."

He moved to sit next to her, his branches catching in her curls.

Horra brushed her hair away and scooted a couple inches over, remembering Rowan's nonexistent understanding of personal space.

He proceeded, oblivious. He held one hand out, palm up, which was devoid of the mossy growth covering the rest of his bark. "Before, in the graveyard forest, my feelers perceived not only the chitterbugs beneath the soil's surface but poison saturating the ground. The elves and I assume the Erlking polluted the Riven with their spells."

Rowan tapped the silver trunk with his wooden knuckles and glanced up at the Ghost Tree's underside. "This tree, and possibly a few others I witnessed as the Riven transported me from place to place, is essentially an island in an ocean of toxic mulch, drenched in hazardous dark spells, proving everything the roods reported about the Riven true."

Horra inhaled a deep breath ford let it out. "That doesn't completely answer how this tree and the other ones you saw are safe havens. Wouldn't the spells seep into them as well? I know they did in the graveyard forest. The chitterbugs came out of the wood in swarms just as I left." She shuddered. "It's not something I ever wish to see again."

He blinked his grayish-brown eyes. "I assume these roots grow deeper than the other trees?" The tone of his voice wasn't as self-assured as normal.

She petted Pidge, who had her beak tucked in her wing while she napped. "Are you asking me or telling me?"

Rowan glanced away. "What else could it be?"

It wasn't often that the woodgoblin druid was off his game. It seemed she'd caught him in one such rare moment. "The Riven is drenched with magic, Rowan. There might be another reason these trees have been spared. Wouldn't Merrow encourage you to consider other possibilities?"

His mouth twitched. "Yes, I suppose you're right."

She bumped him in the arm. "It's okay, Rowan. No one can be right one hundred percent of the time."

This time his cheek ticked, almost like her father's eye did when he was upset but trying to hide it. "I don't like being wrong."

"Maybe you're not. But that's why we should evaluate different possibilities. The elves have kept a pretty tight hold on the Riven for reasons we may never fully understand. As the most developed magic-users in the history of the Wilden Lands, it stands to reason there might be more than what meets the eye going on here."

Though she hated to admit elves were more advanced than trolls, what little they knew about elves pointed to them being incredibly powerful. Horra had always been curious about why they'd pulled out of the Wilden Lands and hidden themselves away from the rest of the creatures and their kingdoms. It never made sense to her.

Rowan's tight posture relaxed a fraction. "You are correct. We should consider other options."

Horra smiled. She loved to plan and search for solutions. "Now we're talking."

<hr>

~Rowan~
A Few Minutes Later

"You cannot be serious." Rowan stared at the queen bearer in disbelief.

"What? It's possible." A twitch of her green lips betrayed her attempt at humor.

Rowan cleared his throat. "I would've noticed if the Erlking was a giantized insect. If you're not going to be earnest in your attempts to figure out the puzzle of the Riven, I won't continue discussing it with you."

A strange look crossed the troll's face before it cleared. "Fine. Maybe he's *not* a bug king from the future who has returned to set up his own Utopia in the Riven and is bent on destroying all other forms of life in the Wilden Lands. Your turn to guess."

"Finally." Rowan steepled his fingers to gather his thoughts. His mind went blank.

"Ha! You've got nothing." Horra's glee fueled his brain stem into gear.

He snapped his fingers. "Time lock. I read one of Merrow's older druid Middle Aged Archives, which mentioned witches used time locks to keep their victims hidden."

Horra's mouth hung open for a moment. "That's ... actually, that's pretty good. Tell me more about this time lock thing."

Rowan frowned and strained to recall what he'd read. He'd dismissed it as hocus pocus when he came across it. Now he wasn't so sure. "It was a spell. There wasn't much information, only a passing mention of a clan of witches who employed it as a means to siphon magic from other creatures."

She stuck her tongue out. "Like the grubby worms?"

He thought about that. "No, grubbies have to attach to their host to gain access to the magic. Witches, it seems, did not. They would strike their victims into paralysis and then seal them in their time locks. There, they stole the other creature's magic. The book called it pooling. They could then seal the magic away and use it at will."

"That's quite a bit of information."

He met the queen bearer's steady gaze. "The text did not mention how they pooled the magic or how they sealed the time locks. Nothing about their spells or the means by which they siphoned magic."

"Huh," Horra huffed. "Pooling magic? That sounds ominous. Good thing you can't steal a troll's magic since we don't have any."

"That only serves to make you worthless in the eyes of a witch." Glory's voice startled them both.

Rowan had forgotten the fairy princess was with them since she'd remained quiet after crawling to the other side of the Ghost Tree.

Horra stood to face the other girl. "Maybe worthless in your eyes, since you came from a magical background. I'd call it being safe from magic thieves."

Rowan shook his head, making his crown rattle. He rose from the ground to stand between the two. "Let's not argue again."

Glory shrugged. "Who's arguing? It's a difference of opinion, log boy. That's all."

Horra tensed.

Rowan stepped in front of her, unsure what Horra found offensive in the fairy's response. "Do you have anything advantageous to add to the conversation, or are you just going to take jabs at other creatures?"

The fairy princess straightened her shoulders. Until then, he hadn't noticed how much the girl slumped when she stood or how humped her wings appeared beneath the tattered cloak. "Matter of fact, I do. Magic pools. Witches aren't the only ones who use them. Though it's not quite the same, we fairies have our own supply of magic reserves."

"What kind of reserves?" Horra asked with a narrowed gaze.

Glory tsked. "I'll only tell you if it'll get us out of here."

Horra flung her arms out. "How am I supposed to know if it will help if you don't tell us first?"

They stood staring at each other, the fairy from behind a shadowed hood and the queen bearer with a darkening face.

"What does it hurt to share your information with us, Princess? Trolls cannot use magic, and I have woodgoblin and druid magics. I don't need fairy magic."

The fairy made a popping noise. "Okay. This is magic 101, by the way, for those of you who don't have a clue."

Horra made a sound behind him.

Glory explained. "There are magical fault lines all across the Wilden Lands. There once were more—before the elves dispatched the witches for their wickedness in creating the worqs. Some disappeared after that. Our history books weren't sure whether it was due to the witches hiding them or the elves moving them when they left."

"Why don't trolls know about any of this?" Horra's voice pitched higher.

"Pshaw. Probably because your kind has never been interested enough in magic to keep those kinds of records. Or maybe it's because, before the War of the Warts, Oddar would never align itself with a creature it couldn't rule over."

Horra knocked into Rowan as she rushed toward the princess. "That's not true!"

He extended his arm and held Horra back, digging his roots in to remain steady against her angry efforts to reach the princess. No matter how hard she tried, Rowan wouldn't let Horra get to Glory.

Horra screamed in frustration. "I should've left you hanging in that stupid tree. See if I help you again." She stormed off as far as she could in the small space. Pidge, sensing her owner's emotional state, tottered after her. They disappeared around the opposite side of the tree.

Rowan straightened to his full height so that his crown tangled with the lowest branches of the mighty Ghost Tree. "We are not your enemy, Princess Toppenbottom. I hope it's not too late once you finally realize that."

~Glory~

Glory watched the log boy stalk off to the other side of the tree. Her satisfaction in telling the troll princess off cooled after his final words. She stomped away just far enough so she couldn't see him or the ridiculous troll. The tree was almost not big enough for the three of them.

"What do I care about his opinion?" she muttered under her breath. Glory chided herself for the prick of conscience he'd unleashed in her.

Her only focus should be on her single mission: to find the Erlking and make him remove his hex.

Glancing around, she found herself alone. Though she'd done it on purpose, that fact also needled her. Before she'd lost her beauty, people thronged to her, vying to hear her musical voice.

Now her voice wasn't musical at all. And she was stuck

with the horrid troll princess and her sidekick, Mr. Mossy-pants-Stickface-Know-It-All.

Again, Glory shook herself. She'd told the troll the truth about her kind. She vaguely recalled their first meeting when she, her sister, and her mother arrived at the castle. During the formal tour, Horra revealed an almost obsessive loyalism to her foremothers and her kingdom's history. Her instructor's frosty support had been evident as well.

She snickered. If anyone had a history to be proud of, it was fairies. Her forebearers had chosen the most beautiful land to build their Shining Kingdom. They remained unmatched in art, music, and fashion. Everywhere they went, they were idolized.

Except for Oddar.

Glory searched the horizon, stepping close to the edge of the roots. Green grass swayed in the breeze. The sky was a dark, night blue. Nothing about the place seemed nefarious, unlike what the other two seemed to think.

Impatience nipped at her gut. She needed to find the Erlking sooner rather than later. Mostly because he held her mother—the queen—captive. She feared for her mother, yes. But it also wouldn't look good if the evil elf took advantage of fairy royalty. Once she had her magic back, she'd use it to thwart the Erlking's music spells. She'd almost managed to the first time. But she'd underestimated him.

She wouldn't make that mistake twice.

The golden bridle was still tucked inside her cloak. Glory took it out, rubbed it, and whistled low. Calliope would hear it and come save her from her current company. Then she could resume her hunt for the elf.

Nothing happened.

She shook the bridle as the moonlight glowed upon the

shiny gold, flickering like a candle on the tree trunk behind her. Strangely enough, the tree was a beautiful creation. She vowed to plant one back home. "Come to me, faithful Calliope."

Silence.

And then a rumble.

Glory's heart hastened with hope.

But it was only the Riven changing again. Her arm dropped, and she closed her eyes against the dizzying spectacle.

"What is that?" the troll princess said.

Glory quickly hid the bridle in the cloak's secret pocket and glanced innocently at the other girl. "What's what?"

Hostility glittered from the troll's awful mud-colored eyes. She let out a small, derisive laugh. "So, that's what the Erlking wants so bad, isn't it? You're going to trade it to get your looks back. Were you trying to summon him?"

Glory stuck her chin out. "I don't know what you're talking about."

Pidge toddled next to the troll and glared at her with beady black eyes. The bird twisted its head back and forth as if sizing Glory up.

Which only irritated her more. "You stay on your side of the tree, and I'll stay on mine." She started to walk off, but the ground rumbled harder, knocking her to her knees.

"What's that?" Horra braced herself against the trunk.

"Princess? Queen Bearer?" Rowan called.

Queen Bearer? Glory had never heard the term before. However, she wasn't curious enough to ask.

A familiar whinny pierced the air. Calliope's midnight form was a shadow in the moonlit sky.

Glory's heart picked up and she rushed to the outside of the root's boundary. "That's my girl!"

"Is that a flying horse?" Disbelief rang in the troll's voice.

"I believe that's a kelpie. Why is it here?" Rowan asked.

Glory waved her hand in the air so the creature could spot her. "Because I control it, and I just beckoned it to come get me."

"But it's not safe out there."

Glory ignored Horra's concern. "I'll be perfectly safe."

Calliope dipped down by the tree, reins dangling from its leafy mane. In an instant, the kelpie was close enough for her to grab the straps. She swung herself onto the kelpie's back. The saddle horn dug into her stomach, but she didn't complain. She was safe now. "Goodbye, losers. Hope you find your way out of here," Glory yelled over her shoulder at the sputtering duo.

Pidge screeched in alarm.

She grinned.

Calliope's massive wings made easy work of flying away. "Good girl." Glory patted the kelpie's neck. "Lead me to the Erlking."

~Horra~

HORRA COULDN'T BELIEVE her eyes. The selfish, good-for-nothing fairy princess had left them behind without a second glance.

Rowan's mouth hung open before he snapped it shut. "Oh dear," he said.

"Yeah, that's too courteous of a response, druid. She left us stranded in this whirly-bird maze without even a thank you for rescuing her from certain death." Horra picked up a stick and threw it, but it wasn't enough to satisfy her anger.

She stomped back to the Ghost Tree and dropped to the

ground with a thud. Her backside hurt, but she wouldn't admit it. Horra welcomed the pain over the harsh sting of the fairy's betrayal. "I don't care what my father says. I won't save her hide again. Not ever." She peeled apart a drying leaf. "Let the Erlking have her. I don't care."

Tears stung her eyes, and she sniffed to keep snot from running out of her nose. Though the fairy was conceited and superficial, nothing could have prepared Horra for what the girl had just done. She rubbed a sleeve across her leaking nose, and traitorous moisture made its way down her cheeks. Pidge danced next to her as if sensing her distress.

Rowan lowered himself to sit beside her. "Are you all right?"

"No, I'm not all right. We may be stuck here forever. And she just calls out to some kelpie thing and is suddenly saved." Horra flung her arm out. "We've been doing everything to rescue her. To save all of us. She doesn't get to leave us like that, without any remorse." She sniffed. "Uncaring about *our* fate." Horra's bottom lip trembled, and she dropped her head on top of her knees. She tucked her legs tight against her body as she fought a wave of anguish.

Rowan sat silently next to her, unmoving. She glanced up at him once her tears dried and she'd swiped away all the snot.

"I was thinking about the magical pool thing the princess spoke about earlier." He stood and shook his leaves. "I meant to ask her questions before she flew off on the kelpie." He turned to peer at her. "There may be some kind of underground magical stream that feeds these trees, keeping them safe from the noxious spells. I need to inquire of the rood."

He placed his hand against the tree. "Master Rood, I have a question for you. Is it possible this tree is rooted in a magical underground stream?" He tipped his head as if listening, but Horra couldn't hear anything. "I see. Would it be possible for you and the others to locate it and travel to the other trees along the border to find your way out?"

Horra waited, eager to hear what they would tell him.

"Ah, good. I have a plan. If all goes well, we'll meet you outside the Riven shortly. Be careful. It might also have traps." He lowered his arm, the moss on his face not as droopy as it had been.

Horra stood and dusted off her bottom. "Well, what did they say?"

A grin split his wooden face. "That they'd never considered a magical reservoir feeding the trees before. He agreed it might exist and they would search for it and try to free themselves."

A spark of hope grew in her chest. "So, what's your plan?"

"You brought the princess here on Pidge's back. Now the princess has left on another flying animal." He reached out and scratched the soft underside of Pidge's chin. "Without a third person holding us back, we should be able to use Pidge to fly us to safety."

She clapped her claws together. "Rowan, you're brilliant! But what about the bugs? The music?"

"I don't have the answers for that yet. It would be better to evaluate the connection somewhere other than the Riven."

She whooped. "I might disagree with you on some things, Rowan. But I couldn't agree more on that point."

Pidge stared at Horra with intelligent eyes. "Ready, girl?"

She screeched.

"Then let's get out of here."

Rowan let out a woodenish, clacking sound. "Let's wait to be sure the tree spirits are safe first. Then we can make our way out of the Riven." He placed his hand back on the trunk.

Though she was impatient to escape, Horra agreed. Seconds turned into minutes. Just when she grew too anxious,

Rowan jerked to attention. "Thank you for reporting back. We'll meet you as soon as we can."

Triumph glowed from the druid. "They found a magic channel at the end of the Ghost Tree's roots. It feeds the trees I saw as well. We'll stop at one of them as we fly over and check on them again to be sure. Congratulations, Queen Bearer. We have found the alternative solution you championed."

"Yes!" Horra pumped her fist in the air. "Let's go."

She swung herself onto Pidge's back, and Rowan sat behind her. Within seconds, Pidge launched them into the air.

They flew over the swamp. Pidge darted her head when the frogs jumped. "Keep steady, girl. We can't stop for a bite to eat right now. I'll get you something on the other side."

They rode on, the land shaking, then shifting, and finally returning to a whole space again.

"There, to our right. One of the trees I spotted before." Rowan pointed.

Horra steered Pidge toward the massive oak with a wide cover of branches. They circled it, then Pidge landed as close to the trunk as possible. Their landing went sideways, knocking both Horra and Rowan off.

They scrambled closer to the tree, and Rowan made it there first. Pidge darted for a snack under the dead leaves.

"Well, two passengers or not, Pidge got us here in one piece. Barely." Horra glanced at the trunk that was Rowan, noting how much he'd grown in such a short time. It wouldn't be long before he wouldn't fit on Pidge at all.

A few minutes passed before Rowan regained contact with the group. He faced her, his arm at his side now. "They made it this far. It looks like we're on the right track. Most of them are eager to get out and far away from here. The rood stated they probably won't wait to greet us when they finally escape. He will have to locate an acceptable tree to reside in first."

The spark inside her chest flared into a fire and traveled across her body, warming her. "I don't blame them, I guess. But it would've been nice to meet with them."

Rowan climbed onto Pidge behind her. "I understand their hesitation to remain close to what has been their prison. But I agree."

Once he settled behind her, Horra tugged on the rope. "Onward." Pidge darted into the air.

They flew past the carnivorous mountainside and then entered the wyvern-infested space.

"Pidge, swing by the wyvern that grabbed hold of me. I'd like to see if I can do something." Rowan clacked out the order.

The pudge wudgie squealed but did as he asked, flying close to a massive, snaking wyvern.

"Now hover over. I'm going to see if I can rescue him."

Horra hesitated. "But it tried to kill you."

"Maybe. Maybe not. I've had time to contemplate, and I think they're stuck here like we are, even if they're able to fly. Their blinking in and out had a rhythmic pattern."

Horra's heart pinched. "What if you get stuck but we're free? Or what if none of us can escape?"

Rowan balanced himself on Pidge's tail. "Come back for me, and we can regroup then." He jumped.

A ball of fear slammed into Horra's throat. It wasn't like the wood boy to take chances.

The wyvern blinked out of sight.

When it appeared again only a few feet from where it disappeared, she saw the druid had landed in the middle of its back, startling it. It shrieked and jerked, knocking itself out of the circuitous path it had been on. It bumped into another wyvern, which bumped into another. This continued until the air was no longer filled with synchronized flying creatures blinking in and out of vision.

None of the wyverns were in sync now. They all bumped into each other, screeches filling the air. Wings fluttered. Tails darted. Dragon heads snapped at each other. And Rowan was in the dead center of it all.

"Vinegar," Horra groaned.

What had they done?

CHAPTER 23

~Horra~
Moments Later

Horra stared at the wyverns. Now material in form, they were larger than she'd imagined when blinking in and out of sight. They blended into the night sky, but because she knew they were there, she could see their flying bodies, grand silhouettes against the starry expanse. Their dragon forms still snaked, but not as jerkily as before. Instead, they gracefully slid through the air. Rowan's blundered landing had freed them from the constraints of whatever spell they'd been under.

Besides their skin, the wyverns were incredible to watch. Horns lined their heads and spiked beards ran down their cheeks and chins. They had two legs instead of four, and their arms stretched out into bat-like wings. Moonlight glowed through the sheer membrane between the sections as they moved about. Most intimidating, however, were their long, curling tails, which ended in what appeared to be stingers, much like a stone scorpion's.

"Stay away from their tails, Pidge," she yelled to be heard over the wyverns' shrill squalls. None of them seemed happy about Rowan bumping them out of their rhythmic flight.

What would happen if they attacked Rowan? Could they swoop in and save him? Horra didn't think so. She guided Pidge lower than the wyverns from what she hoped was a safe distance.

Rowan didn't appear to be the least bit concerned. He held on to the bony protrusions on the wyvern's lower neck and back area.

Horra's thoughts turned to her half-dragon, Nimble. How long had they been in the Riven? She'd left her gulgoyle in his stone state and prayed to the Creature God that he was still safe on the outside. She shuddered to think what would happen to him if he were to stumble inside the Riven's unstable boundary. He'd be stuck inside the shifting place forever.

Irritation toward the fickle fairy who'd left them behind rose once more. "That creature only thinks of herself," Horra mumbled.

The raucous roars of the wyverns calmed. Rowan's ride swiveled and took the lead. Horra lost count at twenty-five as the group of flying dragons trailed after Rowan.

"Follow them, girl, but not too close."

The ground beneath them swirled and changed again. Up in the sky, they were all unaffected by the shift.

Maybe this would work after all.

Then another thought hit Horra. If they did make it out, what would happen to the wyverns? By the looks of their size-able stingers, they were quite dangerous. Would they unleash something upon the Wilden Lands that would cause mayhem and tragedy?

Dragon's fire.

It was too late to stop their progression. One minute, she could see Rowan. The next minute, he went beyond some unseen boundary and disappeared.

He didn't wink back into sight like the wyverns had earlier.

As her heart pounded, Horra's claws were slick against Pidge's rope. She rubbed each one against her cloak. Fear of slipping off Pidge released a ball of angry bungbees in her gut. She twisted the rope around her wrist for good measure.

The area beneath them reformed into a lovely meadow. All but five of the wyverns had made it through the barrier, and Pidge wasn't far behind. Horra let up on the makeshift reins and allowed Pidge full speed.

Before hitting the magical invisible wall, Horra prayed. "Oh, Creature God, I hope we're doing the right thing."

The meadow disappeared.

Darkness greeted them along with the sparse-looking, rocky area.

Could it be true? Had they actually escaped?

The wyverns flew off in different directions. Horra couldn't tell which one Rowan had ridden, but it didn't take long for them to flee once they sensed freedom.

"Rowan?" she yelled, the bungbee sensation climbing up to sit in her throat. "Where are you?"

"Down here."

Pidge screeched and dipped. Luckily for Horra, the bird had great hearing. Though she possessed night vision, it took a moment for her eyes to adjust to the difference in lighting.

What she saw didn't make the bungbees go away. In fact, they grew in intensity.

Rowan stood facing a woodland creature, possibly the

dryad he had told Horra about, though that conversation seemed like years ago. But it could only have been a few days since they'd trapped the worqs and set them free.

Horra shook her head to clear the thoughts.

A long grass dress flowed down the tree-looking creature. Horra's skin itched just looking at it. Branchy hair littered with dead leaves cascaded down her back. Her skin was smooth as if whittled from a tree limb, complete with wood-grain markings. Her trunk wasn't thick like Rowan's. She was fine-limbed, almost frail-looking.

Until Horra met her gaze.

"Join us, troll pseudo-queen." Her voice traveled like the wind, hitting Horra's hide like magic.

No, not like magic. It *was* magic.

Horra gritted her teeth, pinching her lips over her tusks. The Erlking had once tried to influence her in a similar manner. She instantly despised the woman.

A glance beyond the tree woman revealed Glory standing with her arms crossed and her back hunched. Was she pouting? And where was the kelpie that had flown in and saved her?

Pidge scree'd angrily.

"It's okay. Take me down," Horra whispered. She wouldn't abandon Rowan like Glory had.

Pidge landed, and Horra slipped awkwardly from her back. She'd yet to figure out how to not fall off the pudge wudgie when landing.

Horra brushed dirt and dried leaves from her cloak as she stood, fixing a haughty glare on the dryad. Like with Captain Erast, she refused to be intimidated. "I'm not a pseudo-anything. I am Queen Bearer of Oddar, and it would serve you well to remember that." She stepped closer to a stiff Rowan. Either he was assessing the dryad, or he was mesmerized by her. In either case, she would get close enough to make sure the druid was safe. "Why are you here, and what moldy log did you crawl out from under?"

Glory snickered beneath her tattered hood.

Though it felt good that someone laughed at her insult, Horra was still angry at the fairy for leaving them behind.

The dryad gave no sign that Horra's insult affected her. "You are to come with me and meet your fates."

Magic tickled Horra's hide, fueling her ire.

Horra planted her claws on her hips. "Yeah, that would be a no go. And stop trying to influence me. Your magic does not affect trolls."

The tickle turned to a scratch. "Maybe not you, but I assure you the others are not immune."

Pidge screeched and darted for the dryad.

The dryad raised a bony hand, and the air grew heavy with magic.

Her pudge wudgie faltered and squealed. She shook her head.

"Stop that!" Horra rushed toward the dryad.

Tree roots sprang up.

Horra's boot snagged in one and she fell to the ground, helpless to aid her pet. "Knock it off. She hasn't done anything to you."

"The bird intended to attack me. For that, she will die."

The dryad fisted her hands and stepped closer to a cowering Pidge. She sent a bolt of magic at her pet.

"Don't you dare touch my bird," Horra screamed and lunged over the rooty obstacles.

A roar bellowed before fire split the air, aimed at the dryad. Bells jingled and jangled as the dryad's magic hit Nimble's neck, knocking off the alarm he still wore.

Nimble stood in front of Pidge, smoke curling from his

nostrils. Feathers fully covered his wings, and stony scales covered his skin. He looked glorious. Heat radiated off of his body as he stood tall in front of Pidge as if daring the dryad to attack her again.

"Good boy, Nimble." Horra smiled.

The dryad stopped, staring at the gulgoyle while patting out flames on her limby hair. Her affected leaves glowed orange and then faded to black, falling to the ground as ash. The dryad's glare was full of fury. "You have not seen the last of me." She reached out to a nearby tree and vanished.

Horra's eyes widened. Though she knew dryads resided in trees, she didn't realize they could disappear like that. She turned to Rowan and Glory, who stood several feet behind him. "What was that all about?"

Rowan's crown rattled as he shook his head. "I'm not sure. I didn't see her when the wyvern blinked out of sight and dropped me here." He pointed to the grove. "She emerged from that tree, and I was immediately incapacitated."

"Yeah, she has that effect on some creatures," Glory said with a whiny grumble.

Horra glared at the girl. "You," she sputtered, gaining her wits, "left us in the Riven. If I hadn't already known you were a selfish, self-centered—"

Rowan's hand on her shoulder stopped her. "I agree with your anger, Queen Bearer. But we are not out of danger. We need to get away from the Riven. Regroup."

Horra jerked her shoulder away from the druid's hold. "Fine. But I'm not helping her. What happened to your kelpie, anyway?"

Glory straightened. "Nothing. I let it go."

Horra snickered. "Right. Like I'd believe that." She strode away from them and over to Nimble. "Good boy, saving your friend from the evil stick woman." She ran her claws over the gulgoyle's hard exterior. He preened, sticking his chest out as a rumble burbled in his throat. "His hide has changed. What do you think that means, Rowan?"

Rowan stepped up beside her. He bent to pick up the ruined bells, then let the charred pieces fall to the ground. "He's filling out nicely. It must mean he's finally maturing."

Horra hesitated. "Maturing? But he's several centuries old."

The druid twisted his head sideways and ran a hand down the feathered wings. "I don't think he's as old as you claim. My guess is he was a baby when your mother found him and took him in. He's only a little older than you."

Horra was stunned at his proclamation. Could it be? Was that why he'd been so mournful when her mother died? He was still a baby, and she'd been his faithful keeper, almost like a mother to him. She glanced around, seeing only a rocky plain. "How did he find us? It looks like we're far from the Sterling River's bend."

"Yes, I see that as well. No matter. We now have reliable rides out of this forsaken place. I am eager to leave." Rowan moved toward Pidge, stroking her feathers more gently than he'd done with Nimble. "Everything is all right now," he murmured.

"You two can leave. I'm not going." Glory flicked her hand and began to walk away.

Anger rushed through Horra like hot snake oil, sizzling along her nerves. Though it was dark out, her sight dimmed further as the anger overtook her. Before she knew what she was doing, she charged Glory and tackled her. "You're. Not. Leaving. Us. Again." She struggled to get hold of the fairy's flailing arms inside the massive cloak. Her claws snagged on some of the torn fabric, but Horra was determined. "Rowan, get me a rope."

CHAPTER 24

~Glory~

Glory squealed and squirmed, but the troll princess had completely tangled her inside her worn cloak. And though the coat was tattered and threadbare in places, it held like sea glue, which they used to repair holes on boats on the Shining Shore. "Let me go!"

Horra pounced, knocking Glory to the side, allowing the troll a better angle to grab her arms. "Not this time. You're coming back to the castle to meet your sister."

"Argh!" she screamed to no avail. The troll held her in a solid grip. Glory spied the mossy legs of the log boy as she flung her head back, hoping to buck the girl off her.

No such luck.

The scratchy ropes bit into her skin. Horra was stronger than she realized. "Okay, okay. I'll come with you. Just let me go."

"Nice try. I don't trust you anymore." Horra finished tying

her wrists together and pushed Glory's head to the ground as she climbed off her back.

"What was that for?" She spat out the dirt and leaves grounded into her teeth.

"That and much more is penance for you leaving Rowan, Pidge, and me behind. Now get up. You're riding with me."

When she didn't move, Rowan bent down and picked her up. He lifted her so high her feet came off the ground. She stumbled when he set her down. "You guys need therapy, you know that? I'm a royal princess. You can't treat me like this."

"According to Oddar's and the Shining Kingdom's treaties, we are allowed to treat you like a hostile offender." Rowan clacked beside her ear. He was growing tiresome with his support of the troll princess. Just like that other instructor.

Glory jerked away from the branchy creature, but he held her fast. And because her arms were restrained behind her back, she wouldn't be able to catch herself if she fell. She stopped struggling, but she wouldn't give up so easily. "You can't do this. I don't care what any treaty says. I have diplo-matic immunity."

"You're our prisoner until we return to Oddar. Then you're your sister's problem." Horra stood back while Rowan lifted her onto the boulder-like back of the half-dragon. Kicking her feet didn't stop the log boy from plunking her onto the saddle.

Nimble bellowed, and smoke spewed from his nostrils as he turned to look at her wriggling form.

Glory still tried to wrestle away from Rowan, but the twig had grown too strong. She, on the other hand, grew weaker each day that she couldn't access her full magic. It was a wonder she could still put up such a good fight. "This is an act of war. My mother will hand me your head for this."

"Oh yeah? Where is your mother?" Horra dared her.

The troll couldn't know that the Erlking had captured her mother and her two guards. Could she?

Horra snorted. "That's what I thought. You either don't know where she is, or you do and you don't care. My vote is the latter."

Nimble lowered so Horra could climb onto his back.

She leaned forward and away from the disgusting troll girl, pulling her arms tight. Somehow, while she was talking to the troll, Glory hadn't noticed that Rowan had tied the ends of the rope to the frame holding the saddlebags onto the animal's back.

She shrieked and sent Rowan a withering look. Not that he could see it from beneath the hood. But Glory still glowered, willing him to sense her rage.

Nimble lifted a leg, tipping her sideways.

Horra jerked her back onto the center of the saddle. "Let's go."

Glory had no recourse.

The moment she'd left the Riven's border, the dryad enticed Calliope with some dried fish. Had Glory not known the tree creature was in cahoots with the Erlking, it would've been obvious at that moment. Glory hadn't even known what the kelpie ate except the creatures it drowned in lakes and seas.

It was a morsel of information she wouldn't forget.

Now, trussing her up like a criminal, the despicable troll and her log boy lackey were taking Glory back to the one place she never wanted to return to.

She would have to bide her time and flee later when they didn't expect it. Glory was nothing if not a master at sneaking around.

Yes, that's what she would do.

And she'd make the troll princess pay for trollhandling her.

~Rowan~

MOMENTS AFTER SETTLING Glory on Nimble, Rowan took his familiar seat on Pidge's back, thankful to be out of the Riven. The Wilden Lands were harsher than he had first perceived back in the Weald. How he longed to return and sink his roots in.

He mentally shook himself. Whatever these lapses into folly were, he didn't have time to deal with them. They needed to get the princess back to Oddar and restore relations between them and their fairy allies.

And he wanted nothing more than to be free from the squabbling duo.

Horra snapped her reins, and Nimble took off at a fast walk.

Pidge jumped into the air, following closely behind the gulgoyle and its riders.

Though the fairy princess had struggled twice, he assumed she quickly realized his constricting knot would be impossible for her to detach. He'd doubled the knot for good measure and therefore wasn't afraid that she might fall off. The only way to undo the knots was to remove the saddle and specially made frame holding the queen bearer's supplies and saddlebags.

His bark tightened as his roots detected deviant magic nearby. Pidge noticed as well. The bird dipped and circled Horra's group. The mountainous area they traveled over was mostly made up of pastureland with a few thickets of trees scattered about. A full moon broke through a cloudy sky and shone brightly upon the serene area. But they were almost out of the open area and headed toward the lower Iron Mountains if he wasn't mistaken. And he was sure he was not.

"What is it?" he asked the pudge wudgie in a low tone, not wanting to alarm the troll and her gulgoyle.

She cackled.

He caught Horra glancing his way, so he swung Pidge down to her level. "We may want to avoid this area, Queen Bearer. We're near the Erlking's mountain. Head northwest before crossing Hobgoblin's Pass."

"That will take another day's travel." Her gaze was alert. "Are you sure?"

"You told me to trust my instincts. All my fibers are telling me not to continue on this path."

Horra nodded.

Glory snickered. "You're taking direction from a green log with sticks for brains who's been unrooted for what? Five seconds? What kind of royalty are you?"

Horra's boot caught in the rope Rowan had tied, twisting the fairy sideways and stretching her other arm taut.

Glory shrieked.

"Oops. Sorry about that. My boot got tangled in your tethers." Horra resettled herself on the saddle, pushing the fairy into the saddle horn.

Again, the fairy let out a shrill squeal. "When I'm free, I'm going to—"

A blue light on the horizon interrupted the fairy's rant.

Rowan's sap quickened. It looked like fairy-path light.

Last he knew, the Erlking had taken possession of the fairy queen's carriage. Though other conveyances could use fairy magic, it took a strong fairy to create one. "It could be the other fairy princess."

Horra blinked. "Or it could be the Erlking. If he finds us here, it can't be coincidence."

"Hey, over here!" Glory screamed.

Horra jerked the fairy's head back, muffling her voice. "Shut up, you dimwitted dolt."

Rowan knew there was no way to lead the gulgoyle and hold onto a noisy, struggling fairy determined to attract attention. If the light came from the other fairy princess, having Glory tied to the gulgoyle would not look good. However, his intuition told him it was the Erlking.

The fairy continued to make struggling noises, spooking Nimble.

"You're going to get us caught, you ninny!"

Rowan landed Pidge, hoping the cover of land would disguise them from whoever was now coming straight for them. "Use your woodencloak, Horra. Maybe it will hide you both."

Horra removed her cloak with one arm, squealing when the fairy bit her claw. Rowan recalled how troll nails were thick and hard as flint. "Hope that hurt you more than me," Horra growled at the other princess. With a final yank, her woodencloak was free, and she draped it over Glory.

Her screams no longer echoed.

Horra stopped Nimble and told him to lie down. "Rowan, come close. I'm going to see if we can get Nimble to shift and protect us."

"Is that wise?" He climbed off Pidge and rushed to the gulgoyle's side so that they were hidden beside a few rocky mounds. Horra's plan might work, but could they survive staying inside the rocky barrier?

"I don't know. But they're coming in fast. We don't have many other options." She slipped down from the saddle and, with Pidge beside them, jabbed her beast in the gut.

Nimble let out a bellow and everything went dark.

"Rowan? Are you there?" Horra's voice wobbled.

"I'm right here, Queen Bearer."

Though they could still hear the fairy's complaints, the sound was dampened and the air remained still around them.

"I think it worked. Pidge?" she whispered.

The pudge wudgie fluffed her feathers behind Rowan. "She's here."

"How long do we wait?"

"That depends." Rowan dug his roots into the rocky soil to steady the rhythm of the rushing sap in his core.

"On what?"

"On whether the gulgoyle decides to come out of this state tonight or a month from now."

CHAPTER 25

~Horra~

At the Same Moment

A shiver overtook Horra at the thought of being stuck inside the gulgoyle's protective shell for a long time. The warmth from Nimble's fire was stifling.

Nimble shuddered, and the shell tightened around them. Horra suddenly struggled to breathe. "Gah! What have I done? We're going to die." Her voice was breathy, and panic surged inside her gut, spreading out to the rest of her body as quickly as the magical fire had spread across the Weald. "Oh no. Oh no."

Glory's screaming, though the cloak lessened the noise's intensity, did nothing to ease Horra's distress. Horra gasped, and her breaths came quick, making her lightheaded.

"It does no one any good to give in to your panic, Queen Bearer. Take a deep breath. Let it out slowly." Rowan's steady voice only increased her tension. How could he be so calm?

Oh, right. He could get nutrients from the ground. He'd be

fine even if they stayed here a decade. "What do you know? You don't even breathe." Her chest ached from the dread building inside her.

"Yes, but I receive oxygen from my system. I can control it as needed. You can too." He rested his hand on her shoulder.

Horra squashed the urge to jerk away. Her mind knew he was right. Her body, however, didn't agree. "I can't—I can't—"

She couldn't fall to her knees like she wanted, because Nimble's shell was too close. Tears wet her cheeks.

"Then find something to focus on. Don't think of anything else but that until you relax."

Pidge nuzzled Horra's claw. She grabbed her pet bird, yanking her close. The bird's heartbeat was steady, so she concentrated on that and only that. After a few moments, the band around her chest eased. A few more, and her breathing slowed. The dizziness lightened. Pidge purr-clucked, and Horra leaned her head against her soft feathers.

Another couple minutes that felt more like hours passed before Horra let out a deep breath. "Thank you, Rowan."

"You're welcome, Queen Bearer." He was quiet for a few seconds. "I sense through the soil that the Erlking is now gone. Let's see if we can get Nimble to release his shield."

"Right." The only thing she knew would convince Nimble to release his shield was another animal to make him feel safe. She reached behind her to find where she was along the gulgoyle's body. "Come with me, Pidge." She grasped the rope and shimmied past Rowan, closer to Nimble's head. "Hey, big guy. You saved Pidge and all of us. Aren't you a good boy?"

A rumble started in his chest. It vibrated until the shell fell off them like dust. She blinked in the sudden moonlight.

The only sound came from Glory's muffled screams.

A blue fairy path remained, glittering on the ground. It wove in arcs across the open rocky space, several wheel marks coming close to their location. But neither the carriage nor the Erlking were in sight. "We did it." Horra inhaled deeply and let it out. Relief spread through her.

Rowan clacked, clearing his throat. "Yes, but he is now alerted to something in this area. We're going to have to be doubly careful now."

Horra's heart skipped a beat. "Not helping the anxiety, Rowan." She dug into her pack attached to the gulgoyle's side. At the bottom, she found the extra clothes she was looking for. She pulled the first cloth out, revealing another tunic top, and tore a couple strips off the bottom.

Wadding up the second strip, she climbed back into the saddle. Without removing the woodencloak, she dug inside the fairy's tattered hood. Once she reached the fairy buried deep inside, she stuffed the cloth into the princess's mouth. Yanking both the woodencloak and the tattered coat away from the fairy's disfigured face, she wound the strip around her head and tied it tight, snagging it in Glory's hair when she knotted it. "That's for biting me. Keep it up and you might end up tied to the underside of Nimble's tail."

Glory glared at her.

Horra would be glad to be rid of fairies once and for all. But they still faced a long trek across the mountains to Oddar.

Horra placed the woodencloak back over the fairy, tucking it around her arms and her chin. She sat back down in the saddle, her shoulders aching from tension. "Nimble, take us home the long way."

<hr>

SEVERAL HOURS and a blooming headache later, thanks to the princess's relentless caterwauling, they'd made it halfway to Oddar. Golden light glowed from a thin edge on the horizon.

They'd made it past the mid-range mountains and were traveling along the northern edge of the trolls' Iron Mountains.

Horra fought the exhaustion that plagued her. She'd caught herself nodding off more times than she wanted to admit. The druid was wide awake, having received some nourishment to re-energize him when they took cover inside Nimble's shell.

However, she would not last long, and someone needed to keep an eye on the other princess. If her woodencloak fell off for any reason, not only would she lose a valuable asset, but the princess's voice would be loosed again and draw more attention.

A yawn overtook her.

"You need to rest," Rowan stated.

"We have to keep moving." But even as she said it, her body faltered and her head drooped.

"There's no way to know how long we were inside the Riven. Time doesn't seem to be material there. And we exited farther south than I imagined we would've."

How long had they been lost inside its depths? How had they come out so far from where they entered? Horra couldn't even concentrate long enough to ponder either. Another loud yawn yanked her mouth open. "Okay. Fine. I need to sleep. But we'll have to find a good hiding spot. My tent is in the side pack." Her eyes refused to stay open.

"Horra?"

"Hmm?" she murmured before the fairy's jerking movements roused her. She pushed on Glory's back, yanking her arms just enough to get the fairy to sit still once more. "I can't go on much longer. Can you find something adequate, Rowan? Something like when we had the children with us?"

"I'll return shortly," he said as Pidge flew along the rocky ledge. Traveling through Bough Valley would be too far out of the way now. They'd have to take the harder trail through the mountains. Good thing she knew it well from her travels with Torren. Her thoughts stuttered and her head dropped.

"Queen Bearer?"

Horra jerked awake. "Rowan?"

"I found a place. Follow me." Pidge flew toward a break in the mountains.

Horra nudged Nimble, and the gulgoyle picked up the pace. She slapped herself to keep from nodding off. Finally, Pidge swooped down and landed.

She joined them shortly after. A small jolt allowed Horra the energy to slide down Nimble's side, where she unbuckled her tent.

Rowan took it out of her lethargic claws. "Let me set it up." At her raised eyebrows, he said, "I watched Torren last time. And I'm stronger now."

He was right. Horra nodded and untied her packs. They weighed more than she remembered. When she reached the bag with the food, she unwrapped one package of bread only to find it hardened. She broke off a piece anyway and choked it down with the final dregs of water from her pouch.

Rowan returned with Pidge, who pecked at the dry loaf of bread. "I've set the tent up, Queen Bearer."

"Thank you." She tossed the loaf at Pidge and grabbed her two packs. "Can you get the princess and bring her in with us? Hopefully, we can tie her somewhere safe."

Horra didn't wait for his reply. She walked to the tent, which Rowan had strung beneath some mid-sized, stringy pine trees growing along a rocky cliff.

The ground inside the tent was lumpy and hard. Horra frowned. Though she was tired enough to sleep on rocks, she also didn't want to wake up with ten cricks in her body. She stuck her head out from beneath a pine bough. "Rowan? Can we move the tent over a little bit?"

He carried a thrashing and shrieking Glory, held away from his body like one would an angry, prickly cat. Some of the branches on his crown were broken. The woodencloak lay on the ground beside the gulgoyle.

Deep exasperation bloomed inside Horra. "She's more trouble than she's worth. Maybe we should've let her walk away outside the Riven." She rolled her neck, which ached, as did the majority of her tired body. "We need to move the tent first. I can't lie on a bunch of rocks. Put her there and we'll rearrange things first."

Rowan placed Glory beside a tree and fastened her to it. Horra hoped no one was nearby who could hear the princess's smothered cries. How anyone could put up a fight for as long as she had was beyond Horra's understanding.

Between the two of them, they re-situated the tent as Horra explained the finer details of other creature's needs to Rowan. When that was done, they led Nimble and Pidge into the trees and tied them up. Horra gave them the dried-out food, though she knew it wasn't enough. But it was all she had. She tried to hand Glory a canteen, but the princess hissed and spat at her from around the gag.

"You're like a rabid animal. Don't say I didn't try to give you something to eat and drink." They placed the fairy against the rocky mountainside with a blanket beneath her, and tied her ropes to two small trees they'd tacked the tent for sturdiness. Slits in the material would need to be re-sewn, but it was a small price to pay to keep the princess from escaping.

When everything was finally settled, Horra unfurled her sleeping bag and fell asleep almost before her head hit the pillow.

~Glory~

AFTER HORRA LAY down and appeared to fall instantly asleep, Glory kept up her wailing, though quieter now to keep her throat from shredding. She just had to keep the ruse until the troll was truly asleep. It didn't take long for the snoring to begin. A few last screams, and she quieted fully. She needed to concentrate.

First, to test the ties. She jerked her wrists, which were now raw from the ropes, ignoring the pain. Before, the log boy's knots had been impenetrable.

However, these weren't the same as the previous ones he'd used. Glee bubbled inside her. This was her chance. She'd stolen a thread of magic from the silver tree when the troll and the woodgoblin were talking. Though it hadn't been hard, she couldn't take much, or he would've known.

She'd used most of the magic when she summoned Calliope. Much good that had done. She'd never be able to trust a hungry kelpie again.

The rest of the magic was what she would use to leave when the log boy wasn't looking. Glory hid a smile when he didn't stay inside the tent while the troll slept. She assumed he'd sink his revolting roots into the ground as soon as he could. She hoped he'd dive deep enough that it would take time to retract.

Then she'd steal the dried meat the troll princess had been waving about and, along with the golden bridle, and call on Calliope once more.

She gathered the sparkling magic, held it in a ball, and concentrated. Knots were simple most of the time. Locks were trickier. Enchantments were easy to untangle with the right knowledge. Spells were harder. Hexes, like the one the Erlking put on her, were the absolute worst—impossible without the caster to reverse them.

Glory grinned. He'd used a twisting vine knot.

She'd learned how to untie these in her elementary training. Careful though, she chided herself, there needed to be enough left over to call Calliope.

Slowly, Glory worked the magic from the center of her being through her arms and into the ropes. Not too much. She stopped and pulled back. It was not in her nature to limit her magic. Allowing it free rein was habit. But she couldn't now, not in her disgraced magical state.

Taking a deep breath, Glory threaded the magic back into her arms and into the rope's threads. Sweat dotted her brow as she leaked tiny amounts and undid the knot.

Her arms fell as her bonds loosened. She complained a few more times to keep Rowan off her trail. After a few seconds, she trusted the log boy was completely unaware of what she was doing.

Her cackle was a whisper. The troll's saddlebags lay on the other side of the troll. Glory tiptoed over and reached for the one with the meat inside it when the troll snorted and moved in her sleep.

She stood, frozen above the troll girl, her arm reaching for the bag. One second passed. Then two. Finally, she relaxed and grabbed the bag. Inside were several wrapped chunks of food. Magic throbbed at the side of the pouch.

Glory hesitated. *Did the troll princess have a secret stash?*

With an eye on Horra, Glory dug around the bag and found the source of the magic. A jeweled dagger—priceless, if her knowledge of precious metal was correct. The marbled blade was smooth and razor-sharp. Kobold.

Glee filled Glory. She stuck the dagger in her belt, leaving the plain sheath behind. An idea pricked her mind. She'd vowed to make the troll girl pay for jumping her and tying her up. Yes. She knew what she would do.

The woodencloak lay in a pile in the corner by the doorway. Glory snatched the first chunk of meat she found and crept over to the cloak. She undid the fastenings on her abused coat and stripped it off. Cool air washed over her body. Glory hesitated. The dour coat had once been a sheer overlay for her beautiful dress but had changed with the hex.

"Good riddance," she whispered. Glory took the woodencloak and slipped it on, relishing the idea of the troll princess waking up and not having it to hide her horrible self. The cloak shifted larger to account for her wings. A small squeak of laughter broke through her lips.

She stopped and waited, but Horra was well and truly asleep. A pack of wildebeests couldn't wake her now.

New invigoration bubbled inside Glory. She left the bag where it was and her tattered hood where it lay, removed the golden bridle, and made her way to the door. It wasn't sealed.

She pulled the fabric back just enough to glance outside. Surrounding trees shadowed the area, but enough sunlight shone in from outside for her to spy Rowan. He had rooted in close to the edge of the trees and was guarding the tent. He had one arm on the trunk, his eyes closed in concentration.

Pfth. This was too easy.

Glory understood, however, the moment she stepped outside the tent onto the ground, he'd know. She stepped on the loose edge of the tent material, then worked her way across the front to the edge of the side before stopping.

Horra's snores echoed from inside the tent.

Rowan stood still, no movement or alertness to her escape detected.

Her plan was working!

Glory continued on to the side. Thankfully, neither the troll girl nor the green druid was any good at setting up tents. Had it been taut, there'd be no way she could use it to hide her departure.

At the backside of the tent, several feet lay between the tent and the rocky hill. She pulled out the bridle. "Come to me," she whispered as she rubbed the metal. "And be quiet about it," she added as an afterthought. Her mind-link with the creature would alert it to her intentions.

The kelpie's dark form appeared several minutes later, swooping down and landing on the rock. Glory held out the chunk of meat. "Take me to the Erlking, for real this time. And make it quick."

Calliope gulped the meat down instantly and leaned over for Glory to take the reins and climb atop.

She hadn't even touched the ground.

A glance back as she flew away assured her the druid was none the wiser. She tucked her head inside the woodencloak's hood and soaked in the feeling of triumph.

CHAPTER 26

~Rowan~

Rowan unrooted midday, having taken in as many nutrients as he needed and a bit more for storing. Sometime during each quest with the troll queen bearer, he ended up stuck somewhere bereft of nourishment.

In the hours since Horra had lain down, he'd tried everything he knew to connect with the rood from the Riven with no luck. They should've escaped by now. He hoped they hadn't run into the same dryad Rowan had met outside the Riven.

Rowan thought of the wyvern he'd ridden and wondered where it had gone. He'd tried to create a link to its mind, but the creature had been so confused that he couldn't. Riding the wyvern had been much more comfortable than riding either Pidge or Nimble. Too bad it had dispatched him so quickly after leaving the Riven. Rowan would've liked to follow Horra's example and make it his pet.

The sun was still bright as late-afternoon light spread across the rocky plain. In the silence, he wondered if the fairy princess had finally succumbed to exhaustion as well and fallen asleep. Only one way to find out.

He quietly pulled the tent door flap aside and glanced in. Horra lay sprawled across the floor of the tent, mouth open and slobbering, still deep in the throes of sleep. His trunk tightened when he didn't locate the fairy.

He stepped on something with his roots as he entered to search—the threadbare cloak the fairy had worn so faithfully.

But where was the woodencloak? The sap inside his core rushed in a heated path. The princess had escaped!

He stepped toward Horra. "Queen Bearer, wake up. The princess is gone."

"Mnyah?" Horra smacked her slobbery lips. Her eyes cracked open before closing again.

He shook her shoulder. "Wake up, Horra. Glory is gone."

Horra jerked into a sitting position. "What?" She swiped a sleeve across her mouth and chin, clearing the spit.

"Princess Glory escaped. She's gone, and she's taken your woodencloak with her." He held the tattered cloak for the troll to see.

Horra scrunched her face. "How did that happen? I thought you tied her up." Horra rolled to her knees and got up. She checked the back area and picked up the ropes he'd used. "Rowan!"

Rowan's core tightened. He hated being wrong. The knots he used weren't as strong as the ones he'd used on the gulgoyle, because he had no fear of the girl falling inside a tent on the ground. Those knots had kept her secure for her safety. But now he now second-guessed himself. "I was right outside the tent. I would've noticed if she slipped out."

"Well, somehow you didn't." Horra ran a claw through her hair, something she did often when she grew agitated.

He clenched his hands. "She couldn't have set foot on the ground. I had my feelers out. I would've known."

Horra moved over to the bag. "Was this here when I went to sleep?"

"No."

She dug inside the bag. And kept digging until she screamed. "That little sneak stole my mother's dagger."

"And your woodencloak."

Horra glared at him, as angry as he'd ever seen her.

"Prepare the animals. We're going to find that little snake and teach her a lesson she'll never forget."

~Glory~

CALLIOPE FLEW in the opposite direction Glory thought she would. They headed south toward the dwarf lands for what seemed like hours since she'd escaped the tent. Finally, the kelpie dropped to an open space beside a small mountain. If she wasn't mistaken, they were still in Oddar, though she wasn't completely sure where the boundaries were in real-time.

Frustration bloomed in her stomach. Why did this creature continue to bring her to random places? She refused to get down, shaking the reins to urge the horse-like animal to continue on. "I told you to take me to the Erlking. Why are you leading me here?"

"Ah, because I bade her to." The Erlking stepped out from behind a rocky shelf, standing tall and dark against the gray mountain.

"How?" Glory's hands tightened on the reins. "I have the bridle."

"You have a charmed bridle, yes." His voice held a hint of humor. "I have the original cast bridle." He held bony hands up to reveal a grander, more elaborate set of reins. Magic pulsed off of them. "You can remove that troll's useless cloak. I can see you through it, thanks to my captive roods." He let out a derisive laugh. "Have you enjoyed the journey we've led you on?"

So the kelpie *had* been taking her for a ride. Fury at being duped yet again by this elf flashed like water on hot oil inside her. "You knew."

"That you stole it from me? Oh yes. I know about everything you've taken." He stepped closer, his cloak whirling as he moved. "Like that musical spell book of mine."

Glory refused to react and let him see her flounder. "Well, then you know what you have to do to get it from me."

His laugh started small and then grew. "You think you're in a position to bargain with me? That's a mistake, oh fair one. You'll not get what you desire from me, not after all you've done to warrant my displeasure."

She clenched her jaw against the doubt crawling into her mind. Had she handled everything all wrong? How could she turn this around now? "I only have one spell. You need them all to take over the Wilden Lands. I hid the rest of them. Reverse the hex you put on me, and I'll tell you where to find them."

He waved a hand, and the kelpie bucked, knocking Glory off. She landed hard on her backside. Pain exploded, stealing her breath for an instant. Her survival instinct took over, and she rolled to her feet to face him. "Hurt me again and you'll never get hold of the other books I took. Neither of us cares about the trolls. Give me what I want, and I'll return what's yours."

"Thief." He threw a seething ball of magic at her. "You are not in charge here."

The ball hit Glory in her chest, flinging her backward and

knocking the hood from her head. More pain burst through every part of her. She recalled this pain. He'd struck her with it once before. Her body twitched and morphed. "No!" Glory squealed in agony. He was hexing her again.

He stood above her, his black, fathomless eyes staring into hers. "You don't seem to realize I don't need your help to recover what is mine, oh shining lady. Well, once shining lady. You are now but a husk of what you were. And this you'll always remain." He reached inside the cloak and searched for the troll's spell.

But in her haste to leave the tent, Glory realized she'd accidentally left it behind. So even if he had made the deal with her, she couldn't have fulfilled it. Sudden gladness from having forgotten to grab the spell buoyed her.

For the first time, Glory realized he'd never bargain with her. He truly was as despicably evil as that stupid troll princess claimed. She now understood how idiotic she'd behaved, thinking she could bargain with a devil.

"Where is it?" he demanded. "Where is my spell?"

The taste of iron was sweet on Glory's lips. He'd never get it now. Probably never would. Her mistake had foiled his grand plan. "The troll princess has it."

She clung to a sweet thread of satisfaction at his outrage. If she couldn't get her beauty back, it was only right he didn't get his spell back. He'd never be able to take over the Wilden Lands without it. That hope was the only thing she held onto as he cursed her again and again.

~Horra~

As soon as she could pack her tent, Horra allowed Pidge and Rowan to take the lead as the pudge wudgie used her hunting ability to guide them to Glory. A sense of dread that started as a seed grew and took root as they moved.

They were headed directly toward the dwarf mountains.

What if the princess ran into the Erlking? Whatever she had that he wanted so badly couldn't be a good thing for her or Rowan. No doubt, it would be something that betrayed them further. They traveled south for a couple hours, not in a straight line but moving as if following a meandering path. Had the fairy traveled this way on purpose?

Magic made the air heavy.

Nimble shuddered, and Horra pressed into him to keep him moving forward.

"The Erlking is near," she called out to Rowan.

"My roots detect him also," he yelled back.

With the woodencloak missing, she couldn't hide. And without her favorite weapon, the dagger, she was almost help-less against him. She yanked her bow and quiver from Nimble's side. It was all she had, but she was prepared to fight as hard as she could.

Fear that the Erlking had killed the princess grew in her mind.

She shoved it aside. Fear wasn't helpful. It only made her claws shake harder.

The air grew denser, making it more difficult to breathe. She remembered the feeling from the kitchen when the Erlking had tried to capture her the first time. "We're getting close. Be on guard."

"Ready, Queen Bearer." Rowan drew his bow and arrows hidden inside his bark coat.

Horra held back a groan. She'd yet to see him hit an actual

target. The only bright spot was that he might distract the Erlking enough to let her get a shot in.

Nimble trudged through grasses and past blooming trees. Golden sunlight faded to pink, and darkness edged the horizon on the east. They needed to reach the princess and leave before nightfall.

A smooth mountainside came into view—a familiar side that held a concealed doorway to the inside of the mountain. The Erlking's mountain. "Fly around and see if you can find her."

Rowan, riding Pidge, took off in a circle. Horra twisted this way and that, searching. She coughed at the magic thickening the air. It sizzled at her nose and prickled along her hide. A lot of magic had happened here. The area was steeped in it.

Her heart thudded harder.

Pidge screeched. "Over here, Queen Bearer."

Horra directed Nimble to her left, deeper into the trees. The scent of magic hung in the atmosphere like smoke, only more noxious.

What happened here?

And then Horra saw her.

The princess lay broken on the ground. She wore the wood-encloak, which was charred. No hair remained on the girl's head. Instead of a disfigured face, she now had the face of an old crone—hooked nose and all. And she didn't appear to be alive.

Horra jumped from the saddle and stumbled over to the princess's side.

"Princess Glory?" She ran a claw beneath the girl's nose and found she was still breathing.

"Horra?" Glory's words were but a breath before she stilled.

Horra's heart jittered painfully at the state of the girl. "Princess?" she shook Glory's shoulder, praying to the Creature

God that she wasn't hurting her worse. Whatever magic the Erlking had used on her had been devastating. More profound than his first hex.

"I tried to tell you. Why wouldn't you listen to me?" Anger shook Horra's voice. Then compassion tamped it out. Yes, she'd warned the princess about the Erlking. But no matter how much the princess vexed her, Glory didn't deserve this. Horra's loathing of the Erlking rose to new heights.

Rowan stepped next to her and bent over. "How bad is she?"

"It's grave. We need to get her back to the castle so we can treat her." Horra gathered the woodencloak around Glory to delicately lift the husk of the princess's remains. The fairy didn't even move or blink an eye at Horra's touch.

She searched the area for her dagger but didn't find it. Her heart sunk at the thought of the Erlking possessing it now.

"Excuse me," a voice said from behind, startling both Horra and Rowan.

Horra gulped back the knot of fear in her throat before she realized it wasn't the Erlking's voice. She twisted to see who it was, but they remained hidden within the shadow of a boulder.

"Who are you?" she called, reaching to her side automatically to grab the dagger. She winced.

"I saw what he did to her. You might not be able to save her without my help."

The voice was coarse and gravelly, but distinctly female.

Rowan stood and steepled his fingers. "And what exactly can you do to help her that we cannot?"

The shadow person stepped out from behind the wall. It was a hairy, beastly girl—a giant. She held Horra's dagger in her paw-like hand.

Horra gasped. "Grendel?"

CHAPTER 27

The giant girl hugged her arms across her chest, seemingly unaware that she clutched a dangerous weapon. She danced from foot to foot as if wanting to flee. "How do you know my name?"

"Your sister Galumph thought I was a doll—"

"That was you?" She stepped closer to look at Horra before shrinking back into herself.

"That was me." Horra gently removed her arm from beneath Glory. "You said you saw him. Who was it?"

"That strange guy who's been stealing children. He stole my sister. I finally found him, but I was too scared to confront him. And then I saw him attack her." She pointed to Glory, and a visible shudder rippled across the girl's body. "Help me get away from here, and I'll help you heal her. I'm a giant. We're spell-crafters, as you may know. I'm able to create antidotes and spells that do incredible things."

Horra's laugh was short. Though the expanding pastries

and contracting candies had broken Horra's mother's inadvertent spell that kept her small, they also had some powerful side effects. "I know all about giants and their amazing concoctions."

Grendel tilted her chin slightly upward. "They aren't concoctions. They're scientifically calculated formulas created for intentional outcomes."

"Great." Horra glanced at Rowan, who seemed to be taken by the furry girl's show of intelligence. "Another informapedia."

Rowan raised a finger. "Are you a spellist or a chemitrician?"

"I am going to be—" She hesitated. "I was going to become an institutional apothecary. My specialty lies in experimentation." She dropped her head and stared at her hands. Hair covered the backsides of them, their dark tips ending in talon-like nails. "Or it did once. Before this happened." She waved an arm up and down her body.

Horra grabbed at the hand holding her dagger. The girl was going to maim herself with the way she kept waving it about. "Did you find this on the princess? She stole it from me."

Grendel gave the dagger up without a fight. "Yes, I took it when he disappeared. The only other weapon I have is a stick."

Horra tucked the dagger into her belt. "It was the Erlking's music spell that turned you into a beast."

Grendel jerked to attention and gasped. "How do you know about that?"

Remorse nagged at Horra. "I saw it happen when I escaped your sister's bedroom that day. I heard the music and knew he was close."

At her haunted expression, Horra continued. "Look, I'm sorry I didn't stay to help. Not that I could've done anything *to* help since I'm not magical. But I had just escaped from your sister's pets, a giantized torentula and a catterwump, both of which were trying to attack me." She was rambling, but she couldn't stop herself. "I had an important mission, and I was way too lost—"

Grendel held up a paw. "I get it. Galumph loved playing with her experimental bugs and dollies." She sniffed. "But I saw that man and those horrible worqs take her when I was hiding from my parents in the woods. I don't know where they went since they used a fairy path. So I went searching for her. She's kind of a pest, but she's my sister, you know?"

Horra didn't fully understand. The closest thing she had to a sibling was Torren, and he certainly didn't count. However, she saw Grendel's distress. "Your parents are looking for you too. I came upon them hunting for you guys after I completed my mission. They're awfully worried about you both."

Grendel swiped at her face, tears glimmering in the tufts of fur on her cheeks. "They are? Where are they?"

"I don't know. That was weeks ago. I told them to search the Iron Mountains, and they left immediately."

She blustered out a breath. "I was afraid they'd be disgusted by what I turned into."

A noise stopped their conversation.

Horra flicked a glance around, her heart pounding hard and fast. "We need to get out of here right now. We can talk about everything later. Are you coming?" she glanced back at Grendel.

Grendel nodded, her lip quivering.

"Then let's get out of here before the Erlking finds us and does the same thing to us that he did to the fairy princess."

HORRA SAT behind Rowan on Pidge's back as they headed home to Oddar once more. Grendel, who cradled a limp Glory in her lap, rode Nimble. To her surprise, the giant girl wasn't afraid of the gulgoyle but took to him instantly.

Bright light from a waning moon glowed whitish-blue across the forested valley when they reached Oddar's central territory.

Now that they had a chance and Horra realized the girl wasn't a rabid beast out to destroy everything, she had loads of questions for her. "I saw you almost destroy Hobgoblin Pass. Why?"

Grendel hid her face. "The hobgoblins chased me out of Bough Valley with torches. I was scared."

"So you destroyed the bridge?" she asked, incredulous.

"I don't know." Grendel shrugged. "I get violent urges once in a while. Especially when I'm scared. My anger takes over and I do things I wouldn't normally do."

Rowan leaned away from Horra and spoke for the first time since they'd left the spot where they'd found Glory. "It must have something to do with the spell the Erlking placed on you. His spells all seem to differ according to his intent. For instance, he sent a plague of grubby worms not so long ago. It made me unable to communicate, but it drove the infested trolls mad. I would surmise he intends to make you crazed and either divide the lower kingdoms from the giant realm out of fear, or possibly have you carry a contaminate to infect others."

Horra jerked her head sideways at her companion. "Rowan! It's insulting to infer that she's possibly infected. Don't say that to other people."

"No, he could be right." Grendel shifted the princess, wearing an intent expression on her furry face. "It's not that I hadn't thought about it myself. There's no way to test it without another giant. Do you have a lab in Oddar? I could run some tests while we're there."

"Uh, yeah. We have a nice lab in the castle." Horra worked to keep the astonishment out of her voice.

"I propose we set up a series of tests with varying elements that could factor into differing outcomes and see what happens." Grendel's voice took on a quicker pace, her tone chipper.

Horra had been correct about her first impression of the giant girl. She was a bookish intellectual who loved facts and knowledge. "I like potions," she added, wanting to join in.

"Oh, this will be much more complicated than potions or elixirs," Grendel stated, as oblivious to other people's feelings as Rowan.

"Quite, Queen Bearer. This is experimentation in its highest form, not some mediocre magical recipe out of a text-book." Rowan backed the giant girl up, proving they were indeed similar.

And it stuck in her craw. "Well, one of those recipes, as you call it, helped me unmesmerize a bunch of people before you were even planted, druid."

"Mm-hm," Rowan muttered before diving into a deep conversation with Grendel about research, analyses, and how to perform rigorous trials.

Horra groaned before tuning them out. She slumped forward against Pidge's soft neck. Their arduous trip back to the castle just grew infinitely longer.

~Rowan~

Having traveled through the night, Rowan found it refreshing to talk with another, more academic-minded individual. Neither he nor Grendel had stopped conversing the whole time they traveled. He hadn't had so much fun since he and Merrow held educational discussions in the Weald.

Not that the queen bearer was completely uneducated. Uncouth, for certain. But a scholar, she was not.

As morning fell, they rested Pidge and Nimble near a rickety bridge that crossed a small stream spurred from the Sterling River. They were close to the edge of Oddar's capital, only a few hours away from the castle. There they found a small pool of water. The morning bloomed a rich orange on the horizon, which cast golden light through the trees and foliage.

He and Grendel sat on a fallen log amongst tall grasses while Horra took care of some personal needs. "Is something wrong, Grendel? You haven't responded to my last theory about dependent variables."

She stayed quiet for a moment. "I haven't been by Hobgoblin Pass since I destroyed it."

"I don't understand."

"This bridge reminds me of Hobgoblin Pass." Grendel pointed to the weatherworn wood, which tilted to the side. Moss and vines grew over it, possibly the only thing keeping the structure in place.

He nodded as comprehension sank in. "I don't believe it was fully demolished. The giants, I'm told, helped repair it. It was back to functional almost immediately."

"Ugh! That makes me feel worse," Grendel wailed.

Rowan pulled away from her, unsure how to respond.

Horra pushed his shoulder, moving him back toward the giant girl. "She's upset because she caused the damage and others were called on to repair it for her. Her actions probably frightened her as much as it did the rest of us. In other words, she feels bad about it." Horra turned to Grendel. "He was unrooted too soon for his emotional growth to kick in. He doesn't fully comprehend or express emotions."

"Oh." Grendel sniffed, her eyes shining with unshed tears. "I didn't realize he was stunted."

Rowan's fibers quickened. "I am *not* stunted."

"Good for you!" Horra punched his arm. "You're upset. That's progress."

He pursed his lips. "I fail to see how this is humorous."

"And there it went." Horra's voice hadn't lost her teasing note. She did, however, grow more serious. "Rowan, you expressed anger at what Grendel said. That's emotion. Just because you're a druid doesn't mean you won't have emotions. You had other things to put your energy into when you unrooted."

Grendel placed her hand on his leg. "I meant no disrespect by using that term. It's simply scientific. Force something to grow too soon and it will become stunted in some way. There's nothing wrong with that or with your delayed emotional growth. You're not less important because of it. It just makes you unique in a good way."

He wasn't sure what to say to that.

Glory moaned from the spot in the soft grass where Grendel had placed her.

"We should probably keep moving," Horra said as she moved toward the animals. "I'm so looking forward to my favorite meal."

"Your staff doesn't have carrot stew, do they? Oh, or vegetable cobbler? Mother had the best recipe, with lots of onions." Grendel stood and left Rowan behind on the fallen log.

He let them go. Was it anger that had made him speak out?

Torren had teased him openly, and he never snapped at him like he just did with the girls.

Maybe it was anger. He was also tired of needing things explained to him that he should already understand. Complicated mathematical equations weren't so difficult.

The common denominator in the whole confused mess was the fact he was dealing with females. Their emotions swung back and forth constantly. Take the fact that Horra and Grendel went from teasing to serious and now congenial.

Females, he inwardly reasoned, were like the Riven's shifting maze. He never knew when their temperaments would change or where he would end up when it happened, and it always left him unsteady and unsure.

CHAPTER 28

The castle had never looked so welcoming, Horra thought hours later as they clomped up to the stables. Even in the dark, it appeared like heaven. They'd ridden the rest of the way to the castle after their short break. Horra's food resources were gone and their pouches were empty.

Re-energized, Horra jumped off Pidge as the bird landed. She ignored Rowan's annoyed grumbling as he waited for the pudge wudgie to hit the ground and fully stop before he slid off. He needed to sink his roots in the Conservatory as much as she needed a hobgoblin-cooked meal.

Horra took a deep breath of the chilled mountain air. "Ah," she said. "It's so good to be home."

Nimble, with Glory and Grendel on his back, followed not far behind. The giant girl's caution toward the fairy they carried surprised Horra. Her gulgoyle, she knew, was as tired as everyone else and deserved to be pampered.

"Queen Bearer!" Sageel rushed out of the kitchen. "We didn't realize you were coming in so late."

Horra took her servant's chiding in stride. "Next time I'll send a whimsy bird."

Sageel snapped her teeth in jest. Ever since the fairies had taken the castle over, neither of them liked the frilly creatures. "Don't you dare. And who's this?"

Nimble clomped over and Grendel slid down his side. Her hold on Glory never wavered.

"Sageel, meet Grendel Largeness." Horra rushed to explain the girl's furry features. "The Erlking hexed her."

Sageel tittered in sympathy, then turned to Horra. "And the old one?"

"That would be Princess Glory Toppenbottom. She had another run-in with the Erlking."

Her servant squealed. "Ach, no! He needs to be caught and strung up, that one. Come along. I'm sure you're hungry, and the princess looks like she needs some special care. Beware. That other princess has been a'storming the castle gates." Sageel turned on her heel and strode into the castle without looking back, muttering about fairies the whole way.

Horra gestured for Grendel to go first, then grabbed the damaged woodencloak. "I'll show you where to take Glory. Hopefully, we can avoid her sister. Then we can get something to eat. Rowan, can you make sure the stable hands are here to take care of the animals?" She, too, strode on without waiting for his reply.

Sageel had disappeared by the time they made their way inside. The kitchen was tidy, with lingering scents of roasted swamp swine in the air. Horra started to step into the servant's hall when her father burst through the doorway from the dining room on the other side.

Her heart constricted. Would he blame her for Glory's

condition? She had only been concerned with returning to the castle, not with confronting the king. Grendel followed closely on Horra's heels, leaving little room in the maid's preparation space.

"Sageel said you brought Glory back with you?" His bulky body filled the doorway.

"Where is she? Where's my sister?" A shrill voice leaked around her father's form.

Dread dropped like a marble stone in Horra's gut. She was stuck between her father and the woolly giant girl holding the still-unconscious fairy princess.

"What happened?" her father mouthed to her, his body firmly blocking the doorway. "And who's this?" He eyed the giant girl dubiously.

"It's a long story. In short, this is the Erlking's handiwork." Horra waved a claw toward Glory and Grendel.

He squinted. "She looks better than before."

"Not her." Horra pointed to the princess wrapped in her tattered coat. "That's the princess. This is Grendel, a giant girl cursed by the Erlking."

He snorted. "That's worse yet. There's no way Princess Misty won't notice the change," he said over the demanding voice insisting he move out of her way.

"Should we bring her in a different way?" Horra asked, already pushing Grendel back into the kitchen.

The king stiffened. Floral-scented, sparkling magic puffed out around him. "Just a moment, Princess. I'm speaking with my daughter now."

"I want to see my sister."

More flickering magic burst into the cracks around the king's body and the doorway.

Infuriated, Horra motioned to her father. "Step aside, King Fyd," she stated in a bold voice for the princess's benefit. If she could handle Glory, she could handle her imperious sister.

He blinked at her before moving.

Misty stood behind him, her hands in the air ready to send another zinger at the king.

"Your Majesty." Horra bowed her head. "We were just—"

Misty breezed past the king, her massive, gauzy lilac dress squishing as she stomped through the doorway. She flicked a glance over all of them. "Where is she?"

"She's right—" Grendel began, but Horra stopped her with a raised claw.

"Outside. She's helping tend the horses. I'm sure she's just as excited to see you, Your Majesty." Horra bowed and held her arm out toward the kitchen entry. Even so, she didn't miss the confusion on the blonde fairy's face.

"Well, was that so hard?" Misty said, her voice back to tinkling instead of jangling. "Out of my way." She pushed past Horra. Grendel dodged the girl's arrogant arm as the fairy stormed through to the kitchen.

"What are you doing?" her father growled.

"I'm giving us enough time to get Glory back to her rooms and settled in before Miss Prissyface creates a real tirade." She waved at Grendel. "Follow me."

Horra rushed to the guest quarters and opened the door to the princess's former room. Gold greeted her. Veins of the precious metal wound throughout the walls and floor. Horra recalled the golden vial Glory had tried to bribe her with. She frowned and walked to the bed, which had remained untouched by the fairy's spell.

Horra grabbed the blanket's edge and flicked it so they could lay Glory down.

Grendel was quick and efficient. "I used to put Galumph to bed at night," she said as she laid the princess gently upon the mattress, then tucked her in. "It's the small things you miss." She sniffed.

Horra placed the woodencloak over the princess. "Cover her with this if you have to. It still has some magic left to hide her from her sister if it comes to that."

She turned to Grendel. "Now, do whatever it is you said you could to help her. At least try to wake her so she can talk with her sister and explain what happened. I'll try to delay the other princess as long as I can. Lock this behind me."

"But I need ingredients—"

"I'll send Sageel back. She can get you anything you need. Don't open the door to anyone but her, Rowan, or me."

~Glory~
Sometime after All the Pain

GLORY HAD NEVER BEEN SO cold before. Her very bones ached from the torturous piercing sensation. But she was too spent to move or do anything about it. Voices and noises sounded from far off. She couldn't concentrate on what was being said or what was happening.

A song filled her mind, one that her fairy nanny used to sing to her. She couldn't recall the words or the name of the song, only the melody. It soothed her and reminded her of cheerful things like unicorns and pretty flickertail birds.

Oh, how she'd loved those as a young child.

Glory embraced the memory, sinking into it and away from the agony.

~Rowan~

ROWAN HAD HOPED to go directly to the lab once they returned to Oddar's castle. However, he did as the queen bearer ordered.

"Hep," greeted the old stable hand, Murly. "You take'n bird. I'll take'n dragon," he muttered while leading Nimble into the largest of the stables.

Rowan was relieved to lead Pidge into the Conservatory, where he could also re-root and refresh himself. "Come along, Pidge." He grabbed the rope.

The castle's kitchen door slammed open. "Where is she? Where is my sister?" A tall woman wearing a wide, gauzy dress stomped into the courtyard, her wings fluttering wildly at her back. Her crystal shoes crunched against the grit on the stones. She swung her head back and forth, ignoring both him and the stable hand.

Rowan's roots detected a heady scent in the air akin to overripe flowers. He surmised the woman to be a fairy by the sweet notes and the fact she glowed in the moonlight.

Nimble rumbled and turned to stone. Murly growled, which ended in a cough when he raised his head to see who was speaking. "Majesty." He bowed. "Who might'n you be referring to?"

"My. Sister," she screamed.

Rowan would never understand why women screamed and squealed. "Majesty," he said, gesturing an official fairy greeting. "She was with Queen Bearer Fyd inside the castle."

The yellow-haired woman stepped closer to him. Magic probed across his bark. "You're not lying to me. Yet someone is lying." She turned and stomped back into the castle, her skirt billowing out around her as her shoes crunched across the stone walkway.

"Grrr. Now'n I have to bring the dragon about," Murly grumbled.

"Pidge, if you please." Rowan led the bird back to her companion.

With a rumble and a pop, Nimble changed back to his animal form.

"Thank-ee." Murly saluted and marched the gulgoyle inside the stable.

Rowan shook his head, his crown rattling with the movement. "Females."

Horra rushed outside. "Rowan, have you seen the other fairy princess, Misty? Tall, blonde, in a real snit?"

"I don't understand what 'snit' is, but yes. She was looking for her sister. I told her Glory was with you."

"Oh, bother. She'll be trying to get into Glory's room." Horra wrung her claws. "I can't let her see Glory in the state she's in. She's already furious at not finding her here when she arrived. I need you to help Grendel. Do you recall which room Glory stayed in while she was here?"

Rowan nodded.

"Misty can't be allowed in until Grendel has reversed as many of the Erlking's spells as she can." Horra leaned in and grabbed him by the arms. "You have to help me. It's of dire importance to keep peace between the fairies and trolls. Grendel will let you in. She might need supplies for whatever antidotes she's going to mix up. Go check on her. Get her whatever she needs. I'll tend to Pidge."

He was taken aback by her sudden vehemence. "You don't want the other princess to know the truth?"

Horra let him go and waved her claw around. "No. She won't understand how this all happened."

"I see. I would like the opportunity to work with the giant

on the antidotes." He scratched his fuzzy cheek. "I can't lie to her."

"No, just try to distract her or something. That's what I did when she didn't recognize Glory at first. I told her she was still out in the courtyard. But she won't stay sidetracked for long." Horra pushed him. "Hurry. Don't leave Grendel waiting. We need to bring Glory around so she can reunite with Misty."

Rowan dragged his roots for the first couple steps, not wishing to manipulate the second fairy princess. A shriek broke through the castle's thick stone walls, spurring him into motion. The sooner he helped Grendel, the sooner she would stop rampaging about.

CHAPTER 29

Guilt for sending Rowan into a situation he was uncomfortable with nagged at Horra. She knew the Conservatory was the last place Misty would look for her sister, and she needed a moment or two of peace before dealing fully with the fairies.

She threw Pidge another ground-insect ball she'd snagged from the snack jar in the kitchen, a surprising favorite of the pudge wudgie's since Rowan created it before they left to find Glory.

Had it been days, or weeks ago?

Horra wasn't even sure what day it was. She hadn't had time to ask since entering the castle.

She took a deep, steadying breath. Her stomach growled, reminding her she needed to eat as well. But Pidge had saved them more than once, and since Nimble moved faster while following her, the time it would've taken them to return was halved. Her pet deserved to be taken care of first.

Horra sat down in the center of the Conservatory, against the giant Yew tree. "Oh, Pidge. What if Grendel can't do it? What will I do, then?"

The tree creaked and moved.

Horra scooted away from it, her eyes wide.

"Queen Bearer." A woody voice came from a semi-formed face.

"Master Knurl?" she asked. Pidge screeched and landed next to her. The bird preened in front of the tree.

"I am." A branch reached out to scratch Pidge. "I sense the princess and the artifact she took have returned to the castle."

"Glory has returned, yes. I'm not sure what the artifact was, so I can't answer that." Horra twisted around to face him.

Master Knurl clucked, clearing his throat. "A sheet is in the fairy princess's room. It is invaluable to the Erlking. For the safety of your kingdom, do not let the other fairy get hold of it. It is of paramount importance for you to find and destroy it."

"Master Knurl, may I ask you a question?"

"Do so quickly."

Horra picked at her clawnail, dread and hope warring inside her. "The Erlking's spells damaged the woodencloak. Is there a way to repair it?"

After a moment of silence, the rood continued. "I'm afraid I do not know the symbols needed to place the protections."

Dread triumphed. "I see. Thank you anyway."

"Now go, Queen Bearer. Find the artifact, and fulfill your destiny of saving your kingdom."

The tree cracked, and the face disappeared. Pidge pecked at the spot where it had been, a forlorn cackle in her chest.

"I know, girl. But he's not gone for good. At least we can still consult him." Horra stood and dusted herself off. "One more snack, and then I have to go."

Horra plucked the last jar of pickled torentula eggs off a

preparation table and flung them in the air. She rushed to the doorway while Pidge plucked them out of the plants. She locked the door and kept the keys. "Wouldn't want some enraged midnight visit from a certain fairy."

The princess's shrieks and bouts of fizzing magic followed Horra through the castle and into the guest quarters. A peek around the stairway wall revealed Misty standing outside her sister's bedroom door.

Grendel was doing a stellar job keeping the girl out.

Horra tiptoed back to the stairs and went in search of something to eat. Inside the dining room, she spotted her father. Several scrolls sat in front of him, along with other important-looking sheets of parchment.

He grunted. "Where have you been?"

"I was feeding Pidge." She walked over to his chair at the far end of the long wooden table. Beside him was a plate laden with all her favorite foods. "Is this mine?"

Another grunt. "Your favorite hobgoblin kitchen maid takes excellent care of you." He set the scroll he was reading aside. "When Torren returned with a mesmerized Captain Erast and the other knights, I was told you and Rowan were headed for the Riven."

Horra placed a chunk of dense bracken bread dipped in bacon grease in her mouth to give herself time to think of how to approach her father. Maybe Rowan was right. The truth upfront was always better than trying to work around a problem or situation. She swallowed.

"We couldn't find the princess. My captain had gone missing. Everywhere we turned, we ran into some form of the Erlking's messengers." She twirled her glass of spruce juice. "When I ran into Balk, he mentioned we should go to the source of the problem."

Her father frowned. "Meaning the Riven."

She moved her claws to her lap. "Yes."

"And yet here you are." His voice was low but revealed nothing of what he was thinking.

She gazed into her father's handsome green face, and all the panic and fear she'd experienced in the dizzying space came back to her. She wished she could crawl into his lap and let him make everything better.

However, he'd made her Queen Bearer. And he'd put her in charge of retrieving the princess. She wouldn't apologize for her methods.

"The Riven isn't like anything I imagined it to be." She explained running into Glory outside the Riven, all the events that had happened while in the Riven, and the events after they'd escaped.

He sat still and quiet as she detailed all of it, including the part where they'd tied Glory up.

After she finished, she took a deep breath and waited for him to react.

Misty's shrill voice echoing outside the dining room preceded her entry.

Horra shoved as much of the greasy bread into her mouth as she could, knowing this might be the last chance she'd get for a while.

The fairy princess stood at the end of the table, her chest expanding with heaving breaths. "Where. Is. My sister!" She raised her hand, and a swirling, vaporous cloud bloomed in her palm. "Tell me now, or I'll—"

Her father's chair scraped against the stone floor. "Or else you'll what? Attack an ally in their own castle, declaring the next war started?"

Horra gulped.

Sageel rushed into the dining room. Her eyes widened at the two royals facing off. "Majesties," she squeaked.

Everyone turned to her.

A figure glided in behind Sageel, capturing everyone's attention.

Glory walked through the doorway, her footsteps graceful. Her skin was no longer alabaster with a tinge of death. It was a muted gold, not as robust as it had once been but also not the pallor the first hex had created. Her gray hair had regained its auburn color. And her face was no longer disfigured, though she also didn't have the delicate beauty she'd once had. She looked normal and startlingly plain. "Sister?"

The cloud dissipated from Misty's hand. The princess broke out into a loud sob and ran to Glory, pulling her into a tight embrace.

Horra's father put his claw on the back of Horra's chair and gave her a surprised but meaningful look.

Behind the two princesses, Grendel and Rowan entered the dining room.

"Where's the food?" Grendel asked loudly. "I'm famished."

Sageel sidled up beside Horra. "What do giants eat?"

"Probably whatever they want," she said distractedly. "Mostly vegetables, from what I gather. Oh, and make sure Glory has something to eat as well. There's something I must do."

Sageel pinched one eye closed and tsked. "Sounds to me like you need a distraction."

Horra was thankful once again for her keen-minded maid. "Keep them all busy." Horra walked over to Rowan. "I need your help."

GLORY's golden room appeared as she'd left it, with a few of their lab's glass jars sitting around in obscure spots throughout the room.

"Queen Bearer, what are we looking for?" Rowan asked.

Horra rummaged through the dresser, finding it empty. After the fairies had invaded the castle, they'd filled the rooms with gossamer fabrics, pastel dresses, and all kinds of frippery. Somehow, that had changed when the Erlking hexed Glory.

"When I took Pidge to the Conservatory, Master Knurl warned me to retrieve the artifact Glory had stolen from the Erlking. He said it was of utmost importance to find it if we wanted to keep the kingdom safe."

"I see. Did he say what the artifact was?" Rowan lifted the bed and glanced beneath it.

"A sheet of paper. We just have to figure out where it is, remove it, and put it in a safe place." And Horra knew just the place to put it—the passageways. No one would find it there. "But we don't have much time. I can't alert Misty or Glory to what we're doing. Glory could still be bent on making the trade with the Erlking. There's no way I will ever trust that girl again."

They spent several frenzied moments searching the room, to no avail.

"Where haven't we looked?" she asked Rowan, who stood scratching the green moss on his cheek.

"You said she returned with it. Could it be on her person? What else did we return with?"

Horra's eyes widened. "The woodencloak!" She grabbed it and searched the hidden pockets inside. No luck.

"What about her torn coat?"

"You're a genius." Horra rushed to where the hobgoblins had placed the folded tattered cloth. Horra furiously searched it, hearing the crackle of paper before locating the hidden pocket. "I got it," she said.

High-pitched, chimey voices from the hallway leaked into the room.

Horra shoved the sheet into her pocket. "Act like we're cleaning her room."

Rowan twisted in a circle, a confused expression on his fuzzy face.

"Just stand aside," she said as she pushed him. When she straightened the bedsheets, her claw hit a book hidden inside the pillow.

"Rowan," Horra whispered. "Take this and hide it." She shoved it into his hands, which were tucked behind his back. His limbs jittered nervously.

Horra stepped back from him, hoping to draw their attention away from Rowan.

The two princesses strode into the room.

Misty stopped and glared. "What are you doing in here?"

Glory didn't look very pleased either.

Horra donned the innocent look she'd used on Woodsly, mostly unsuccessfully. She silently prayed that she would be more successful now. "I knew the hobgoblins wouldn't be able to get back in here to clean up your rooms, so I had Rowan come help me." She patted the rumpled blanket she'd pulled crookedly across the bed.

"Wow. You're as good at making beds as you are at cleaning your castle." Misty flicked her narrow fingers at Horra. "I've got it now. You can leave."

Rowan joined his hands behind his back and stood tall. The book, Horra noted, was outlined inside his shirt along his backside. "Your Majesties, must I remind you that you are here in this castle at the goodwill of the trolls? And the queen bearer went out to great lengths to rescue Glory from the Erlking. I would think instead of the animosity you're showing toward your hostess, you might instead show a bit more respect."

Tears pricked Horra's eyes. It was moments such as this that Rowan reminded her so vibrantly of her late instructor Woodsly. However, now was not the time to get melancholy or fall into a bickering match with the two fickle fairies.

"That's all right, Rowan. I'm sure this has been an ordeal for them both. I just want to make them comfortable." She locked onto Rowan's arm and directed him around the two princesses and toward the door.

Rowan walked stiffly as she led him, turning as he went through the door and bowing at the princesses, effectively hiding the book.

Horra turned, smiled, and waved. Both Misty and Glory held her in their squinted gazes, suspicion clear in the tilt of their heads. "Sleep tight." She shut the door behind her. "This way," she whispered to Rowan.

She steered Rowan to Woodsly's old room. After the fairies had gone through the castle on their cleaning spree, the room was left spotless and empty. For now, this was the best place she could think of to store their pillaged items. She made her way straight to the fireplace. "Hand me the book, please."

She reached in and flipped the switch to Woodsly's hidden storage shelves. It popped open soundlessly.

Rowan gave her the book. Taking the sheet of paper, she placed them both inside the unit. It locked automatically when she closed it, and Horra heaved out a sigh of relief.

She spun and faced the druid. "You did a fine job of misdirecting them, Rowan." She didn't mention Woodsly. Every time she'd done so in the past, Rowan acted strange, and she didn't want to ruin the moment. "I'll come back at a later time and hide it. Until then, let's try to keep tabs on the fairies' movements. I don't trust them, and both of them are far less diplomatic than their mother."

"Did you honestly think Glory knew of her mother's

whereabouts?" he asked, referring to Horra's conversation back in the Riven.

She shrugged. "I honestly don't know, but it wouldn't surprise me. By her actions so far, she's out for herself alone. I'm surprised she welcomed her sister after Grendel healed her. What did she do to Glory to restore her to such a good condition?"

They walked back to the door.

"Grendel mentioned something about a rejuvenating elixir the giants used in their hospitals for ailing citizens. I didn't see everything she put in it, but I memorized everything I saw." He closed the door behind them.

"Good." She handed him the keys to the Conservatory. "Take these and go rejuvenate yourself. Keep them hidden. I don't want anyone who shouldn't be there to wander in."

"Good evening, Queen Bearer." He took the keys and strode off. Something wiggled along his backside, catching her attention.

Horra stared. Was it her imagination, or was he growing a nubby tail like his predecessor?

CHAPTER 30

~Horra~

Horra stopped pacing in the hallway outside the royal bedroom suites. Earlier in the afternoon, she'd grabbed a snack since she'd barely had the chance for a proper meal. Then she showered. After that, she visited Nimble to make sure the stable hands had fed him and that he was comfortable. Chores mixed with wasting time to throw the fairy princess' off.

She glanced around before entering Woodsly's old bedroom. In moments she had the sheet and book. They barely made a dent in the knapsack she'd snagged from beneath her bed earlier. Once secured, she was ready to put them where they would remain safe from the Erlking's reach. She closed the door quietly behind her.

Relief flowed through her tired body. The task was almost complete. She entered her bedroom.

Glory sat on her lumpy bed with her hands crossed over

her knees, waiting for Horra. The princess had changed out of her singed, tattered clothing into something not quite pastel, but also not the mourning clothes she'd worn before. Her hair was styled, not wild, and a healthier pink tint glowed from her ivory skin.

Horra fought the dismay and her pounding heart upon seeing the fairy in her room. She clutched the bag tighter to her shoulder, praying the girl wouldn't realize what was inside.

This wasn't the forlorn girl she'd had to deal with lately. Horra wondered what the giant put in her mixture to work this kind of miracle.

Blood rushed through her body, and it took all her formal etiquette training to remain calm and not show her shaking claws. "Princess Glory. Is there something I can do for you?"

"You could return what you stole from me." She took the woodencloak out from behind her back and dropped it on the floor. Her wings unfurled and fluttered at her back.

Teeth gritted, Horra smiled. "I'm not sure what you mean. But thank you for returning one of the items you nicked from me. Don't think we're even. We're quite far from it, Princess Sticky Fingers."

Glory waved her hand dismissively. "I'm sure you believe I should be grateful to you for bringing me back to life, but I'm not." She laughed and glanced up to the stone ceiling. "I thought for sure when the Erlking was attacking me I had breathed my last." She tipped her face back down and snagged Horra with a glare.

Horra didn't know what to say, so she didn't say anything.

The fairy smiled condescendingly. "Even if your politeness hadn't clued me in, I would've figured it out very quickly."

Horra took a moment to consider how to proceed with the conversation. She didn't think being honest and forthcoming with Glory would work. The princess was far too devious.

Horra settled on her eye-to-eye approach. Back her opponent into a corner.

"Why didn't you say something in front of Princess Misty? She is your sister, after all. Blood is thicker than water and all that." Horra walked over and picked up the woodencloak. "Hiding something, perhaps? Possibly she and I need to have a one-to-one. You know, princess-to-Queen Bearer conversation." Horra emphasized her title. Technically, she was higher royal than they, even if Misty had been ruling in her mother's stead during her absence. "I mean, so much has happened lately, and I'd like to clear the air between our two kingdoms. Make sure no wars break out. And it would behoove us all to find your mother. Don't you agree?"

Glory's lips puckered. Horra had hit the bullseye of the fairy's vulnerability. The fairy rose gracefully.

Though some of her beauty had returned, the hex and the other spells she suffered lessened her stature. The intimidation Horra had once experienced from the fairy princess was now long gone. Her sympathy had dried up as well. She stepped back and gripped the bag's canvas straps in her pinched claws as the fairy moved toward her door.

"You won't get away with it," Glory sneered.

"Get away with what?" Horra asked with a defiant snarl. She held the other girl's gaze.

Glory blinked first. With a "tsk", she sailed through the still-open door and down the hallway.

Horra slammed the door behind her and locked it for good measure.

She slumped to the floor with the bag at her side. "Ah! That was too close. And what's up that fairy's sleeve now?" Different scenarios of how Glory might seek retribution bombarded her mind. She shook her head to rid herself of the visions. "Stop it. You're a troll warrior. You can handle whatever that spiteful snit sends your way."

She rose, emptied her bag onto her bed, and hung up her woodencloak. Ruined or not, it still held some power, and she wouldn't leave it in the fairy's hands any longer. She moved to the stones by the secret doorway and pressed them.

Rock dust sparkled in the air as the doorway opened silently. Horra knew exactly where she was going to hide the book and paper. She stepped into the familiar safe space and closed the doorway behind her.

~Grendel~

LATER THAT EVENING, after healing the fairy princess, Grendel couldn't sleep. Instead, she knocked on the Conservatory doors. The keys she'd been told were hanging on the wall outside were curiously missing.

"Who is it?" Rowan's muffled voice came from the other side. The doors were clouded over from the humidity inside the garden space, and water dripped down the glass.

"Grendel," she called.

The sound of a lock being tripped echoed before the door swung open. "Welcome!" Rowan looked around as if expecting someone else. "Isn't it late? Shouldn't you be asleep?" He stood on a platform above a wide expanse of a mini forest and meadow all rolled into one. A stately Yew tree branched out from the center of the glassed-in space. Moonlight glittered over everything, allowing enough light to see.

"Couldn't sleep." She stepped inside. Rich humus scents washed over her, as did a sticky warmth that clung to the fur on her body. She'd grown accustomed to being over-warm, so the heat from the humid air didn't bother her. "This is beautiful."

Rowan locked the door behind her.

"Are we locking ourselves in or locking others out?" she asked.

He stowed the key ring inside a pocket she wouldn't have noticed had she not seen him use it. "Locking others out, I'm afraid. The fairies once killed most of the plants inside these walls and the lab as well, I'm told. Horra doesn't trust them to not do so again in their current moods."

Shock made her stop before she moved down the small stairway. "Why would any creature destroy something so magnificent?"

Rowan steepled his fingers. "The fairies were mesmerized at the time. They were doing the Erlking's bidding."

Grendel winced. The evil creature hadn't mesmerized her, but she had suffered from his magic. "That's awful."

Pidge screeched from somewhere in the depths of the Conservatory. "Ah, so this is the pudge wudgie's home as well." She bent to examine the flora, finding a night crimson flower in full bloom. The flower couldn't grow in the giant lands since they were too far north and too cold for it to survive. "You have some unique plants here."

Fingers still steepled, Rowan clacked out a cough. "The trolls pride themselves on their variety. The Weald, of course, had many more." He dropped his hands. "Most of that is gone now, thanks to the Erlking."

His words, though gently spoken, held sadness on a level she didn't know he could express. Though she'd heard of the Weald in the central part of the Wilden Lands, she'd never studied it much. Giants never visited the Weald, nor did her kingdom have anything to do with the druids. But losing any kind of rare plant upset her anyway. "What happened?"

"Come, I'll explain. Horra has a bench by the pond where we can sit and discuss."

Grendel followed him into the heart of the Conservatory, marveling at everything. Her parents had a small garden in the back of their house like all good giant families did. But this was more than she'd ever imagined a troll kingdom having. They weren't as civilized, after all.

However, after the troll had helped her and trusted her to heal the princess, Grendel reconsidered her opinion of trolls. They weren't the small buggish creatures her kind thought them to be.

"Here we are." Rowan waved her over to a wooden bench. It was out of place among the mostly stone-furnished castle, though she had spied wooden tables in the dining room.

The bench was polished and had intricate designs carved into it. It looked inviting. "This looks too finely crafted to be something a troll made."

Rowan remained silent for a moment while she made herself comfortable. He sat next to her, leaving no room for anyone else on the bench.

He placed his hand on the armrest. "Hm. There's magic in it. It must be elven made."

"I'm surprised," she said, running her hand across the design's smooth surface. "How can that be?"

"The trolls filled the Conservatory with soil from the former Elf Lands. When the elves departed for Endwylde, the trolls assumed ownership of the lands and mountains they deserted and built this using that soil. I'm sure this was among the things the trolls took for themselves."

"It's so odd, don't you think? The way the elves left? Our textbooks only document the move, not the motivation behind it. What could've inspired a whole race to leave everything behind and take up residence behind an impenetrable magic wall?" Her heart quickened from discussing an intellectual subject with Rowan again. She'd missed this since she was changed. Talking with someone who didn't run away screaming in fright was refreshing.

"Indeed. It's one piece of the puzzle that might explain a few things about the Erlking we have yet to figure out." Rowan crossed his legs, his roots dangling in the air. "I've been rethinking everything we know about the elves. You see, when we found ourselves in the Riven, it was far different from anything I imagined it would be."

Grendel's eyes widened. "You were in the Riven? What's it like?"

"Confusing. Like a time-space maze that shifts and changes just when you get your wits about you. It's filled with music and mesmerized creatures." Rowan's crown moved as he shook his head. "It is nothing I ever want to return to."

Though the view of the pond was lovely, she shifted to face him. "I always pictured it like one of the giant fairytales where the forest is dark and full of boogie creatures."

"Bug creatures, yes. Boogies, no. It was scary nonetheless. I wasn't sure we were going to make it out. But I found a Ghost Tree that was occupied by several woodland spirits. When Horra found me after rescuing the fairy princess from a hanging death, we figured out there was an underground magical channel running through the Riven."

That intrigued her. "Are you certain?"

He gestured with his woody hand. "That's how we allowed the spirits to escape. Then we helped some wyvern break free from their thralls."

"Oh, it all sounds so exciting. Much better than running from everyone and hiding." She sighed. "I never wanted to leave the giant lands. I thought nothing could be as grand as my home. But I now realize all areas have their beauty and their share of dangers as well."

"If I may ask, giants are, well, giant. How did you become so small?"

She clutched her hands tight in her lap. "The spell changed me completely. One minute I was sitting on my chair in my yard reading. The next thing I knew, I heard music, and the pain began. When I came out of the spell, I was a fraction of my original size, and fur covered my body." She held out her hands. "When I ran into the bathroom, I climbed up to see myself in the mirror. That's when I saw what I'd become."

Rowan tipped his head. "But why did you run away? You could've stayed and explained to your parents what happened."

"My sister Galumph saw me." She raised her hands to emphasize her next point. "She loves bugs and all kinds of icky stuff. But when she saw me, she screamed in terror. She ran off to tell our parents a monster was in the house. That's when I knew I must leave."

"That was hard for you?" he asked.

"The worst. Until a few nights later when the Erlking and the worqs appeared and stole her." Her shoulders sagged at the memory. "I needed to find her. I still do. The Erlking has to be stopped."

Rowan placed a hand on her arm. His brown eyes gleamed, but something foreboding laced his tone. "Something is coming."

"What?" She glanced up, thinking someone had entered the Conservatory.

He squeezed her arm, his eyes staring into space. "The Erlking is coming. We need to warn the king and the queen bearer."

CHAPTER 31

Seconds after entering the passageway, Horra's forehead grew damp as she waited for her bedroom's hidden door to seal. Once locked, she turned to head toward the hallway leading to the library.

A squeak made her freeze in place.

Roaming along the dust-laden path were a half dozen mice sniffing around, not scurrying as they used to. The memory of the mesmerized rat flashed in her mind, and she hesitated.

She and Rowan had discussed the link between the creatures in the Riven and the Erlking.

Images of all the creatures she'd encountered since the Erlking showed up crossed her mind in vivid detail.

The mesmerized rat in the passageway before Woodsly found and warned her, another tiny mouse in the giant girl's bedroom, a suspicious rat on the peddler's wagon while she was lost and headed to the Weald. Then the gang of rats outside the Weald when they'd fled the fire-struck forest, and the mouse at the Inn when the bells on the building weren't working.

Could it be the Erlking was using the creatures as spies?

Horra hugged the bag tight to her chest, her heart racing at the realization. Anger boiled in her gut.

"Get out of here," she screamed at the vermin. She chased them, swinging the bag so that they scurried off in different directions.

But not until after they made eye contact with her.

Which only cemented her new belief that these vile critters were spies. Possibly, they were how the Erlking stayed one step behind her for so long.

She stood alone in the dark passage, her chest heaving from darting back and forth. "I need Pidge."

But first, she needed to hide the book and paper in a hidden room beside the library's far wall. Then she'd head to the Conservatory.

The doorway to the library didn't open as smoothly as the other doors. Horra hadn't used it since her mother was alive, because it was too painful. Her mother had dubbed it her nest where she could sit and read for hours when she wasn't being tutored or fulfilling royal duties—which at the time merely consisted of making appearances.

The quilt her mother had the hobgoblin seamstresses make for her sat scrunched in a corner. Stitched frogs and lily pads over a mosaic, blue-water background. Her old troll dolly lay on its side next to a hay-stuffed pillow. Picture books lined a small, half-full bookshelf. Her mother had promised to help her fill it as she grew.

Horra climbed over her "nest" to reach the bookshelf. Its side backed the library wall where the dullest academic informapedias were kept. She slid the panel open and dropped the book and sheet there. Dust plumed as they fell into the void.

No one would find them here. They were as safe as a treasure in a cronkodyl-laden swamp.

With a glance back at her childish hiding spot, Horra closed the door on that chapter of her life and made her way to the Conservatory.

No mice appeared on her way back through the passageway. The Conservatory's doorway panel slid open silently. Horra heard voices in the distance, first Rowan's and then Grendel's.

She hesitated. Should she close the door so no one would discover the passage's entry, or should she keep it open so she could sneak Pidge in to feast on the spying mice?

In the end, she closed the door and snuck beneath the creeping briar.

Pidge squealed.

Vinegar! She'd hope to sneak in and out without Rowan's knowledge. Which was probably a false hope. Once she set foot on the soil, the druid would know.

"Queen Bearer?" he called.

Horra hoped she could avoid explaining how she ended up in the Conservatory without entering the front doors. "Coming," she yelled back. She found the path she normally used and walked over to the smallish pond area. "Couldn't sleep?" she asked the giant girl.

Grendel shook her head.

Rowan wrung his stick-like hands. "Queen Bearer. We have a situation."

Horra's heart constricted. "What is it?"

"I've received a message from the dryad." He pointed to the back wall of the Conservatory. "She has warned that the Erlking is coming."

"You heard from the dryad from the Riven? They survived?" Anxiety danced with hope in her gut.

"Not that dryad. From your dryad, the keeper of the weeping tree." He pointed once more at the back wall.

Horra narrowed her gaze. "*My* dryad? I—we don't have a dryad." Then she recalled Rowan mentioning dryads when they'd been trying to figure out how the Erlking had set the Weald on fire. "We have a dryad?"

"You do. You just didn't know it. She told me how she moved the tree for you to escape to the Weald with my seed." He gestured wildly with his hands, which he only did when he was excited or afraid.

She grabbed his hands. "When did you know for sure we had a dryad?"

His hands moved despite the fact she held them tight in her claws. "When you brought me to the Conservatory the first time. I sensed her presence, and Master Knurl verified that she lives in the Weeping Welter tree."

How could that be? Of course, they hadn't known Master Knurl lived in the Yew tree before Rowan came, either. Horra shook her head. "And she—this dryad—said the Erlking is on his way?"

"Yes. We have time to prepare, but just. I was on my way to find you and the king." He yanked his hands from her clutch. "We must ready our weapons."

Horra jerked her head back. "What weapons? Last time we had mud bombs, but they were for getting rid of the grubby worms. How are we supposed to stop him in the middle of the night without our knights here?"

"If you don't know, that's a question for the king."

Pounding sounded on the glass doors.

Horra, Grendel, and Rowan glanced at each other with startled expressions.

Grendel spoke first. "Are you expecting someone, Queen Bearer?"

"Rowan, are you in there? Horra? It's Torren."

Horra's shoulders relaxed. "I'll get it. You two follow me. We need to wake the king."

They made it to the door quickly, but not in enough time to stop Torren from pounding on it again. "Stop or you'll break the glass, you dunklehead!"

Horra undid the lock, and Torren blasted into the space. "The Erlking is on his way. I was on watch duty and caught sight of him. It took me a few minutes to go around them so they wouldn't hear me, then I kicked my horse into high gear to arrive ahead of him.

Torren met Horra's eyes. "He's riding a flying horse. The fairy queen and some other woodland creature are with him—tied up and gagged. And he's angry."

The band around Horra's heart tightened again. She knew exactly what he was after. And she silently vowed to her fore-mothers and her Creature God she would not let that evil elf get hold of it.

⸻

~Glory~

LATER THAT NIGHT, Glory stared at the newly placed bed next to hers where her sister snored in her sleep. They'd insisted the hobgoblins bring in the extra bed since neither of them was good at sharing.

"This is why," she mumbled to herself. Not that her words would rouse her sister. Misty slept like the dead. Always had. Which was why Glory snuck around their palace so easily without getting tattled on.

She groaned, which did little to ease her frustration.

Glory walked over and covered the mirror with a spare sheet. Her sister had constructed the offending mirror—against Glory's will—from a pile of rocks, which she then hung from the center of the wall. Candles flickered and glowed with a rich golden light reflecting off the walls her potion had affected. The light held off the darkness that reminded her of the nightmares she'd suffered after her last visit with the Erlking.

Her reflection wasn't something she wanted to see. No, her face wasn't piggish now, but it also wasn't as beautiful as it once had been. She dug her fingernails into the palms of her hands to keep the tears from falling. If only the troll hadn't snuck up here and taken the book and the music sheet when the giant bullied her into meeting with her sister.

And what would she do with them? The Erlking wouldn't bargain. She possibly could've found someone—another giant, maybe—whom she could've traded the music spells to in return for some of their unique healing treatments.

She'd told the giant girl she didn't want to see her sister. But the horrid, beastly girl had forced her to go anyway. Though the girl had some talent with elixirs, Glory wouldn't forgive her for that slight.

Unable to stay away, she lifted the small cloth she'd hung over the mirror and glanced at her reflection. She didn't recognize herself. Plain as a bocan woman—that's what she was now. She flicked the cloth back over the gleaming surface.

Glory bowed her head. How had her plan gone so awry? By now, she should be basking in her beauty once more. Instead, she was halfway healed, Horra had stolen the Erlking's spells, and her sister thought they were going back to their Shining Kingdom on the morrow.

It was all inconceivable.

Thumping on the stairway broke the silence of the sleeping castle.

Curious, Glory padded over to the door and opened it enough to hear anything that might drift her way.

"Do you want to do it, Queen Bearer, or shall I?" A hobgoblin's gravelly voice was the first she heard.

"Let me do it. He won't be happy to be woken for such news," came Horra's answer.

Glory's heart raced. Something was going on, and she needed to know what it was. She crept down the short guest's hallway and peeked around the edge toward the royal side. It skewed to the left, though. Out of sight.

She tiptoed past the stairway to spy on them.

A loud knock made her stop.

"Father?" Another long knock. "I'm sorry to wake you, but we have dire news."

What could that be? Did they run out of snake oil or spruce juice? Glory wrinkled her nose and held back a snicker.

"What is it?" the king snarled.

"Father." Silence.

Another troll voice continued. "King Fyd. I've spotted the Erlking. He's on his way to the castle. And he has hostages, Majesty."

CHAPTER 32

he Erlking has hostages?

Glory's knees faltered, and she almost fell to the floor. Images of her mother trussed up by her guards marched through her mind. Her mother was a strong woman, a regal ruler. Glory hadn't doubted the queen would find a way out of her precarious situation.

The Erlking knew she had his spells, and she'd made the mistake of telling him the troll princess had them.

What had she been thinking to give away the location so carelessly? Glory wanted to kick herself. It was a simple rule of engagement. Never give away too much information. And yet she had, after her plan to bargain with the Erlking failed.

He was going to turn the tables on them. He was going to use her mother as a bargaining chip. What would the trolls do in return? Would they give everything up to keep their castle safe?

No. She knew they wouldn't. They were much too stubborn for negotiations.

Her mother was doomed.

The air in her lungs caught, stealing her breath. She must get her sister. Misty had full use of her magic. She could help free their mother. Save her from what Glory had put into motion. She rushed toward the guest hallway.

"Princess Glory?" She stumbled at hearing the king's deep voice. "Is that you?"

Glory ran into the wall, recovered, and turned around. "King Fyd." Her lips faltered as she smiled, but her heartbeat created a presto chorus in her chest.

Horra stood beside her father, another troll they called Torren stood a step behind, and Rowan and the giant girl took up the rear of their procession. She ignored the hobgoblin maid.

The king crossed his arms over his chest. "I take it you heard our conversation?"

Glory smoothed her hair. "On accident, yes. I was unable to sleep, you see, so I was walking the hallways."

Horra plunked her claws on her hips and jutted out her lower lip. "Put a cork in it. You heard us coming up the stairs, and you followed us to eavesdrop."

The king raised his arm. "Let our guest explain herself."

Glory blinked and grinned, hoping it would be enough to smooth things over. "I do apologize. My sister snores. I was heading to the kitchen for some of the hobgoblin's delightful sugared rose petals when I saw you all."

Rowan clacked to clear his throat. "Your Majesties, we don't have time for fairy follies. We need to plan."

A loud bang rattled the castle.

"What was that?" The king's eyes darted around.

Horra rushed past them. "Sounds like a ballast to me. We

need to get downstairs. Follow if you want, fairy, but do so at your own risk."

Her unspoken "I won't save you this time" rang in Glory's ears.

The group ran down the stairs. Grendel was the only one who glanced directly at her. Glory waited for them all to leave before bounding back to her room and pouncing on her sister. "Misty, wake up. That fiend is here, and he has Mother."

"What?" Misty yawned and spoke at the same time.

"Wake. Up." Glory lifted and pounded her sister back against the lumpy mattress. Magic zinged her fingertips, snapping her sister's ire back at her.

"Okay, okay. I'm awake." Misty sat up, her blonde hair ruffled and her face creased. "What's the emergency?"

"The Erlking is here, and he has Mother. Get up. Unless you want Mother's life hinging on the trolls' decisions alone?"

That got Misty moving. In the blink of an eye, she magicked herself back to rights. "Lead the way, sister."

For once, Glory was thankful for her sister's presence. It was almost like old times, before the Erlking led her astray. She guided her down the stairs, and they followed the voices to the throne room.

"How do we fight off a rock creature?" Rowan asked as they stepped into the room.

"We fight rock with rock," King Fyd said. "Princess Toppenbottom? Would you do us the honor of defending the castle?"

Misty clicked her tongue. "What do you need from me?"

Horra stepped in front of her father. "They've got ballasts. Can you remove the charm? Or can you create another ballast army to fight them while we confront the Erlking?"

"Fine. Step back." Misty waited for the others to move out of the way. "I'll have to use what we have here." At the king's nod, she made a circle with her hand and magicked the thrones into small stone creatures. When she breathed the spell, they came alive. "Go fight. Defend the castle to your last pebble," she ordered.

The new ballasts, each about the size of a large troll, walked through the open door before pounding on the closed outer door until it broke and fell into a heap of rubble.

When another boulder hit the castle, Glory knew her sister's magic wouldn't be enough. "Where's Mother?"

Torren, who stood vigil at one window, pointed. "Over there. He has her wrapped up and her mouth gagged. There's some sort of band around her hands."

"Magicuffs. They keep the wearer from using their magic," Glory said as she stepped up to an empty window that looked down onto the courtyard. Covered in green grass with trees around the edges, a few boulders stuck out of the courtyard soil. Memories of being there under the Erlking's spell pricked at Glory's mind. "He has that despicable dryad with him."

Whatever hope she'd kept alive dwindled. If the Erlking had enough power to transport a dryad without their tree, they might never free her mother. And that left their Shining Kingdom vulnerable.

She should've tried to rescue her mother the first time the dryad showed her face. She'd been so determined to meet up with the Erlking, though, to get her beauty back. Why did she have to be so single-minded? She knew beauty was in her fairy genes, and losing that had been like losing everything. Now she saw the error in her thinking, how her selfishness affected others. Glory bit the inside of her mouth to keep from showing too much emotion.

"I worried, but I never truly thought the Erlking was a match for Mother. How could this happen?" Misty turned angry eyes on the trolls. "Ever since we came here, nothing has been as it should be. Why is it when things go wrong for the fairies, trolls are always at the center?"

Horra growled and bared her teeth. "Your mother was out looking for Glory when the Erlking overtook her. She wouldn't have been out had Glory not escaped from her on the way back to your kingdom with items she'd stolen from the Erlking. I wouldn't have been lost in the Riven had she not escaped from our castle after we rescued her from the Erlking. She was in possession of some musical spells she thought she could trade in exchange for her beauty. If you want to blame anyone, look no further than your sister."

Misty spun and faced her. Fury twisted her sister's lovely face into something ugly. "You are the reason for all this?" Her voice went shrill at the end. "I should've known."

The accusing note in the troll's voice coupled with her sister turning on her whisked all the regret and contrition from Glory's mind. She couldn't admit to her part in this fiasco. Instead, she settled for misdirection. She pointed a finger at Horra. "It's the trolls he wants. It's their fault he's targeting the fairies. We were just pawns in his ballad to take over the Wilden Lands."

The tilt of her sister's head revealed that Glory hadn't persuaded her. "Why didn't you tell me about his magical spells? And how did you get hold of them? We were all mesmerized at the same time. At least, I thought so." A confused look crossed her sister's face.

If she remembered everything, Glory was sunk.

Rowan held up a finger. "Don't forget Glory had the golden bridle for the Erlking's pet kelpie."

Fury glowered from Misty's gleaming eyes but quickly cooled to an icy understanding. She'd finally put all the pieces together that Glory had tried to hide from her. All the lies. The truth finally dawned in her sister's mind. "I see."

"We have no time to argue about who's to blame for what. We need to stop the ballasts and free the hostages," Horra said.

Misty turned and walked away from Glory, which was a subtle act. One only a fairy would notice. They had always been inseparable, until the Erlking. Seeing her sister's change of attitude stung more than she'd imagined.

"Sir Rowan." Misty approached the log boy. "Do you have any woodland tricks you could use to distract the Erlking? The only way to defeat him and get my mother back is to work together."

~Rowan~

ROWAN RUSHED to the Conservatory moments later to approach Master Knurl for advice.

Grendel followed. "What's your plan?"

"That remains to be seen." He opened the doors with the keys he still kept in his pocket. Pidge screeched when they entered.

Rowan stopped and scratched a spot on his cheek. "I didn't think to ask Queen Bearer Fyd how she got inside the Conservatory."

Grendel shrugged. "Is there a back entry?"

"There is, but that's not the direction she came from." He jerked himself into motion again and made his way directly to the Yew tree. "Master Knurl. We need your help once more against the Erlking."

A face took shape on the trunk. "Young Master Rowan. How can I help?"

"We need a diversion, something to distract the elf so we can retrieve the hostages he is holding."

"Rowan?" a woman's voice called out through the roots. *"Is that one of my daughters I sense?"*

Rowan hesitated. Daughters? "There is a dryad with the fairy queen, yes."

"She must not remain with the evil one. Allow me to help you free my child, please."

Grendel sent him a questioning glance, but he didn't stop to explain. "I welcome any help you can give, Lady of the Willow Tree."

"I see you have the help you require. If you need me, I'll be here." The rood's face faded back into the shape of bark.

"What help is that?" Grendel asked.

"The Conservatory has a resident dryad willing to fight," Rowan explained. "You mentioned another entrance earlier. It's more of a hole. Follow me if you'd like to join us."

After grabbing the pot holding the strangler vine, he led the way to the break in the fencing. Pidge flew down and darted through before he could stop her.

Rowan dug into the tree roots, which shifted and moved to allow them close to the Weeping Welter Tree, its ropy limbs dangling around his shoulders. With a mighty wrench, he broke off a piece of the tree. "Are you there, Lady?"

"I am."

Rowan turned to Grendel, tucking the broken root aside. "Be careful," he warned as he crawled on his knees and one hand through the tight spot. He didn't recall it being this small before, but he had grown. After a couple minor scratches on his bark, he was finally out.

Grendel had much the same trouble squeezing through the opening since she was almost as big around as he was. Her orange hair snagged in the metal fence, and she squealed. "Ugh. You need to redesign this opening."

"It might be recommendable to Queen Bearer Fyd, yes."

Once outside, the Erlking's shouts rose above the boisterous calls of birds in the trees growing along the ravine's edge behind the castle. A glitter of sunlight lightened the horizon, signaling morning.

Pidge flew straight for the front courtyard.

Grendel snorted. "That bird is a go-getter, isn't she?" She dusted herself off. "Where to now?"

He pointed to the edge of the castle where Pidge had disappeared. "Wait for me there. I'm going to put the Lady of the Tree down over here so she can gather any resources she needs to help us."

He walked to a stray yew tree, still young but big enough to harbor any other spirits in the area. There must be others nearby if the Lady knew of the Erlking's arrival. He hoped they were the spirits he and Horra had freed from the Riven.

When he joined Grendel at the castle's edge, the Erlking jumped off the kelpie. His magic suspended his two hostages in the air. Rowan considered what magic it could be but realized they were moving like grass in the wind. He inserted a finger in his ear and moved the detritus growing there.

Musical notes carried on the breeze.

He quickly tucked the fuzz back into place. "He's using music to keep them afloat," he told Grendel.

"Ah, music. I've never cared for it. Galumph was the one who liked lullabies and such." She frowned. "It must be too low for me to hear."

"It could be your ears aren't suited for music now that you've changed," Rowan reasoned. "Let's see what we can do." His roots ripped apart the grass as he dug them deep into the ground.

It was comforting, yet he wasn't here for comfort. "Lady of the Tree? Are you ready?"

"Ready and eager," came her steely reply.

Rowan broke the pot and held the strangler vine out to the pudge wudgie. Without a tree to grow it on, it had languished in the Conservatory. The vine wiggled in his grasp, searching for an object to latch onto. "For the ballast. Don't get close to the rock beast yourself, or I'll have to answer to Queen Bearer Fyd."

Pidge chirruped and fluttered into the air. In a quick darting motion, she grabbed the choker vine and headed into battle.

CHAPTER 33

~Horra~

Horra spied Rowan, Grendel, and a tall woman at the side of the castle. Like Rowan, this woman was more tree than creature, with her branchy hair and barkish-looking skin. Even the dress she wore was green like a meadow. She was more majestic than the dryad outside of the Riven.

The ballast standing on the edge of the courtyard knocked Misty's smaller boulder creatures aside as if flicking away flies. It picked up a boulder it had just smashed and threw it at the castle. The stone sailed through the air and hit a spot above the entry doors.

The worqs accompanying the Erlking but standing away from the ballast ran for cover as stone shards flew in their direction.

Horra and her father ducked as pieces rained down on them. "We need to stop that thing first," she shouted, not mentioning the fact they would need to have new thrones carved.

Pidge was a blur as she glided over their heads. Some kind of vine dangled from her talons. She circled the rock creature before letting the vine loose.

"What is she doing?" Horra asked. The vine hit the charmed boulder creature and wrapped itself around it, growing as it wound around and around. In the blink of an eye, the vine covered the ballast, disabling the creature's ability to toss stones. "Rowan, you brilliant druid! It's a strangler vine."

The ballast toppled, breaking into small pieces. The vine crawled over the remains and engulfed the rock corpse, gorging on the magic. Worqs, who had ducked for cover, peeked out from behind boulders and trees. Horra noted they didn't join their master right away.

Unfazed by his rock beast's demise, the Erlking strode closer to the castle, yanking the two women with him.

Thanks to the stuffing Horra now kept almost permanently in her ears, the music accompanying the elf was muted. Only a few notes broke through, but they didn't affect her. She clenched her jaw when the Erlking pushed both women ahead of him like prized trophies.

Anger simmered in her gut, spurring her to confront him. She shook the rock dust and pebbles from her thick hair as she and her father marched out of the castle and onto the courtyard grounds.

"Let those women go," Horra demanded with a confidence she didn't completely feel. Dew dampened her boots and slicked her steps across the grassy yard. She adjusted her quiver strap across her chest, holding her bow tight in her other claw. She'd nocked an arrow and held it in a ready position. Her wrist brushed against the dagger sheathed at her side.

Golden light bloomed in the distance, dancing happy circles around the fairy queen, but there was nothing happy about her expression. Horra couldn't see any bruises, but she'd lost weight. Her once-lovely face was devoid its plump features, allowing her bone structure to be highlighted instead.

Torren, the knights, and the hobgoblins formed a semi-circle behind Horra and the king. They held any weapon they could find, though Horra knew it wasn't enough to battle dark magic. Possibly, they could hold off the worqs should they decide to join in.

"Ah, a welcome committee." The Erlking's snide remark was met with the dryad's elbow in his gut. Her muted screams were hoarse, and the web across her mouth puckered where it stretched too tight. The elf's hood fell down, revealing the pale globe of a bald head. The red, puckered scars where his ears should be only made the gaunt elf look more hideous. He struggled to breathe for a moment before straightening again.

He jerked the dryad around as a haze of magic oozed from his bony hands. The spell snapped at the tree woman, and she squealed. "Uh, uh, uh. You're nothing more than a bargaining chip, my friend."

Horra admired the dryad's fearless rebellion. But her admiration faded as the Erlking turned his solid black gaze on her. Chills swept across her hide, and she fought to conceal them. Sucking up every ounce of indignation she could, she straightened and met his look with defiance. "Your dryad friend doesn't seem so friendly right now, fallen elf. Maybe you should un-friend her."

"You think you're so incredibly witty, don't you, young would-be queen?" A sneer lifted the corner of his thin upper lip. "The days of your sarcasm have come to an end. Give me the book, including the spell I know the damaged princess had, or these women won't live to see the full sunrise."

"Hand over the queen and her companion, or it's you who won't survive this fine morning," King Fyd uttered in a deadly quiet voice. Attached to his side was the golden sword he'd hastily retrieved.

Horra longed to stab something, but she couldn't move without fear of the hostages getting injured.

Pidge screeched as she flew a wide circle around the group. Horra spied Rowan and Grendel peeking out from behind the castle's corner. She wondered what the druid was up to besides taking the ballast out of action.

The Erlking zapped the dryad once more with his magic. Worqs snickered and cheered their master as the bravest ones gathered around the dark kelpie.

The ground rumbled, reminding Horra too much of the Riven, and the grass moved like a wave. She gulped back the fear-riddled memories.

"Stop! Let my daughter and the queen go," a woman's voice blared, startling the birds in the trees around the courtyard. They flew off in a loud frenzy.

Horra swiveled around to find who had spoken.

The majestic dryad stepped out from behind Rowan. Power radiated from her in waves. Her hair was ropy and knotted, but not in a messy, tangled way like Horra's. Her wooden face held a beauty that wasn't obvious at first glance.

All heads turned to the new dryad, including the worqs, who recoiled at the sight of the woman.

Horra's mouth dropped open in surprise. Besides the Erlking, the worqs rarely cowered from anyone.

King Fyd's eyes were wide, and he stuttered, "That must be the Grand Lady of the Tree. All the stories I've read say she perished when the elves cut down her tree and fashioned their carriages from its wood after fleeing to Endwylde."

Horra gritted her tusks at the thought of such an atrocious

act. Her hair reminded Horra of the Weeping Welter Tree. Could it be possible? "Is this the dryad from the Weeping Welter Tree?" She remembered Rowan mentioning a dryad that had taken refuge in the Conservatory. Suddenly, the truth hit her. If this was the Grand Lady, she must've been hiding in the castle since her foremothers built it.

Had they known? Did they create the Conservatory to hide this dryad's presence until now? And how could she disguise such power? And then, Horra realized: The Conservatory had always been powerful, seeped in elven magic. It would've been easy for her to take shelter inside its glass walls.

A wide black grin spread across the Erlking's translucent face—a garish sight. "Ah, so you *are* still alive. The Sylvan Council believed you hid in the Weald. Imagine their surprise when you, as my prisoner, inform them they were wrong."

"You won't be taking her anywhere." Princess Misty's voice came from right behind Horra. She and Glory stepped up beside her and her father. A crystal gleam floated above Misty's hand. "And you won't be taking Mother anywhere again either."

A flush spread across Glory's pink cheeks, and her gaze flickered to Horra. She leaned slightly Horra's way and whispered, "Where's the book? We could end this standoff if you give it to him. Keep the sheet holding the troll's spelled sonata if you must, but Mother's life is at stake here. We can't risk losing her for one stupid spell book."

Outrage flushed through Horra. "That's rich! Where was that reasoning when you were bent on trading it in return for your beauty? He wouldn't be here if you hadn't stolen the book from him in the first place, so don't blame me for your misdeeds." Spittle flew from her lips. "And just so you know, I'm not about to upend the balance of the Wilden Lands just to appease a tyrant who will then turn our kingdoms into a wasteland like the Riven."

The Erlking's laugh sounded like a little girl's giggle, alarming Horra. "See the little princesses all in a row? Dressed and blessed and ready for the show. One fell prey, one left betrayed, but the last little princess chose to go astray." His giggle turned to a cackle.

Her father straightened. "*The Music Man's Curse*," he muttered, naming a fable her mother had read to her once or twice until Horra had begged not to hear the absurd tale again.

Horra tried to recall it now. It was an obscure account about a musician who stole the show and the hearts of children with his songs. She'd never understood why the story's characters were so captivated by the lyrical tunes. Music wasn't something she'd ever been interested in.

But then the Erlking showed up with his charmed instruments spewing their mesmerizing notes.

A flash out of the corner of Horra's eyes revealed Pidge attacking the distracted Erlking like the good huntress she was.

Princess Misty followed suit and sent her shimmering spell flying.

The Erlking jerked, taking the dryad and the queen with him. They stumbled as roots burst through the ground.

The princess's sphere hit the queen in her chest. Sparkling light exploded around the regal fairy, but instead of affecting her, the spell worked its way over to the Erlking's hand, which held her in a tight grip.

He screamed and flung the regal fairy to the ground. In a fury, he cast a dark spell on the queen.

"No!" Misty and Glory screamed at the same time.

Glory jumped to stand in front of her mother, but it was too late. The spell hit its target.

Queen Stella Toppenbottom jerked around on the ground, muted screaming around the gag covering her mouth. Glory dropped over her mother's body and wailed as Misty screeched and attacked again.

Horra lifted the bow and aimed at the Erlking, but she couldn't get a clear shot with the Erlking holding the dryad against his chest like a shield.

Another shriek echoed, and the Grand Lady joined in the fray. "Let my daughter go!" She stretched her arms out, reaching for the Erlking and the dryad. He rushed backward, away from her reach, and ran into his horse.

With a flick of his free hand, the music changed and the worqs bounded into battle.

"Knights, attack!" Horra shouted.

Torren, with their meager group of knights, ran at the worqs.

At the edge of the courtyard, dirt flew as Rowan dug deeper into the ground. Roots broke out around the Erlking.

They had him cornered.

"Get the golden bridle," Glory yelled. "It controls Calliope, the kelpie. Don't let him escape."

Dark magic crackled around the Erlking. He held the dryad's throat, choking her. Bugs crawled out from his sleeves and swarmed the dryad in a frenzy. She thrashed, but they covered her quickly.

Horra refused to let him take another life. She nocked an arrow and aimed for his head. The arrow flew true, and for a moment, hope glimmered in Horra's heart.

Glory stood and sent a golden flash at the arrow, knocking it sideways. It nicked the side of the Erlking's head, splitting the scar on his ear open.

A shriek blasted from the Erlking, and the bugs quivered and fell from the dryad.

But the damage was done. All that remained of the dryad was a husk of a tree. Visions of Woodsly's wooden body crashed inside her mind, clogging her throat.

"No," she cried out.

The Grand Lady let out a shrill wail. Branches, like arrows, sprouted. She flung them at the Erlking, but he'd already mounted the kelpie.

Horra was torn. Should she shoot an arrow at the Erlking, or kill an innocent animal?

"Don't kill him!" Glory shouted. "He has to heal Mother."

Horra ignored the fairy's screams. With tears in her eyes, she nocked the arrow, aimed, and let it fly.

The thwap she usually loved to hear when using her bow was not thrilling or comforting this time.

She was too late. The horse was too quick. Her arrow hit the kelpie in its haunch instead of its chest where she'd been aiming, and it didn't stop the beast from using its wings.

With a powerful arch, it cast off the ground, dragging its hind behind it. The kelpie was now too far away for her to try again.

Horra slumped to the ground, holding her bow in a limp claw. "What? No!" Her distressed cries joined in with the Lady's wailing and the fairy's weeping.

The worqs made a hasty retreat into the thicket of trees that grew along the ridge above the swamp. Torren and the other knights cheered.

The king glanced at her, concern etched across his green face. He knew.

This was not a defeat to be celebrated. The Erlking had taken one, possibly two more creatures' lives.

Horra hung her head and wept.

CHAPTER 34

~Horra~

Moments Later

A claw fell on Horra's shoulder and squeezed, jerking her from her misery. "Come along, Daughter. There is much to do."

Horra sniffed and swiped a sleeve across her dripping nose. She didn't want to be Queen Bearer at that moment, bound by duty to regroup and assume leadership. Her long red curls swung as she shook her head. "I can't."

Her father took a deep, audible breath. "This is what being queen actually means. It's not all about ceremonies and Goblin Courts. It's about making the hard decisions and living with the consequences. Putting others above yourself and your needs when the circumstance calls for it."

Horra's heart squeezed tight, making it hard to swallow the spit gathering in her mouth.

Her father kneeled next to her, his claw still firm on her shoulder. "Maybe I was wrong to give you responsibility of the

Queen Bearer title. I've known all along you would become an excellent ruler. I never doubted it, even before you broke your mother's spell and would've remained my darling little princess."

Horra glanced at him. "You've never called me your darling anything before."

A lopsided grin crinkled his cheek. "We're trolls. Fierce and unmoving. It's not something one should hear coming from a cold, hard king." He wiped away a tear trickling from her chin. "But I do—we do—have feelings. I know you care about the dryad and Queen Toppenbottom. We both have to suck it up and take care of business first. It's what your foremothers expect. It's what your mother would've done."

"King Fyd, Queen Bearer Fyd," Rowan interrupted. "Grendel has offered to attend to the fairy queen. The Lady of the Tree wants to perform their sacred rights for her daughter."

Horra swiped the last of the moisture from her heated face and rallied her inner strength. Her father was right. She was a troll, fierce and brave. She gripped her father's claw tightly as he offered to help her stand. "Yes. Thank you, Rowan. I'll work with the staff to ready the Conservatory for a service to honor the fallen dryad. Can you have Torren ready the knights to stand guard?"

Rowan struck a fist to his trunk in salute. "Yes, Queen Bearer."

Understanding shimmered in the depths of her father's clay-colored eyes. His smile was assuring.

Someone pushed Horra from behind, and she stumbled into Rowan. Luckily, the druid was prepared, and he caught her with two sturdy hands. "What?" She turned to find a red-faced Princess Glory pointing at her.

"You! All you needed to do was get the book. My mother

wouldn't be—" Glory's breath caught on the last word. She pounded her chest. "Are you happy now?"

Misty glided over and shoved her sister. "Oh, put a shell in it. Don't blame her for things that are your fault. It was you the Erlking approached in disguise. And you fell for his lies and brought us along for that fun little ride." She moistened her lips, her chest heaving as if she'd just run a long distance. "Yeah, I know. I found your diary when I returned to our castle. I read all about how you thought you could control him." She waved her hands in front of her. "He ended up controlling *all* of us. This, sister dear, is all because of you. Mother has been hexed, and it's not anyone's fault but yours."

Misty turned and stormed to her mother's side.

Glory's face slackened and then crumpled. Her chest rose and fell with quick gasps. "She's right," the girl uttered around her sobs. "It *is* my fault. I didn't want to admit it, but there's nothing I can hide now. Why did I think—?" She screwed up her lips, and her eyes glazed over. "Because I always think I can control everything. It wasn't just my beauty I wanted back. He bested me, and my pride couldn't handle it." She shook her head and fell to the ground, covering her mouth with her hands. "It was me," she muttered over and over as she rocked back and forth.

Horra wasn't sure what to do with an inconsolable fairy.

Her father looked as ill at ease as she was, as did Rowan, who quickly scurried away. With a pat on her shoulder, her father stepped back. "Comfort the princess. I'll take charge of the cleanup."

"Cowards," Horra grumbled, not worried the grieving princess might hear.

Sageel hobbled over. "Good grief. What's the matter with this one now?"

Horra held a claw up to stop the maid from continuing. "What is it?"

"The giant girl wants to use the lab as some makeshift hospitable room. I wanted your permission before I let her turn it upside and down." She twisted her apron around her gnarled fingers.

Horra nodded. "Get her what she needs for Queen Toppenbottom. Call for our healers as well. Maybe ask Princess Misty if she'll send a whimsy bird entreaty to their Shining Kingdom for anything she thinks they'll need."

The hobgoblin hesitated.

"Is there anything else?"

Sageel twisted the apron tighter. "Um, there seems to be a dangerous dragon creature wot landed in the stable area. Nimble busted out to reach it. The stable hands are too afraid to approach."

Horra blinked. *A wyvern?*

"Get me a hunk of meat and some rope." She stopped before restating her request. "Lots of rope." Horra turned away from the sobbing fairy and the maid. "Rowan? I need your help."

~Rowan~

ROWAN RELUCTANTLY FOLLOWED the queen bearer to the back courtyard, where the stables were located. They'd left the fairy princess on the front lawn, muttering to herself and bouncing back and forth like a madwoman. "What is it you need my help with, exactly?"

Pidge swooped down ahead of them and landed next to the dark wyvern and the rock-gray gulgoyle. "This," she answered.

Rowan stopped, his roots tickling the dirt with the desire for comfort. Though he'd ridden the creature out of the Riven, he still recalled how it dumped him after clearing the magic spells hiding the Riven. "How did it find us?"

Horra placed her claws on her hips. "Beats me. But it must have followed us and concealed itself until we were all gone. Aw, look at it. It thinks Nimble is its best friend."

Rowan noted the behavior of the wyvern. It tipped its head toward the gulgoyle, its tail lying relaxed on the ground. The sap in his fibers rushed through him. "You don't think the others are nearby, do you?"

Horra sent him a dismayed glance. They stood at the end of the castle, far enough away from danger but close enough to watch the two dragon creatures checking each other out. "That would not be good. Would it?"

The wyvern glanced up at them. In the blink of an eye, its muzzle was next to Horra's face. It sniffed, blew a warm, snot-laced breath out, then winked out of sight.

"Wha—" Horra wiped the moisture from her forehead. The wyvern sat once again at Nimble's side. Its skin rippled, changing to match the dirt background before changing back again. "So that's how my wyvern skin tent works. Huh."

"It seems they have the ability to travel long distances and change to match their surroundings at will," Rowan said. "What else do we know about wyverns?"

Horra's throat moved with a hurried gulp. "They were extinct, and now they aren't? They can fly. And they have deadly stingers on the ends of their tails. No wonder my ancestors hunted them." She shivered. "They could sneak up on you and sting you with their tail before you even realize they're there."

Rowan clacked and cleared his throat. "And you once told me *I* stated the obvious."

"You are the captain of obvious information."

The conversation grew tedious. "What is it you want me to do, exactly?"

The queen bearer's eye twitched. "You have a way with animals. You can speak to Pidge. Can you try speaking to the wyvern? Maybe get it on our side before it annihilates us?"

Rowan considered. "I can speak with the pudge wudgie because of her link with the rood in your Conservatory."

"Oh yeah. I forgot that." Horra crossed her arms and studied the two dragons and Pidge, who danced around them, preening. "It seems harmless when it's by the other animals, but can you try to connect with it anyway?"

"Only if you accompany me." He made no move to get closer. "The wyvern was a great means of escape from the Riven. That doesn't mean it will be amendable to my nearness."

Horra inhaled and let out a loud breath. "Let's go."

They made it halfway to the stables when the Grand Lady stepped around the far end of the castle and approached the wyvern.

The wyvern squeal-bellowed and lowered its head for her to pet it. She crooned to the creature in a soothing tone, then turned to look at Rowan and Horra.

"Friends. May I borrow your magnificent beast?"

"He's not ours," Horra said.

Rowan was confused. "If you can tame the beast, My Lady, you may indeed use him, but for what purpose?"

"In the brief moment I connected with my daughter, she informed me what the Erlking has been up to. Not only has he used the wyverns and their magic to create a shifting maze in the Riven, but he's locked many creatures—some my own children—away in that awful, cursed land. She mentioned he used her to attack the Weald as well." She bowed her head to

Rowan. "I apologize for my daughter's actions but pray to the Creature God you understand she was under his hold when acting upon that request."

"And what was his hold, Lady?" Horra asked.

The dryad's face changed from lovely to fierce in the blink of an eye, and then back to lovely again. "He cut her off from her home, used her wood in his vile instruments, and manipulated her into doing his evil deeds. Now that the wyverns have broken one of his foundational spells, I will head to the Riven to free my other children and any who have wandered into that vile place. But I must do it swiftly before he realizes what is happening. If he changes the tempo spells, or destroys the instruments which are attached to my children—" She lowered her head and shook it fiercely. When she looked up, her eyes were glazed. "I cannot let him destroy anything else."

Rowan's wood tensed, and his core heated.

Horra stepped in front of him, her face puckered. "Rowan, are you okay? Your limbs are shaking."

They'd guessed that the dryads had been involved in the fire that destroyed the Weald. But hearing it validated affected him in a way he hadn't anticipated. "Did she mention the magic used on the Weald?"

"I'm sorry, no. However, once I rescue my kin, we will help you rebuild. I promise you that." She lifted her hand in a sign of a solemn vow.

"The Riven is dangerous." Rowan explained about the critters guarding the different sections. "They will fight for their master."

"I can handle them. Thank you for your assistance." She turned her face to the clear blue sky. "I've hidden myself away for far too long. Hazel would not have died had I been a better leader." She hung her head. "It's too late for her, but I will seek the rest of the dryad prisoners, which should help you maintain the balance of good and evil." She gave the wyvern a last scratch on its neck. "I'll leave after laying my daughter in her final resting place. Thank you, Queen Bearer, for allowing me to use your Conservatory in this manner. You do us honor." After a deep bow, she turned, and with a wide billow of her verdant mantle, strode off in the direction she'd come from.

CHAPTER 35

~Horra~

"Well, that was unexpected," Horra said as they watched the Lady disappear. She turned to Rowan, whose branches still jittered. "I'm worried about you, Rowan."

He twisted his head as if trying to ease his tension. "I'm fine."

She didn't believe him. "Let's get you back to the Conservatory to replenish your resources. Sending out your roots like you did must've depleted you." The fact he didn't fight her on anything or give her a running commentary while they walked through the kitchen, into the dining room, and past the Hall of Monstrosity spoke volumes.

Though she needed to get Pidge wrangled into the Conservatory as well, she knew the druid was in shock. She wasn't sure what part of the Lady's speech had stunned him silly. But she needed every member of her band of heroes, however unlikely they were, to be in tip-top shape. The Erlking was missing once again. And she was in charge of the whole mess.

Horra left Rowan next to the Yew tree. She sent a silent prayer to the Creature God to watch over him while she went in search of Grendel to check on the fairy queen.

She found them in the lab, which had indeed been turned over. The tall tables sat against the wall, and a large bed had been placed in the center of the room. A burner sat beneath a glass vial with a pearlescent green liquid stewing above a flame.

Princess Misty sat vigil in a chair beside the bed, holding her mother's hand. Grendel stood on the other side, mixing powdered ingredients into a large mortar. Horra avoided the princess, maneuvering around the high lab chairs to reach the giant girl.

"How's it going?" she whispered.

Grendel glanced up and adjusted her glasses. "It's going to take time to find the right combination. I think I can reverse most of the spell, but the hex was powerful and the queen already in a weakened state. Normally a fairy could fight most magics off, given time and enough natural nourishment." She shrugged.

Horra was afraid of that. "Has Glory been in?"

Grendel frowned. "Not yet."

"I'll be back later. Rowan's in the Conservatory, but he's a little off his game right now after something the Grand Lady told him. I'm not sure if he'll be much help, but call on him if you need something and can't find me."

Grendel touched Horra's arm. "Um, I've been meaning to ask you about something, and forgive me if I'm overstepping."

A rock of dread dropped in Horra's gut. "Speak freely."

She inhaled and let it out slowly. "The book the princess

had. Could I look at it?" She waved her hands and rushed to continue. "Strictly for research. Maybe I could figure something out that no one else has about the Erlking." She paused. "I want to take him down, but only after I find my sister and possibly all the other children he's stolen. What I need to discover is the link between the science of his music and the methods by which he uses it. Maybe coming at it from a scientific viewpoint, we can unravel the mystery?"

Horra turned her back on the unconscious queen and the princess who'd suddenly glanced over at them. She leaned closer to the giant girl. "Talk to Rowan about what the Lady told us first. Then we can see about the book."

With a nod to Misty, Horra left the lab. She wasn't sure if it was a good idea to give the giant the book. However, if it helped them take down the Erlking, Horra wouldn't hesitate to use the giant girl's intelligence in their favor.

Horra went to the dining room and found her father sitting in his usual spot with a hearty breakfast in front of him. "Everything cleaned up?"

Her father wiped his mouth with a cloth napkin. "I put Torren in charge of setting the courtyard to rights, sending a small search party for any worqs that might still be close by, and for wrangling an actual wyvern."

Horra nodded. "About that. The Lady requested use of the wyvern. It seems tame enough so far. I was just on my way to put it and Nimble back into the barn." She grabbed a chunk of swamp-swine sausage from his plate and ran from the room as his laughter followed her.

Back outside, the wyvern and Nimble had wandered over to a grassy patch of land where they nibbled. Since they were content, she wiggled the sausage at her pet. "Here, Pidge. I have something for you."

Pidge, who had been sun-dozing on the barn's roof, fluttered down and snapped at her claw. Horra broke a greasy sausage chunk off and tossed it to her. "This way." Horra led her to the last barn where they used to keep Nimble.

Before reaching the secret doorway, Horra ran out of sausage. "Are you still hungry, girl? I have some mice ripe for the picking." With a glance to make sure no one was around, Horra tripped the door, which she always kept unlocked in case of an emergency, and entered the passageway.

Curious as always, Pidge stayed close on Horra's heels. Once inside, Horra closed the hidden door and headed across the hallway leading to the castle. With a happy screech, Pidge located her first prey and darted off. Horra left her to it and headed back to the space by the library.

Back at her nest, she set the Erlking's spellbook aside and dug around in the stack of books her mother used to read to her. After sorting through a dozen books, she located the one she was looking for, *The Music Man's Curse*.

"There you are. Let's see what this has to do with the Erlking." Horra dusted the cover off to reveal a picture of an elf-like man. He played an elaborate flute and danced while little elf children, both boys and girls, followed in a trance behind him.

She flipped through the pages, but several had been nibbled on, maybe by mice. Almost entire pages were destroyed. "What in the Wilden Lands?"

When Horra slammed the book shut, dust billowed in the air. "I don't know what he's trying to hide, but I'm going to find it, and I will use it for his downfall," she promised.

She gathered the book and the music spell book and left her hidden nook. Pidge waited for her. "Done eating all the rodents?"

The pudge wudgie gave her a sideways glance.

"Back to the Conservatory, then."

~Rowan~

Pidge's screech reached Rowan's ears before he sensed the bird entering the Conservatory. He'd recovered from the conversation with the Lady of the Tree.

She'd returned carrying the root they'd removed from the Weltering Willow tree so she could leave the Conservatory.

With silent ministrations, she prepared for her daughter's consecration ceremony. "Rowan, hand me those pots of flowers, please?" she asked.

Pidge flew in circles above them before landing on the limb that held her nest.

Horra arrived, carrying two books.

Rowan couldn't hold his curiosity off any longer. "How did you enter the Conservatory without coming through the double doors? I know you didn't use the hole in the wall."

Horra held his gaze. "That's a royal secret."

"Curiosity almost always burns the log." The Lady slid by him to gather the pots herself. She leaned over, and tears fell from her eyes into the pots, bringing forth stunning blooms.

Rowan stamped one rooted foot against the stone platform.

Both Horra and the Lady turned stunned faces toward him.

The queen bearer shifted into her "hands on her hips" stance. "What was that?"

He jerked his arms wide in front of him. "Can't a druid get angry or frustrated?"

She laughed, and the Lady joined in.

He stuck his hands on his hips and glared at them. "I fail to see the humor in my discomfort."

Horra strode to him and grabbed him by the arms. "You're growing in emotional maturity, Rowan. You never used to get this upset when I evaded your questions. It's a good thing, and we don't mean to belittle you by laughing. It's an action creatures use when someone is being a bit obtuse or otherwise dramatic when it isn't called for."

The doors to the Conservatory flew open, and Glory entered. Rowan frowned. He'd left it open for the ceremony, not to allow errant fairies in at their whims.

Rowan clacked in his throat and addressed Horra again. "I was not being overly dramatic."

The fairy stood beside them in two strides. "I'm sure you *were* being dramatic, log boy. Horra, may I speak with you?"

The queen bearer jabbed two books against his chest. "Don't let anyone else have these, or your life is forfeit."

Horra held her claw out. "After you," she said to the fairy. "I'll be right back."

Rowan waited for them to leave before turning to face the Lady once more. While his back was turned, she'd brought several more pots to bloom.

"There, that should do." She clapped her hands. "Did we bring the strangler vine back in from the courtyard? I'd like to drape it across the Weeping Welter I lived in."

"But you won't survive without the tree."

She offered a sad smile. "I have lived a coward's life. This is my penance for my sins of inaction that led my children right into the Erlking's hands. Don't worry, young druid. The tree will live long enough for me to do what I need to do. My daughter suffered because of me. I cannot make up for it, but I can give her what I have and honor her in death."

Rowan picked at the edge of the dusty book the queen bearer had asked him to guard. Though he didn't like it, Rowan understood what the Lady was saying. The code of the roods was much the same—honoring those who came before with their deaths. "Then I shall not stand in your way, My Lady."

~Glory~

GLORY WALKED two steps behind the stiff troll princess as they left the Conservatory, her heart a heavy stone in her chest. Remorse hung like a thick cloud around her. They ended up outside of the troll's monstrous hall of infamy. Once, she would've tsked at the terrible location. After her sister's redress and the guilt that broke through Glory's wall of pretentiousness, she now found no need to express her dislike.

Horra turned and crossed her arms. "Yes?"

Glory braced herself. Facing off with the troll princess after how awfully she'd treated her wasn't going to be easy. She'd done horrible, unforgivable things. But she needed to speak her mind even if the girl didn't like or accept it. She gathered all the humility she knew how to muster and spoke. "I wanted to apologize to you for my actions. You were right all along about the Erlking. I didn't want to listen, and I went out of my way to be a menace to you, the king, and the staff."

Horra's mouth dropped open. "You're apologizing. What's in it for you?"

The words were like daggers to Glory's chest. The truth hurt, and the troll didn't realize Glory had a change of heart.

Glory slowly inhaled a deep breath. This kind of reaction was to be expected. The air hissed out of her clenched teeth. "I deserve that. I left you in the Riven and snuck away when you were trying to keep me safe. Then you let that strange orange girl heal me anyway instead of leaving me to die. For the second time."

Horra's look was one of "I told you so," but Glory contin-ued. The sooner she got it out, the sooner things could start to improve. "I am truly sorry. Not the kind of sorry you have to say in order to get out of something and you don't mean it." She clasped her hands over her heart. "But a real one. I was wrong." She'd never admit to anyone how difficult this was, not only as a fairy but as the spoiled princess she now knew herself to be. "I did so many things that were terrible and self-ish. The Erlking preyed on me because I was an easy target."

Glory glanced down at her clenched fingers and worked to hold her tears back. "He wanted a way into Oddar that would enable him to take over the Wilden Lands, and I was a conve-nient means to do so. I didn't care who I hurt along the way, at least not until now. Stupid, selfish, arrogant me." She glanced back up at the troll princess and prayed her sincerity showed. "I'm going to try to change. I'll be better. If you'll let me." She prayed for possibly the first time to the troll's Creature God that Horra would give her another chance. She didn't deserve it, but she hoped for it.

A look of distrust wavered on the troll's expressive green face. Before, Glory would have been gleeful that she'd tricked her into believing her lies. But she was genuine this time. And it was more unpleasant than she thought it would be. Vulnera-bility was not something that came easily to her. And after all she'd done, she was going to have to work to gain people's trust again.

Brows furrowed, Horra dropped her arms. "Is that the truth?"

Glory held up a hand. "Completely."

Horra danced from one foot to the other. "Fine. But don't think you're totally forgiven or that I'm going to trust you completely."

Relief flooded Glory's chest. She tried to hide the tears stinging her eyes. "I wouldn't either," she admitted.

"I have to get ready for the ceremony. Go visit your mom. Some of us don't have that option." Horra spun and walked into the Hall, leaving Glory standing in the hallway alone, a band of solid guilt squeezing her heart.

CHAPTER 36

Horra despised funerals, but the consecration ceremony for the dryad later that day was lovely. She worked alongside Rowan, placing the pots of blooming plants back at the front of the Conservatory. As promised, the Lady took her leave once the strangler vine had been placed and began to curl around the tree guarding the back entrance.

"I wonder why they call it a weeping welter willow tree and not just a willow tree or a weeping welter tree," Horra mused.

Rowan steepled his fingers. "It is a hybrid of the two trees, which creates the confusion. The ropy limbs come from the willow and the sap from the weeping welter. It is a rare tree indeed."

Horra caught a note of something off in his voice. "I know I keep asking, but are you okay? Ever since the Lady told us about the Erlking using Hazel the dryad to attack the Weald, you've been acting funny."

"Have I?" A grin tugged at the fuzz on his lips.

Horra hesitated. The druid never smiled unless he was learning something or imparting what he called wisdom upon someone. "Yes."

His grin widened. "Tell me how you get into the Conservatory without using the two entries I know about, and I'll tell you what's bothering me."

Horra dusted her claws off after laying the last pot down. "I liked you better when you didn't have emotions."

"Hmm."

Horra pursed her lips. She wasn't used to the druid playing pudge wudgie and mouse with her. "By the way, did you keep those books I gave you safe?"

Rowan walked over to the edge of the dirt and sunk his roots in. He dug inside his bark coat and retrieved the books. "I did." He handed them to her. "Why was I keeping a chewed-up book safe?"

Horra swiped a claw across the picture of the Music Man. "I think this book holds the secret of why the Erlking does what he does. He quoted it this morning, but as you can see, his pet mice have chewed it to pieces. I'd like to find another copy and see what he was referring to."

"I see. What if there's not another copy? The Erlking has sent his vermin in every direction across the Wilden Lands."

"I'm pretty sure there's a copy somewhere. Maybe in the Riven? It's important to him, so it's important to our success in removing his magical power." Horra walked over to the double doors. "One thing I do know is that he won't stop until he gets his musical spells back. And for that, we need Grendel."

The giant girl opened the door, startling her. "What do you need me for?"

Horra smiled. "This." She held out the Erlking's book to the giant girl. "Keep it safe. Though Glory seemed contrite, we can't let it fall into the wrong hands."

"I wonder which spell he used on me?" Grendel flipped through the pages. "Would it be easier to destroy the guy's instruments? Would that break the spells?"

Rowan clacked to clear his throat. "We can't do that. The Lady said those instruments are directly tied to the dryads." He explained to Grendel briefly what she had told him about Hazel. "So, you see, lives are linked to the items he's charmed. I don't know how many. And though the Lady has vowed to free them, the magic of the Riven is unstable at best. It will be up to us to find the answers these books hold and save the Wilden Lands."

"And the other question is why he's stolen the children." Horra held her book up.

The door to the Conservatory opened once more. Glory hesitated before entering. "Can I join this soiree?"

Irritation bloomed inside Horra, but she squashed it. "Sure. We were just trying to figure out why the Erlking has taken all the children and hidden them away inside mountains."

Glory flicked her hand. "Oh, that. I can tell you why."

Horra gaped at the girl as anger flared inside her. "You know why the Erlking is stealing children? Why haven't you told us before? You've seen the kids we've taken from him."

Glory shifted, glancing at all of them. "Well, one, you didn't ask me. And two, it never mattered to me before."

Frustration over the fairy's callous disregard for anything other than herself roared inside Horra. "Tell us now, if you please," she muttered through gritted teeth.

Glory blinked, then smiled. "See? All you had to do was ask."

Horra waited for the fairy to continue, but her skin prickled. "And?"

"The elves, as I gather from what he told me when he thought I was mesmerized but I wasn't, used to lure creatures into the Riven to experiment on. The Erlking isn't fully elf, you see. Like the worqs, he's half one thing, half another. And don't ask me what, because he wouldn't say. Anyway, after they finished experimenting on him and his family, the Erlking was banished to the Riven for crimes they said he committed, which he claims he didn't commit. He said they set him up, rigged the court, then tossed him out on his ear." She laughed. "Or not his ear. They cut that off."

Horra snapped her claws, causing a spark to fly. "Maybe that explains how he can still hear things."

"Pardon me, Princess, but what does that have to do with the children?" Rowan asked.

"He's going to use them in his own experiments to create the perfect creature." Glory emphasized her next words by using her fingers to quote him. "One that has all the best properties of each kind of creature to form a flawless race. One we could never win against, and he's sure the elves couldn't either. His newly formed army will take over the Wilden Lands and then invade Endwylde to overthrow the very people who abused him."

Horra couldn't believe her ears. "And he said all this in front of you?"

"He had these critters he'd blended together, a kind of super race of rats." She shook her head as if they understood. When no one said anything, she explained. "They understand small commands, and let me tell you, they're good at fulfilling his orders. I overheard him talking to his pet rats one day."

"You eavesdropped on him, you mean?" Horra clarified.

"Well, yeah. Anyway, he was going on and on about how

he was going to seek revenge against everyone who'd done him wrong, including the trolls who had murdered his grandfather —the first Erlking who was also a mixed experiment of the elves."

All the pieces fell together in Horra's mind. "He's a madman. Completely insane." She gazed into each of her three companions' somber eyes. "We have to stop him."

TO BE CONTINUED ...

Acknowledgments

I thank God for the gift of seeing stories in my mind and then giving me the courage to figure out how to write those visions down and make a book out of them.

And to my husband and family who root for me, lift me up on those dark days, and help me brainstorm when I need help —I will always love you more.

For my friends who have supported me even when my writing was cringe-worthy, thank you, and I love you for it.

Thank you, Scrivenings Press and ScrivKids. I'm so blessed to know each and every one of you.

To my readers, I want you to know how much it means that you take precious time out of your lives to read this story. I hope it doesn't disappoint.

About the Author

Winner of the 2016 ACFW Genesis Award, Dawn has been recognized for her published and non-published works. Her flash fiction stories have been published in *Havok* magazine under both her real name and pen name, Jo Wonderly.

As a child, Dawn often had her head in the clouds creating scenes and stories for anything and everything she came across. She believed there was magic everywhere, a sentiment she has never outgrown. Nature inspires her, and her love for the underdog and the unlikely hero colors much of what she writes.

Dawn adores anything Steampunk, is often distracted by shiny, pretty things, and her obsession with purses and shoes borders on hoarding. Dawn lives in Iowa with her husband, a chef and food service business owner.

MORE FROM THIS SERIES

Woodencloak

The Band of Unlikely Heroes—Book One

Thirteen-year-old troll princess Horra Fyd's life changes forever after an unexpected visit from the fairy queen and her two daughters. Tales of fairies gave Horra nightmares as a young troll. Before evening falls, however, a real nightmare unfolds. Horra's father, King Fyd, goes missing. Her woodgoblin instructor is poisoned and uses his magic to revert to a seed. And a mysterious, gaunt man wearing a cape and playing a panflute joins the fairies in trying to capture her.

Horra flees but is instantly lost in a world she's never had to travel alone. A letter hidden in her knapsack from her late instructor informs her that a power-hungry Erlking seeks revenge against her kingdom and their allies for a two-generation old war. She is tasked with getting his seed to the Weald, a magical forest. There it can regenerate into a druid, the only creature with the power to hold the balance between good and evil, and who is able to defeat the Erlking.

However, the Erlking is always one step behind her. Horra must fight to protect herself, but she has no magic. She accepts a gift from a dead druid spirit of a charmed woodencloak to disguise her. But magic failed her mother, how can she possibly trust it?

Can Horra have faith and courage enough to trust a power she can't see, and become a warrior heroine her foremothers can be proud of? Or will she allow fear to rule over her and lose everything that matters—including her life?

Get your copy here:

https://scrivenings.link/woodencloak

Mossycoat

The Band of Unlikely Heroes—Book Two

Troll Princess Horra Fyd may have succeeded in getting the druid seed to the magical Weald forest in time to sprout, but she's finding that getting her kingdom back in order is not as easy as she hoped. Oddar's subjects are rebelling and trolls are mysteriously disappearing without a trace. Horra and her father King Divitri are at a loss on what's happening, but they know who's behind it all.

When Horra's summoned back to the Weald to meet Rowan, the new druid warrior, she finds the woodgoblin a know-it-all stick in the mud. Rowan's not impressed with the troll princess, either. However, after a suspicious magical fire destroys the Weald, they're forced to rely on each other to venture out in a kingdom that's becoming more dangerous by the day.

Will Horra and Rowan be able to set their differences aside to become a strong team? Or will they fall into the Erlking's traps, stopping their mission before it even gets started?

Get your copy here:

https://scrivenings.link/mossycoat

ALSO BY DAWN FORD

The Girl with Stars in Her Eyes

Firebird Series—Book One

Eighteen-year-old servant girl Tambrynn is haunted by more than her unusual silver hair and the star-shaped pupils in her eyes. Her uncontrollable ability to call objects leads the wolves who savagely murdered her mother right to her door.

When she's fired and outcast during a snowstorm, her carriage wrecks and she's forced to find refuge in an abandoned cottage. There, her life is upended when the magpie who's stalked her for ten years transforms into a man, Lucas. He's her Watcher and they're from a different kingdom. His job is to keep her safe from her father, an evil mage, who wants to steal her abilities, turn her into one of his undead beasts, and become immortal himself.

Can they make it to the magical passageway and get to their home kingdom in time for Tambrynn to thwart her father's malicious plans? Or will Tambrynn's unique magic doom them all?

Get your copy here:

https://scrivenings.link/thegirlwithstarsinhereyes

The Girl with Fire in Her Veins

Firebird Series—Book Two

Former servant girl Tambrynn struggles with her new firebird abilities, especially the internal fire she cannot control. So, she, along with her Watcher Lucas, and her grandfather Bennett journey to a hidden mountain keep to find the answers she seeks before she sets the kingdom aflame.

But there's a new dragon who's targeting Tambrynn, a mergirl who wishes to manipulate her, and the froggen king, Siltworth, who hasn't forgotten that Tambrynn destroyed his watery reign. When her father, the evil mage Thoron, attacks someone she loves, Tambrynn's group is separated and she has to face another powerful foe alone.

Is she strong enough to withstand the deluge? Or will she drown in the fire and the flood?

Get your copy here:

https://scrivenings.link/thegirlwithfireinherveins

The Girl with a Dragon's Heart

Firebird Series—Book Three

After being injured while reversing the froggen's flood on Anavrin, Tambrynn travels to the depths of the mysterious Bloodthorn Forest for a cure. There she finds what she's looking for, but she also finds more trouble than she can handle. Thoron, her dark mage father, has found her and he's brought the Hulda, a villainous spirit Guardian, along as well. Tragedy strikes during the ensuing magical battle, leaving Tambrynn reeling from one loss closely followed by the death of a loved one. Shaken, Tambrynn barely manages to escape to her grandfather's mountain sanctuary to hide.

Burgeoning with power siphoned from dragon bones, Thoron is only a few steps behind her, making that sanctuary a prison. When unrest spreads across Anavrin, threatening all the Anavrinians again, Tambrynn must race to unlock the hidden power of her firebird abilities in order to defeat her evil father. But time is of the essence, and there's no way out of the mountain in sight.

With time running out, and hidden dangers around every corner, will a fairy tale and a secret pathway lead Tambrynn to find a true dragon's heart, the only power pure enough to take on Thoron's enhanced malevolent magic? Or will her father do what he set out to do since she was born—steal her abilities and destroy all that the Kinsman has created?

Get your copy here:

https://scrivenings.link/thegirlwithadragonsheart